"Non-stop action, well-researched, fun reading."
—*Mobile Press Register*

"Highly recommended . . . A page-turner that is impossible to put down."
—*Under the Covers*

"Showcases Wilson's talent for evoking horror by weaving a tight, scientifically sound plot around realistic dialogue, sympathetic well-developed characters . . . a believable story, also quite possibly a true one."
—*Northside Sun*

FERTILE GROUND

"Charles Wilson tapped into daily newspaper headlines for his latest scientific thriller, and he walked away with gold."
—*The Arizona Republic*

"As they say, the book is 'unputdownable.' "
—*Montgomery Independent*

"Provides fast-paced suspense."
—*The Memphis Commercial Appeal*

"Wilson makes the science understandable even to readers who don't know the difference between a bacterium and a virus."
—*Hattiesburg American*

"Brilliant!"
—Neil McGaughey, author

"Adrenaline-pumping action that doesn't let up until the last page."
—*The Sun Herald*

"If you enjoy a good whodunit, you'll like the latest scientific thriller by Charles Wilson."
—*Northeast Mississippi Journal*

"Wilson has written another medical thriller to keep readers of that genre engrossed."

—*Brazosport Facts*

DIRECT DESCENDANT

"Move over, *Jurassic Park*, the really dangerous prehistoric creature has been brought back . . . Man. A terrific read, one done better with your door locked—for all the good that would do."

—*The Clarion Ledger*

"A story as technically correct as Tom Clancy, as terrifying as Stephen King . . . genetic experimentation that not only could take place, but will someday—with the results only to wonder about now. A surefire best-seller."

—Johnny Quarles, author of *Brack,*
Fool's Gold and *Spirit Trail*

"Readers will be hoping for a sequel."
—*Memphis Commercial Appeal*

"Lean, tight, and compelling. You barely have time to catch your breath—and they're back again."

—Greg Iles, *New York Times* bestselling author
of *Spandau Phoenix*

"Wilson is a skilled storyteller—carrying the reader from one dramatic event to another with lots of surprises in between."

—*The Mobile Register*

NIGHTWATCHER

"Splendid . . . A lean, tight, compelling story that was over much too fast. I wanted more."

—John Grisham

"Wilson throws one curve after another while keeping up the suspense like an old pro. The whole book rushes over you like a jolt of adrenaline."

—*Kirkus Reviews*

"A striking book. Quite an achievement."

—*Los Angeles Times*

"A neat mix of mystery, police procedural and terror."

—*Publishers Weekly*

"Told at a breakneck pace that doesn't allow the reader to pause for breath."

—*Mostly Murder*

"Wilson sustains the suspense to the very end of the story."

—*The Houston Home Journal*

"One of the best."

—*Richmond Times-Dispatch*

SILENT WITNESS

"Uncommonly well-plotted."

—*Los Angeles Times*

"Wilson spins an entertaining yarn; a straightforwardly written story of sexual obsession, guilt and cover-up."

—*Chicago Tribune*

"An involving, twisted tale of passion and murder . . . Features appealing characters, strong situations, and fast-moving prose."

—*Kirkus Reviews*

THE CASSANDRA PROPHECY

"Wilson works on a wider canvas than before with equally readable effect."

—*Los Angeles Times*

"Masterfully plotted, breathlessly paced . . . Sparkles off the page . . . Charles Wilson is a born storyteller."
—*The Clarion-Ledger*

"The twists and turns never stop in this tale of murder, deceit, and treachery in the Deep South . . . Will keep you guessing until the very end."
—*Mostly Murder*

"A high-voltage jolt of tension and terror."
—*Memphis Commercial Appeal*

WHEN FIRST WE DECEIVE

"Tightly plotted suspenser that is also a subtle examination of the role trust plays in relationships, both personal and professional."
—*Chicago Tribune*

"Long on characterization, suspects and suspense."
—*The Tulsa World*

"Steadily accelerating suspense, deft plotting and a broad cast of likeable suspects."
—*Publishers Weekly*

"The climax will rattle your teeth."
—*Mostly Murder*

"I will sing the praises of this novel from the highest mountain."
—*The Village Voice*

EMBRYO

CHARLES WILSON

St. Martin's Paperbacks

EMBRYO

Copyright © 1999 by Charles Wilson.

ISBN: 0-312-96824-8

Printed in the United States of America

St. Martin's Paperbacks edition / February 1999

St. Martin's Paperbacks are published by St. Martin's Press, 175 Fifth Avenue, New York, NY 10010.

10 9 8 7 6 5 4 3 2 1

TO LINDA,
ESPECIALLY THIS TIME FOR THE IDEA FOR
MY NEXT NOVEL

ACKNOWLEDGMENTS

My special thanks to those many people whose knowledge, research, and advice made this novel possible.

In particular: William T. Branch, M.D., F.A.C.S. Clinical Professor, Division of Urology, Department of Surgery, University of South Florida College of Medicine. (In addition, Dr. Branch has been Chief of Staff, Memorial Hospital, Tampa, Florida; Governor-at-Large, American College of Surgeons; Chairman, Board of Governors Nominating Committee, American College of Surgeons; and is listed in *Who's Who in the World* among educators.) LeDon Langston, M.D., Gynecology Staff Physician, Southwest Mississippi Regional Medical Center. Dr. Craig Lobb, Dept. of Microbiology, University of Mississippi Medical Center. William S. Cook, M.D., Gynecologist, Jackson, Mississippi.

Also, Colonel Mike Simmons, U.S. Army, Vienna, Virginia. Newspaper columnist Alice Jackson Baughn of *The Sun Herald* and Ocean Springs, Mississippi, who allowed the story's characters to pull from her knowledge of past tragedies along the Mississippi Coast. Billy Watkins, feature writer of *The Clarion Ledger* and

Ridgeland, Mississippi, for his help with the newspaper archive articles that appear within the story. Tony G. Lee, of Pearl, Mississippi, for allowing me the benefit of his extensive knowledge of Mexico and her peoples. Brian Lipson, my film agent of Los Angeles, California, for his help in guiding the story's characters around that city. Ellis Branch of Ocean Springs, Mississippi, real estate broker and friend who found the perfect house in which to set this novel; and Frank and Lynn Burger, the house's owners, who then graciously let it be used by my characters throughout this book. Dwight Rimes, Ocean Springs, hospital administrator. Jeff O'Keefe of the Bradford–O'Keefe funeral homes. Jerry and Karen Saucier of Biloxi. Jim Fraiser, author, friend, and Mississippi Special Assistant Attorney General, who helped me with the legal circumstances the characters had to endure. Neil McGaughey, author and friend, who has been kind enough to read and then give me the benefit of his opinion on this and past manuscripts. Donna Marshall of Brandon, Mississippi. And, not the least of my thanks to Destin Wilson, my youngest son, whose intuitive feel for what plays right once again helped me to set the tone at the beginning of this tale.

Also, my thanks once again to Tommy Furby of Brandon, who from my first novel has been a helpful critic.

And lastly, and again far from least, my thanks to Alison Orr of Brandon, whose many hours of reading succeeding drafts of this manuscript and her insightful comments after each reading, was more of a help to me than I can possibly convey in this acknowledgment.

After the aid of these highly knowledgeable experts, it goes without saying that any factual errors that the text might contain are strictly attributable to me.

EMBRYO

PROLOGUE

Cheryl caught the look on Billy's face. To anyone else it would be unnoticeable—simply the expressionless face of a seven-year-old framed in the warm morning sunlight shining across the breakfast-room table. But she was his mother.

She laid her hand on his forearm. He didn't move his arm away, but she could feel the tension in the muscle beneath her touch.

"Honey, you're going to like soccer." He hadn't liked T-ball. He didn't even like roughhousing with others his age. More and more he was content simply to be by himself. She didn't know what to do about it. But she knew she had to do something.

"Billy, look at me."

He lifted his face. There was still the lack of expression. But there was beauty there, too; his blond hair thick and soft, a firm chin beginning to develop above the collar of his shirt, the deep blue eyes. He was going to be a handsome man. He was highly intelligent. He was everything she could have imagined wanting in the child she had waited so long for. *Except maybe so introverted he could suffer socially.*

That worried her deeply.

"Billy, you're *going* to play soccer."

He moved his forearm from under her fingers. She dropped her hand back to the side of her robe. She felt her determination waver. But she couldn't back off. Not again.

"You know Coach Alan promised you that you would like soccer fine."

Alan had said the sport would bring Billy out of his shell. Alan said he would work with him until he was comfortable with the other children, and the other children comfortable with him. *Alan had promised.*

Billy stared out the window now, past the big magnolia rustling gently in the summer breeze to the wide expanse of water making up the Mississippi Sound spreading out toward the barrier islands. There was no more to say; all she could do was make it as easy on him as possible.

"I'll take a quick shower and then we'll go to practice," she said. "I'll stay with you every minute until it's over. Okay?"

He kept staring at the Sound, glistening in the sun's rays.

"Okay?"

He continued to stare toward the window for the longest moment and then, still without looking toward her, nodded.

She smiled down at him. "Fine, baby. Give me just a minute. You want to see if Oscar has plenty of water? I don't think I filled his bowl yesterday."

As Cheryl moved toward the bedroom, Billy slipped from his chair and walked toward the door at the far side of the kitchen.

"I'll only be a minute," Cheryl repeated as he opened it and stepped outside into the garage.

Near the rear of a pickup truck, a large poodle, his hair clipped short for the hot Mississippi summer, lay curled in a black ball. His bowl was empty. As Billy walked toward him, the poodle rose and, looking back across his shoulder, moved out of the garage and disappeared around a bush at the corner of the house.

Billy stopped in front of the bowl. His gaze went to a baseball glove hanging from a nail in the garage wall. Below the glove, a five-gallon can of gasoline sat in front of a riding lawnmower.

Billy's gaze fixed on the rusting can.

Cheryl let the water from the showerhead pelt her face. *Is the soccer for Billy or me?* she thought. Alan was so nice. So polite. And there was no question he was attracted to her—the first time he saw her, his gaze told her that. But he didn't keep staring like other men usually did. When he shook her hand his grip hadn't lingered more than a polite moment. He loved kids. Despite a very busy veterinary practice, he volunteered every year for the summer youth programs. Handsome. Educated.

Cheryl turned her back to the spray. *Five years,* she thought. Five years since her husband had been killed by a drunk driver weaving across Highway 49. Five years without a husband and trying to raise Billy while running her dress shop. Billy had been deprived. She caught her lip in her teeth.

She noticed the odor.

The smell quickly grew stronger.

Gasoline?

She pulled the shower curtain back.

From under the crack at the bottom of the bathroom door, the shiny, orange-tinted liquid rushed across the tile toward her.

A flame jumped under the door and the bathroom exploded in a yellow flash. Cheryl was blown hard against the rear of the shower, knocking her unconscious; her body flamed into a torch. She slid down the tile wall. The shower curtain melted into fire and fell across her legs. Flames and black puffs of smoke alternately rose from her skin as the showerhead continued to spray her body, and the water began to turn to steam . . .

CHAPTER 1

Bailey Williams is here, Ross."

Despite the excited tone in his secretary's voice, Ross Channing continued to search through the papers on his partner's desk. "Have you seen those summonses I gave Mac?" he asked.

"Ross," Dorothy repeated. "It's *the* Bailey Williams— the model. She says she wants to speak to you."

He looked back at Dorothy. Heavyset in a flowered dress, she stood in the office doorway. She had a serious expression across her face. She wasn't kidding. "I saw her just last night on the David Letterman show," she said. "She's even more beautiful in person."

Bailey Williams, he thought. *Coming to a bail bond agency? For what?* He buttoned his collar and pulled his tie in place as he walked across the floor toward the door. "What did she say she wanted?"

"Only that she wants to speak to you privately. She's waiting in your office."

Dorothy followed him as he stepped out into the compact reception area and walked past her desk toward his office door.

Inside the office, Bailey Williams stood at a window she had opened behind the desk. Wearing a short, plaid skirt that displayed her tight legs, with her jacket loosely gathered at a small waist, and with her full, dark hair resting gently against her shoulders, she gave off a striking appearance even from behind. As Ross came inside the small office, she took a puff from a Virginia Slims, blew a cloud of smoke through the screen, and then walked around to the front of the desk.

She held the cigarette out. "I don't see an ashtray," she said.

He took the cigarette and stubbed it down inside an empty coffee cup sitting next to the telephone on his desk.

Her gaze had fallen on the stack of books sitting on the front of the desk. She used her slim forefinger to trace their titles. "*Constitutional Law. Legal Ethics. Federal Court Procedure.*" She turned her face toward his.

Dorothy spoke from behind them. "Mr. Channing has just taken his bar exam. We're waiting for the results now. Mr. McLaurin graduates at the end of the year."

"More lawyers, huh," Bailey mused, looking back at the books.

"Moving up in the world," Ross said, smiling. "Or down. Whatever your perspective is of attorneys."

"Would you care for a cup of coffee?" Dorothy asked.

Bailey didn't respond. She was looking at Ross's aging English bulldog. He had come out from under the desk and now stood at its far side, his stubby legs braced as if it took an effort to support his thick body, his wrinkled face looking up at the model.

"That's Cooper," Dorothy said. "Mr. Channing's dog. I'll get him out of here."

"He's fine," Bailey said.

"Would you care for the coffee?" Dorothy asked again.

"No, thank you."

Dorothy smiled politely, grinned at Ross, and closed the door behind them. Ross waited for the model to say why she had come as she stepped to the straight-back chair in front of the desk and settled into it. Now, she crossed her legs and looked up at him.

"Mr. Channing, I have heard that you have extensive connections in Mexico. Do you remember Meg Levine?"

He nodded as he started around the desk toward his chair. Meg Levine had come unannounced to the office nearly three years before, her appearance nearly as surprising as Bailey's. She had been sent by a friend who was aware he had spent part of his youth in Mexico. Meg had quite candidly told him that her big break in life had come when she parlayed a bit role in a low-budget film into a quickie marriage to the film's director several years before. The marriage's subsequent breakup had left her well fixed financially. Then she had made "the big mistake," as she called it. She had married a producer thought to be as wealthy as her first husband, but actually deeply in debt from gambling and drug addiction. He had been arrested after trying to pay off the debts by financing a delivery of cocaine into the country. Meg, at first convinced of his innocence, had put up his entire bail in cash, and he had immediately fled Los Angeles. Since then, he had been living in Mexico, with the authorities there either unable or unwilling to track him down—and Meg no longer with any doubts about his guilt. Ross recalled flying to Mexico City, joining with Manuel, a friend from his youth there, and finding the man in only three days, living with his mistress in a luxury beach home not far from Acapulco, his former "favorite" vacation spot. They had flown him back to Los Angeles on a private plane, and Ross had received the largest fee he had ever made from bringing a bail jumper back to stand trial. He remembered seeing in the newspaper where Meg had gone through a third messy divorce since then—and was rumored to be in love again.

Bailey had finished lighting another long cigarette and stuffed the pack back inside her purse. "There's a story I'm interested in," she said. "I know tracing the source of a story is not exactly what you do—but I doubt you're averse to making money."

As she paused, waiting for a response, he nodded, and she continued. "You might call it more of a tale than a story. It's been bandied about the party circuit for years; out-of-womb birth. It's been laughed about as what every young model or starlet needs—a baby delivered straight from a test tube, without time off from a career for pregnancy, no stretch marks. No man to put up with for that matter. The process was of course developed by some eccentric scientist—isn't that always the case? Supposedly his lab was in South America; he had been experimenting with tree seedlings and evidently had nothing better to do with his free time."

Despite her words being almost lighthearted, her expression was serious and she had stared directly into his eyes as she spoke. Now she took another drag off her cigarette and ran her gaze across his desk. Ross slipped the saucer from under the coffee cup and slid it toward her.

"Thank you," she said, setting the makeshift ashtray into her lap. She flicked an ash from the cigarette into the saucer. "As I told you, all I had ever heard was a scientist somewhere in South America. Then I met a model from Mexico City last week. A cute young thing, kind of, not the type who's going to make it in this business, but friendly. She was quite certain this wasn't just a tale. And the process had been experimented with—she said successfully—in Mexico some years ago.

Mexico—not South America. She even said where in Mexico. I'm not so certain she's much more than a child mentally, but there *was* something in her sincerity. I'd like for you to check out the rumors for me and see what you can learn about this . . . like if it's even conceivably possible."

As she finished speaking, she stubbed her cigarette out in the saucer and leaned forward to slide it onto the desk. Cooper, now sitting at her feet, watched her movement.

Out-of-womb birth? Ross thought. Los Angeles was the place where celebrities could discuss how they were kings and queens in a former life and be listened to with a straight face until their looks or money ran out. Yet he also knew Bailey Williams wasn't the typical brain-dead celebrity who dropped out of school to move to Hollywood and lucked into making it big with her face and body. She had been spotted by a modeling agency scout when she appeared on a talk show as one of a group of fourteen- and fifteen-year-olds already accepted to college due to their high IQs. And what did he care anyway?—here was a client wanting to find out something, and with enough money to afford a battalion of information seekers if she felt like it. "My source in Mexico charges four hundred dollars a day plus expenses. Additionally, I will require a set fee of five thousand dollars for myself."

Having never done a straight private-detective-type investigation before, he had picked his fee out of the air. It was a steep price when all he had to do was make a simple telephone call, and then sit back and wait to see if Manuel could come up with anything. But he suspected that Bailey Williams couldn't care less what it cost.

He was proven right when she said, "Agreed."

"You said she knew where this experimentation took place?"

"The Sierra Madres."

They ran much the length of the country. "Nothing more specific?"

"According to the girl, experiments were conducted on Indians."

Where in Mexico weren't there Indians? Over three quarters of the population were of Indian ancestry. "I'll see what I can do." He watched the model pull her cigarettes from her purse once again and, with her gaze directed toward the pack, he took the opportunity to study her face. Unlike many of the faces in Hollywood that appeared beautiful to the camera but garishly made-up in person, she really was beautiful.

Camera, passed through his mind again. There was constant speculation about when Bailey Williams would accept a movie role. She had referred to the legend as a story. Maybe a story around which a movie could be built? About out-of womb birth?

Then Ross's partner, James McLaurin, a broad grin across his brown face, opened the door and stepped inside the office. He carried an ashtray. Where he got it Ross had no idea—probably the delivery dispatcher from the business next door in the building. He was always standing out in the hall puffing on a cigar, sending great clouds of gray smoke into the air.

McLaurin stopped beside Bailey's chair and held out the ashtray. Of a slim build and several inches shorter than Ross's slightly over six feet, and with the grin still across his face, he looked like a Boy Scout proud of a good deed. Bailey smiled politely as she took the ashtray. Then she pointedly looked back at the door and up at McLaurin again. As she continued to stare, his grin disappeared and he turned and walked toward the door. Cooper watched him go.

"That's my partner," Ross said.

"I would rather you kept this as discreet as possible," she said.

"It will only be our office—the three of us—and my source in Mexico."

Bailey placed the pack of cigarettes back in her purse without taking one and leaned forward to deposit the ashtray next to the saucer. She reached down to pat Cooper on the head, and came to her feet.

"Your office is full of surprises, Mr. Channing," she said, looking down at Cooper again and then the law books on his desk. "And now I have one for you. As I said, discretion is important to me. The tabloids pay a lot for information on anything I do. Meg said you were smart. We'll see. If within twelve months of your either verifying that such experiments took place or proving the story baseless, and I have seen nothing in the press of my being here, I will pay you a fifty-thousand-dollar bonus in addition to your fee. So you see how important discretion is to me."

She laid a small business-size card on his desk. "That's my private number. I want to be informed nightly of your progress—every night."

Moments later, as Bailey Williams, now wearing a scarf and sunglasses, stepped from the reception area at the front of the office and walked down the steps toward the exit from the building, Ross turned back to Dorothy.

"Anything from the bar in the mail?" he asked.

"They said they would mail the results next week," Dorothy reminded him.

He nodded.

"You know you passed the exam, Ross. As many questions as you had me read to you, I could have passed."

"She flirt with you?" McLaurin asked.

Ross smiled a little and shook his head no.

"Every talk show I ever saw her on she flirted with every man there," McLaurin added, "young, old, or ugly. She didn't do anything but give me a cold stare."

"File a discrimination suit," Dorothy said. She turned to Ross. "Now, what in the world did Miss Williams want with a bail bondsman?"

"Work for Manuel, really—information on a legend out of Mexico. It might have to do with a movie idea. But she doesn't want anybody knowing about it. If in the next twelve months it doesn't leak out from someone bragging that *the* Bailey Williams was here—" He looked at McLaurin.

McLaurin crossed his heart with his finger.

"—If it doesn't leak out that she was here, there's a fifty-thousand-dollar bonus in it for us, on top of a five-thousand-dollar fee I quoted her."

McLaurin's eyes widened and he quickly crossed his heart again.

"Twelve months," Dorothy mused. "That's long enough to already have a movie in production—and then with that lead it's too late for anybody else to steal the idea."

Ross nodded.

He didn't know what else to think.

In a supermarket parking area across the street, Bailey Williams entered her Mercedes and backed it from its spot. At a corner of the supermarket, a thin man dressed in jeans and a hooded pullover snapped shot after shot of the famous model through a telephoto lens. Then he pointed his camera at the sign in front of the small two-story building she had stepped from, and snapped several more quick shots.

WEST COAST INSURANCE
PACKAGE DELIVERY EXPRESS

SUNSET TRAVEL AGENCY
MCLAURIN/CHANNING—BAIL BONDS/PROCESS SERVERS

Ross leaned back in his office chair, turned it to the side and lifted his feet up onto the edge of his desk. He reached to his telephone, pushed the speaker button, and punched in Manuel Alvarez's office number in Mexico City.

He listened as the number rang, and then a young, feminine voice answered pleasantly in Spanish: *"Detectives y Seguridad Alvarez."*

"Estelita."

"Ross. Gosh, you catch a woman off guard."

"How do I sound different?"

"Pardon me?"

"Everybody knows it's me as soon as I say something over the telephone."

"You have a strong voice," she said.

What's a strong voice? "I'm loud?"

Estelita laughed lightly. "Sometimes. Your voice is very distinctive."

"There goes my chance of taking up a career making obscene phone calls."

"I don't know," Estelita said in a soft voice. "I could pretend I don't know who you are."

Ross smiled a little. "Maybe later."

"Am I speaking to an attorney yet?"

"Haven't received the results of the bar exam. Keep your fingers crossed."

"With your mind, you don't need that. You said you were coming back down here before the summer was over."

"It's not fall yet."

"It's your turn," she said. "I was in Los Angeles last. Wait a minute, Manuel is on the other line. I'll tell him you're holding."

Manuel must have finished his conversation immediately, because it was only a few seconds until his deep voice came across the line. "Ross."

"Hey, *amigo*. How would you like to make four hundred dollars a day U.S., plus expenses?"

"Who do I have to assassinate?"

"It's a wacko story, Manuel, but I don't want you to kiss it off lightly—it might eventually lead to work from a movie studio. A woman just in here says she's heard a story out of your area of the world about what she calls out-of-womb birth. Supposedly, some tree-seedling scientist somewhere in the Sierra Madres experimenting on Indians came up with the idea of test-tube babies. I mean test tube all the way until birth—he's supposed to have succeeded. I want you to see if you can find the source of the story, if there is one."

"Do I get paid if I already know it?" Manuel asked, and chuckled. "It wasn't a scientist, but a medical doctor from your country. A devil disguised as a doctor, anyway, who stole eggs from the Indian women he treated and created demons without the benefit of any of the enjoyment that comes with good old-fashioned sex. The Indian spiritual leaders rallied their people, and with the help of the good gods overpowered the evil, sending the demons back to their fiery hell. The big battle took place close to Taxco. I'll give your client credit for one thing, Ross, she's up-to-date on her legends. This supposedly took place in the last couple of decades." Manuel chuckled again. "Guess the medicine men decided they didn't want their grandfathers to have all the legends to themselves—they had to dream up recent victories to prove their worth."

"You have any idea what's really behind the story?"

"Why does there have to be something behind it other than a tale somebody told which grew bigger and bigger?"

"I want you to do some checking around anyway.

You said an MD, not a scientist—that's specific. See what else specific you can find out. There has to be some basis—something that happened to start the legend."

"Like the alien crash at Roswell? That started something, didn't it? Okay, for four hundred dollars a day U.S., I'll trace the story in any direction it goes; if need be all the way back to the first little devil with balls big enough to have fathered the mother of all demons."

Manuel was still chuckling when they ended their conversation.

CHAPTER 2

Manuel, his sleeves rolled up his strong forearms, his elbow stuck out the driver's window of his old pickup, guided the vehicle slowly along a narrow dirt road that closely followed the edge of a cliff. To his left, the sheer precipice dropped toward a tree-covered valley hundreds of feet below. Ahead of him the road dropped toward another valley. He had to constantly touch the truck's brakes to counter the pull of gravity trying to force it faster down the steep grade.

Coming toward him in the deepening afternoon shadows, an old Indian man dressed in a blue shirt, baggy white trousers and sandals led a donkey burdened with large, round wooden kegs of fresh water alongside the edge of the road. Manuel edged the pickup as close to the other side of the road as he could and stopped alongside the man.

"*Buenas tardes, amigo.*"

The old man acknowledged the greeting by tipping his sombrero.

"*Donde está la residencia del Capitán Bández?*" Manuel asked.

The man pointed back across his shoulder down the

road to where it curved abruptly to the right, disappearing behind the thick pines that covered the mountainside.

A few minutes of slow driving and constant braking later, the pickup emerged onto a flat plateau mostly cleared of trees. The adobe home of the area's head of police, Enrique Bandez, sat at the right of the clearing.

Manuel stopped his pickup at the side of the road. A mixture of small rocks and sand ground under the soles of his boots as he walked toward the house. Two lean Indian men in white blouses, trousers, and sandals sat on short stools to the side of the door. They stared at him as he came toward them. Captain Bandez appeared in the open doorway. He was stocky and short and looked to be in his mid-twenties, younger than Manuel would have expected a head of police to be even in a rural area. Dressed in a dark blue uniform with his shirt open across his brown chest, he had his hands stuck lazily in his trouser pockets. He leaned his shoulder against the side of the doorway and nodded pleasantly.

"*Señor* Alvarez," he said.

Manuel smiled politely. "*Mi capitán.*"

"They say you speak English," Bandez said.

"Yes."

"If you don't mind then, that is the way we shall converse."

Bandez nodded lazily across his shoulder at the Indians sitting on the stools and now staring stoically ahead into the thick pines that climbed sharply up the slope of the mountain past the far side of the road.

"Their legends are as sacred to them as the stories in the Bible are to a Christian. I do not wish to insult them by giving an interpretation different from their belief." Bandez looked at the silver chain dangling around Manuel's neck and disappearing down into the shirt covering his broad chest. "You are a Christian?"

"Yes."

"I am, too," Bandez said. One of the Indians shifted his eyes toward the captain, then returned to staring toward the road.

"What were you told in Taxco?"

Manuel had heard basically the same legend that he had already known, with slight variations, "That forty years ago an evil man—a devil disguised as a medical doctor from the United States—came to an area a few miles south of here and offered to treat the Indians. He implanted the women with his seed to bring forth demons' helpers. These helpers were then able to call forth demons from beneath the mountains."

Captain Bandez smiled, then took up the story, "And there was a great battle led by the Indians' spiritual leaders against the Yankee and his demon helpers led by the demons themselves. Many perished, but good won out."

Manuel nodded.

Bandez shifted his shoulder against the door, slipped his hand from his pocket and used his forefinger to smooth his heavy eyebrows, then slipped his hand back inside his trousers. "The doctor came here with a Catholic aid mission when I was a little boy," he said. "He remained here when the others left. He was a good man. He subsequently tended my mother when she became sick after bearing my brother. My mother died, but the doctor did all he could. I was only a little boy, but I know that. I watched the tears in his eyes as he suffered with my mother. Shortly after that, some children were born with deformities. Several of them over a period of the next few years. Doctors say now that the deformities can be traced back to three main families. Those three families likely go back to an original father—the trait can undoubtedly be blamed on the intermarriages of those closely related to one another. But the Indians know nothing of scientific explanation.

The beliefs of good and evil are strong among the rural Indians in particular. It is not something outsiders would understand—but very strong. Not far from here, only a few years ago, a *curandero*—a man of folk medicine—is said to have performed bad medicine several times. All of the sick he worked with for weeks died. It was undoubtedly a virus, a plague; maybe an illness borne by insects in the area; the answer will never be known for certain. They burned the man to death. Twenty years ago they burned the doctor from the United States." Bandez suddenly slid his hand out of his pocket to slap the side of his face, squashing a large mosquito. He looked at the spot of blood on his palm.

"See, insect-borne," he said, and smiled.

"What was the doctor's name?"

"Dr. Post."

"His first name?"

Bandez shook his head. "No one knew it."

"There would have been others who worked with him I could speak with, some locals—nurses, aides?"

Bandez said, "No."

It was the same thing Manuel had heard in the town—nobody worked with the doctor but demons.

Twenty minutes later, Manuel drove his pickup back up the steep road leading toward Taxco. As he bounced across eroded ruts and washed-out spots along the narrow passageway, spurts of sand shot out behind the truck's rear wheels and an occasional small rock was propelled backward bouncing down the road and tumbling off its steep edge to fall scores of feet toward the tops of the tall pines in the valley below. Manuel switched on the pickup's headlights to dispel the darkening shadows creeping over the mountains as the sun disappeared behind the high ridges to the west. A young Indian boy walked up the edge of the road toward the truck. Thin, barefoot, and without a shirt, he wore only a pair of baggy white trousers. He held a two-foot-long iguana by its tail, the scaly lizard hanging down by the boy's side and swinging gently back and forth in rhythm with the boy's stride as if it were dead. No doubt it was the last remaining iguana that the boy would have carried to the town early that morning to sell to the tourists as pets. Manuel nodded at the youngster as he drove slowly by.

"*Señor. Señor.*"

The boy ran rapidly to the truck as Manuel released his foot from the accelerator and stopped.

"*Señor,*" the boy said in an excited tone. He held the lizard in front of Manuel's open window. "*Señor,* good for pet for your children." The boy caught the lizard under the neck and held its head up where its eyes stared directly at Manuel's. "Very gentle," the boy added. He used the tip of his forefinger to trace a path around the iguana's half-open mouth. "No bite," he said emphatically.

Manuel smiled. "No, thank you."

"Only five dollar, U.S." the boy said, nodding as if to emphasize how cheap a price that was.

Manuel, still smiling, shook his head no.

"Three dollar," the boy said.

Manuel wondered how many dollars the boy had made that day selling the easy-to-catch lizards to the tourists. Manuel was certain the highway leading from Taxco was swarming with the lizards, turned loose by tourists who wondered why they had done such a stupid thing as listen to their children and buy one in the first place.

"One dollar," the boy said. Still holding the lizard up in the air by its tail, the boy stuck his other hand in his trouser pocket and pulled it inside out.

"No money to eat, *señor.*"

Manuel reached into his pocket and pulled out a small wad of folded peso notes. He peeled off a few and

held them out the window toward the boy. The youngster beamed as he took the bills into his hands and
quickly rifled through them with a practiced thumb. His
smile grew broader.

"Thank you, *señor*." He held the iguana forward.

Manuel shook his head. "Turn it loose."

The boy stared at him a moment and smiled, a cap-
tivating smile, bright and gleaming against his brown
skin. He nodded and turned and walked to the side of
the road where he laid the lizard over the edge of the
slope on its stomach.

The reptile slid a couple of feet down the incline,
then, its muscular legs scurrying, caught a grip in the
dirt and lumbered toward the concealment of a clump
of tall weeds.

The boy turned back toward the truck, smiled, and
even bowed slightly.

"Son, what do you know about the doctor from the
United States who brought the demons out from under
the mountain?"

The boy's smile went away. He stared at Manuel.

Manuel repeated the question in Spanish.

The boy shook his head slowly. Manuel pulled the
rest of the peso notes from his pocket and held them
out the window toward the boy.

It wasn't miles away, but close by, and it wasn't south
of Taxco as Captain Bandez and those in Taxco had
said, but west. The narrow road that led in its direction
dead-ended before they reached the spot, and the Indian
boy, Tony, as he liked to be called, and Manuel, covered the last mile walking through thick pines.

It sat in a once-cleared spot, now grown high with
weeds and dotted with tall, slender pines much younger
than those in the surrounding forest. *It* was the remnant
of the burned-out, one-story clinic and living quarters
once occupied by the doctor from the United States. The

partial walls and the sections of the tin roof still left standing, were covered with long vines snaking in every direction. It loomed as a dark, forbidding place framed against the bright moon behind it.

"*Señor.*" Tony held his hand out for the peso notes.

Manuel started to hand the folded bills over but hesitated. "Where is the doctor's grave?"

The boy didn't respond, and Manuel started to repeat the question in Spanish. But then the boy said, "He no dead."

"Not dead?"

"No. *Señor*, the pesos, please. I go now."

"Where is he? *Dónde está?*"

"*Lo llevó un helicóptero al Seguro Social en Mexico.*"

"He was taken to the hospital in Mexico City?"

"*Sí. Señor* . . . please." The boy held out his hand again.

Manuel saw it tremble. He handed the boy the folded bills. Tony immediately hurried back into the trees, breaking into a trot.

In a moment he had disappeared into the dark.

Then, a shout from the boy. "*Señor*, no say I show you, *please.*"

The words echoed through the dark as if they were coming from a cave. Off to Manuel's right, a gust of wind rustled the tree limbs and swept through the undergrowth. A moment later, the gust passed across him, gently ruffling his hair. In the sky above the clinic, a wide cloud began to pass across the moon. It was nearing late summer, approaching the rainy season in the mountains.

Then the tall weeds surrounding the charred remains ahead of him quit swaying and became still. He walked forward through them to the clinic.

Through a wide opening in its wall he stared into an area so black that little could be distinguished. But inside the space to his right, a thin shaft of moonlight coming through a hole in the roof dimly lit a long table of some kind. Close to it sat something that appeared to be an easy chair. He stepped into the ruins.

Walking slowly, careful where he placed his feet so he wouldn't trip over something, feeling his way along with the tips of his boots more than seeing where he was stepping, he moved toward the dim shaft of light.

A soft scraping sound came from his left, and he froze with one boot in the air, about to step over a thick, charred rafter lying on the concrete floor.

The scraping was joined by the louder sound of something sliding—and an enormous iguana appeared in a circle of moonlight and passed through it, dragging its thick tail behind it. Manuel stepped across the rafter.

The object in the shaft of moonlight was the remnants of a long table, as he had thought it to be. One side was blackened with cracks running through the char, while the other side looked untouched by the blaze. The other object wasn't an easy chair, but half of a couch, blackened into a crisp shell.

A few feet away, there was an open doorway. A glow of light filled a room beyond the doorway. He walked toward the light.

The room past the doorway was intact, each of its four walls still standing. Dim moonlight flowed inside through a jagged hole in the roof above the far side of the room. Back to his right, a waist-high cabinet of some kind stood against an otherwise bare wall. An object sat on top of the cabinet. He heard the dragging sound again and ignored it.

As he drew closer to the cabinet, he saw the object on its top was rather several pieces, grouped close together.

He realized he was looking at a half dozen small silver crosses arranged in a tight circle. At the circle's center, stainless-steel tools he recognized as surgical instruments were heaped in a small pile. A scalpel and a pair of forceps were obvious.

The instruments in the center, the crosses arranged tightly around them—it was obvious that he was staring at a shrine.

CHAPTER 3

Manuel stared at the silver crosses arranged in a circle on top of the cabinet in the burned-out clinic. There was only the faintest gleam of moonlight filtering through the jagged hole in the roof above, but enough that the crosses reflected a dim glow. Everything else in the clinic was covered with ash, charred and dull, but the crosses shined.

He reached out his hand and touched one, ran his fingers along its surface. There was no more corrosion apparent to his touch than there was to his eyes. Silver left exposed in the open air for only a few days in the tropical climate would have certainly been corroded. He was not only staring at a shrine, but one that was being faithfully maintained.

Yet not a shrine to the doctor's memory, he didn't think. With the surgical instruments arranged in the middle and the crosses tightly surrounding them, it was more likely the shrine was meant to keep the doctor—or the demons—from returning.

And what else was represented that might not be obvious at first? The crosses? A religious symbol in a nation full of deeply devout Catholics being used to help protect from evil returning—or did the crosses represent something else? Manuel knew he stood in the mountains bordering an area different in its population from anywhere else in Mexico. Slavery had been voluntarily abolished in Mexico years prior to the Civil War that tore the United States apart. The Mexican military had transported the slaves to the country's west coast and ordered them to build boats to return to their homeland. Many had—and ultimately faced death in trying to navigate the countless treacherous miles of the Pacific. Others had seemed to leave, but had stopped their boats out of sight offshore and waited until the soldiers left, and sailed back to the coast. They had spread throughout the coastal plain into the mountains and intermarried with the local Indians. A few of the descendants of those marriages had adopted symbols of the Christian religion while retaining their original African religions. No Catholic could now stand in a hut of one of those descendants and be certain a cross hanging on a wall had anything to do with the Christian religion, as far as the hut's owner viewed the symbol. Did the crosses he stared at now represent Christ's protection against the demons, or did they symbolize something maybe more fearful than the demons themselves?

Something ongoing—given the continuing maintenance of the shrine?

Ross had said he wanted to know all he could.

Now Manuel noticed a charred bundle of postcard-size pieces of paper lying underneath the instruments.

He reached out his hands and moved the instruments aside. As he did, they made a metallic sound like a chain being coiled atop itself.

He slid the bundle out from beneath them.

It was a stack of letters, bound with a string, one end of the small bundle burned and crisp. Ashes flaked off as he held it in his hand.

He felt a gentle breeze pass across his face, and thus wasn't startled when he heard a door somewhere in the darkness creak as it moved slowly on its aging hinges.

He thought about leaving some of the letters on the shrine out of respect for the Indians, but they would know somebody had taken the rest anyway. Then the thought that they had tried to burn a man to death because of their superstitions took away any concern he might have for their beliefs.

With the letters held gently in his hands, he walked past the cabinet to the doorway at the far side of the room.

Beyond it, lay another wide room. Its far side was completely caved in with only a solitary door frame and its door still standing. The door creaked and swung gently in the wind. Beyond the door, the tall weeds swayed and then became still again.

Manuel turned, and still being careful to hold the stack of letters gently, retraced his route through the clinic and stepped outside into the moonlight at the same place he had entered the building.

He held the letters closer to his eyes. There was the faint outline of an address on the charred half of the first envelope, but it couldn't be read in the dim moonlight. When he untied the string to loosen the envelopes, their charred ends crumbled into ash and drifted to the ground.

Again holding the stack gently between his hands, not wanting any more of the envelopes to crumble until he could get to where he could shine a light on the addresses and maybe read them, maybe even read the letters inside, he turned his gaze into the trees, finding his bearings, then started in the direction of his truck.

Even though the wind was gusting stronger now, and more often, and the mountain temperature had dropped into the low sixties, Manuel, concentrating on holding the fragile envelopes gently between his hands as he moved through the trees, felt perspiration forming on his forehead as he neared his truck.

Once inside the cab, he left the door open, letting the interior light shine down on the small bundle. The return address on the top envelope consisted of only one word—MARY.

The envelope was addressed to DR. SEBAS . . . The rest of the name and the address was charred black and couldn't be read. He gently slid the envelope to the side and looked at the one beneath it.

MARY again.

Each of them, all six, were from Mary. He used his fingertips to gently slide the remaining half of a letter from the first envelope. As he unfolded it, flakes of black ash fell into his lap.

The letter was written on a sheet of notebook paper, now turned a faded yellow, turning to brown near where the right three quarters of the sheet had been burned away. Only the first couple of words at the beginning of each sentence could be read. He saw the words *missing you*. Five sentences down in the handwritten letter scribbled in pencil was the word *love*, but the paper was so badly charred he couldn't tell what word was next or would have been in front of it in the previous sentence.

Each letter in turn had similar words: *Missing you . . . together soon . . .*

The last letter was the least charred, and contained a few partial sentences along the left side of the notebook paper on which it was written. . . . *they still talk . . . the pranks you used to . . . would never graduate . . .*

Three nearly complete lines could be made out: *It's difficult knowing you're there and I'm . . .* and, . . . *not that much longer until we're together . . .* and, . . . *said he was proud you're a Tulane Medical Schoo . . .*

The envelope had a full address: Dr. Sebastian Post, Post Medical Clinic. It had been delivered care of the

Holiday Inn in Taxco. Years ago there had been a Holiday Inn high on a mountain top overlooking the city. It was now the Hotel Montetaxco.

Love letters from a wife for some reason separated but expecting to be back with her husband soon? Or from a woman who planned on becoming a wife when she could join him? Join Sebastian Post—the doctor who had not died in the blaze, but had been helicoptered to a hospital in Mexico City.

Manuel looked back at the words ... *said he was proud you're a Tulane Medical Schoo* ...

The school where Dr. Post graduated?

Manuel leaned forward, used his ignition key to unlock the glove compartment, and lifted out a cellular phone.

It received its signal from a satellite, the only type of cellular phone that could be used in the majority of the country, but now the signal was faint, barely registering.

He looked at the trees around him, and at the top half of the mountain rising directly off to the side of the pickup. He extended the phone's aerial as far as it would go and punched in a number.

To his surprise, the cellular signal locked in, and in a moment he heard the phone ringing at his secretary's home in Mexico City.

"Bueno."

Manuel told Estelita all he had learned—that the legend of the evil scientist and the demons had grown up around a Dr. Sebastian Post who had come to Mexico forty years before with a Catholic aid mission and had remained to operate a charity medical clinic west of Taxco. There was nothing of any talk of experimentation on out-of-womb gestation. Indians in Taxco had told him the doctor implanted demon seed in the women of a nearby area, and demons had come from that, but Captain Bandez had said the whole story could be traced to a rash of births with deformities from women under the doctor's care. The Indians had blamed him and had set fire to his clinic with him inside it twenty years before, but he might have survived—at least long enough to be flown to a hospital in Mexico City. In addition, despite what Bandez and the others he had questioned had said, there had to have been locals who worked at the clinic—nurses, aides, even laborers. He would try to find one of them and see what they could tell him. When he returned to Mexico City, he would check records to see if Post had ultimately survived—and if he had, if there was any record of where he might have gone after he left the hospital. One other thing, Post possibly graduated from Tulane Medical School. If that were the case, and if he had indeed survived, there could be someone there who might know his current whereabouts. With Ross's connection to Tulane that would certainly be easy enough to find out. Finally, there might or might not have been a wife or a lover with the doctor at the clinic when it burned. There were letters indicating either a wife or a woman obviously in love with the doctor, a woman who signed her name Mary, intended to join Post. Yet with the postmarks burned off the envelopes there was no way to know if the letters had been received shortly before the clinic was burned, and the woman hadn't yet arrived, or if she had been there when it was destroyed. The letters, along with several surgical instruments, had been found arranged between silver crosses in a manner that suggested a shrine meant to keep the doctor's or the demons' spirits from returning. He told Estelita to tell Ross that he would talk to him in the next couple of days.

After Manuel replaced the cellular phone in the glove compartment, he sat a moment thinking about the polished crosses. Finally, he shut the door, switched on the truck's headlights, and turned on the ignition key.

Five minutes later he reached the crest of the mountain and started down its other side.

The pickup began to increase speed along the steep grade. The road was slightly wider here, and not running close to any precipice, so Manuel let the truck gain speed for several seconds.

When he did step on the brake pedal, it went all the way to the floor.

Manuel's hands tightened on the steering wheel. He pumped the pedal, stomped on it, pumped it again.

The speedometer read sixty kilometers an hour. The trees were beginning to speed by. He pushed hard on the brake pedal.

Seventy kilometers an hour.

The road was wide and only moderately rutted. He was a third of a way down the mountain already. If he could keep control of the truck another minute or two.

He remembered the sharp curve at the bottom of the mountain.

Eighty-five.

It was too late to jump.

Taking one hand off a steering wheel now beginning to vibrate, he clasped the cross at his chest, squeezing it so hard the small points dug into his palms. He asked for forgiveness in Jesus's name. Then he placed his hand back on the steering wheel.

The truck bucked like a horse. Its front bounced in the air and slammed back onto the dusty road again. The sharp curve appeared in his headlights. The tree trunks to its far side quickly grew bigger. The pickup sped into the turn at over a hundred kilometers an hour.

The truck's front wheels, following shallow ruts like sunken railroad tracks, started to follow the curve, the vehicle fighting against the centrifugal force trying to pull it to the side.

The weight of the truck shifted to its left. The rear wheels threw a shower of dirt. The right wheels lost their contact with the road. With a lurching spring, the truck flipped to its left, turning a complete, spinning revolution before it slammed broadside into the thick tree trunks at the far side of the road in a crash of metal against wood.

The sound, loud as an explosion, reverberated through the trees along the mountain.

A *clank-clank-clank* sound of a hubcap rolling across small rocks. A vibrating metallic sound as it fell to its side and quivered as it came to rest.

Then all was quiet.

Incredibly, a low moan came from within the crushed cab.

Manuel, his face a sheet of blood, stared through a red film at the thick tree branch protruding through the windshield. His right arm hung limply by his side. He lifted his left hand, felt the burning pain that crossed his shoulder, but fought through it, pressing his palm against his door. It was partially open, but twisted and jammed, and would open no farther.

He pushed harder, the effort causing a pain to rip through his shoulder and a wave of nausea to pass over him. At his side, a dark shape appeared at the broken window.

Manuel saw the face as it leaned to look at him. A large Indian with straight black hair hanging down past his shoulders. Manuel blinked his eyes, trying to force away his double vision. But it wasn't double vision; a side of the face was swollen out in a half-moon shape. A wide hand came into Manuel's view and caught the pickup's door. A thick muscled arm, protruding from a skimpy leather vest, tightened as the man pulled on the door. Metal squeaked, resisted, the muscles bulged and the door gave way with a loud metallic ripping sound and fell to the ground.

The hand caught Manuel's shoulder. He looked into the dark face, saw the one glazed, gray eye and the one staring eye. The hand tightened. Pain ripped through his shoulder and down his spine. He was dragged out of the seat and slung harshly to the ground.

Above him the thick upper body of the man leaned into the cab. Manuel's vision blurred, darkened. He blinked his eyes. His vision cleared. The man looked at the bundle of letters he now held in his hand, and then tucked them into the waistband of his baggy trousers. He turned away from the pickup and walked toward the road.

Manuel tried to speak, found his tongue swollen and his plea for the man not to leave him coming out broken, almost unrecognizable. "Come back, for God's sake! *Regresa, por Dios!*"

The strength Manuel had to expend shouting the words caused a wave of blackness to settle over him.

The man suddenly stood over him again.

He held something wide and chalky-blue in his hands. Manuel blinked his eyes.

The stone raised high in the moonlight.

Manuel lifted his hand and spread his fingers to try to protect himself. He saw then that the face was not that of an Indian, but of a Caucasian, heavily tanned.

With a loud grunt, the man drove the stone down hard into Manuel's face.

Manuel's feet kicked spasmodically, and he lay still.

The man stared at his handiwork for a moment, then placed his hand against the letters at his waist and turned and walked back into the trees.

A FEW MILES AWAY

The small dwelling was more a shack than a house, its mud-block walls cracked with age, its tin roof rusting and loose in areas. A pair of chickens, roosting at the edge of the rickety wooden door leading into the house, popped awake and scurried out of the way as Tony approached the house. He pushed on the door. It creaked open.

His mother's squat form lay dimly illuminated by candlelight flickering against a mattress at the far side of the one-room structure. A blanket covered her to her waist.

"*Mamacita,*" Tony said softly.

The woman stirred and looked across her shoulder. She started to speak, but coughed. The cough came again and again, one deep sound after another until her brown face began to drain of color. Finally she stopped and regained her breath.

Tony held out the folded peso notes. "*De las iguanas,*" he said, stating simply that the money came from the iguanas, including the amount he had received from Manuel.

His mother stared at the money in disbelief. She couldn't believe even the richest tourists would care so little for money they would pay sums so high. She looked into her son's eyes. She hoped he hadn't become involved with something that would bring shame on them. She coughed again, bringing the back of her hand to cover her mouth this time.

Tony raised his eyes toward the medicine bottles on the shelf above the mattress. Most of them were empty. He forced a smile to his face, knelt, leaned forward, and pressed the pesos into his mother's hand.

A tear came to her eye. "*Gracias, Tonito.*"

Tony leaned forward and placed a kiss on her forehead. Then he blew out the flickering candle and walked toward the window at the back of the shack.

Outside, the full moon was dimmed by the trailing edge of a dark cloud passing across it. Tony could hear the faint gurgling of the creek that ran behind the house. It was a sound that always relaxed him no matter what else was wrong. His mother's sickness, when he was hungry—no matter what, listening to the bubbling of the shallow water as it ran across the rocks somehow always made him feel better.

Then the last of the cloud cleared the moon, its bright light shone down, and he saw the figures moving through the trees toward the house.

He knew instantly why they were there.

He turned and stared in the direction of his mother's dark form.

He started toward the door to meet them. It flew open. Two lean Indian men burst inside.

"No!" his mother shouted behind him. She coughed, came up from the bed and rushed toward the doorway as one of the men grabbed Tony's arm and yanked him out the door.

"Nooo!" she screamed.

The other man placed his palm in her face and shoved her violently backward. She landed on her back on the dirt floor, the blow knocking the wind from her body. She tried to rise, but couldn't breathe. She tried to call Tony's name, but couldn't. She tried to turn onto her stomach, to push herself to her feet, and felt her head spinning.

The room grew darker to her eyes.

She wouldn't quit. Still half-blinded by the lack of oxygen in her diseased lungs, starting to cough again, then coughing deeply, she rolled over, pushed herself to her feet, and stumbled to the door.

It stood open. Beyond it, there was only the dark night.

CHAPTER 4

"Gin," Ross said.

He spread his cards out before him on his kitchen table.

McLaurin frowned from across the table. "You cheated."

"How? You shuffled the cards."

"But it's your deck."

"You never know," Ross said. He added the points to the notepad at his elbow. "You're now seven hundred and fifty points down. You owe me seventy-five cents heading toward a dollar before the night's out." He scooped the cards together and began shuffling them.

McLaurin watched him carefully. Ross smiled. It was the same way with their business—McLaurin carefully keeping up with every dollar they spent. Keeping up with each dollar and agonizing over it. Someone who didn't know him would think he grew up destitute and bad memories made him grasp every penny. But he hadn't come up destitute. His father, a barrel-chested man with a neck to match, had run a one-man detective agency and made a better-than-average living with it, a good enough living that McLaurin had never worried about where his next meal was coming from, or about spending money, despite admittedly being rather free-spending as he grew up. Then the healthy, strong, barrel-chested man had died of a sudden heart attack the same month McLaurin had graduated from college. The only thing he left behind him other than McLaurin and a former wife living in another state, was a ten-thousand-dollar life insurance policy—and, of course, the detective agency.

McLaurin had looked at the small insurance check, and panicked. The next week, eight thousand dollars came in on a case his father had completed earlier. McLaurin saw the agency as a way to live. But at five-foot-five-inches tall, a hundred and thirty pounds, and nervous at his own shadow, there were very few cases he had the stomach to handle. The average client of a small detective agency wasn't exactly a soft-spoken lady or gentleman. The work was often for people wanting divorces and angry, or wanting someone against whom they had a grudge tracked down, or it involved the serving of subpoenas in the type of neighborhoods into which normal messengers working for a law firm refused to go. There was always the risk of bumps and bruises. And McLaurin didn't like the idea of bumps and bruises.

Ross, still uncertain of what he wanted to do with his life during that period, and working part-time for Manuel in Mexico, remembered coming back to the States to check the court records of a man who had committed felonies in Los Angeles, and was at that time being prosecuted by an American business subsidiary in Mexico City. McLaurin had testified for the prosecution at one of the felon's earlier trials. Ross had gone to talk with him. Ross believed they had hit it off well partly because both of them were still searching for what they wanted to do with their future.

Ross ended up remaining in Los Angeles, deciding he

wanted to be an attorney. McLaurin liked the idea of that kind of life, too. They decided they would help each other to make it financially through the years of education that lay ahead of them. McLaurin closed his detective agency; there was no way he could put in the type of hours that most investigations required and attend law school, too. They opened the bail-bonding and process-serving company together; they would put up bonds on the safest of cases to make what income they could, and use the weekends when they were not in classes to serve the subpoenas and summonses.

There was one more thing. They flipped a coin. Ross remembered feeling a little guilty when he won. He would start law school first, while McLaurin devoted his full attention to the company to provide support for both of them. The next year Ross cut his classes back to a bare minimum and McLaurin entered law school with a full load. Continuing to juggle their classes this way, struggling to keep what income they could coming in, studying in the office when they could, they had somehow made it work out. Ross now had his Juris Doctorate. Mac was a semester away. A fifty-thousand-dollar bonus from Bailey Williams and a chance to do later work for a movie studio was going to be a big help in giving them the necessary capital to convert to a full-time law practice. The money couldn't have been more timely. Ross began dealing the cards.

The telephone on the counter dividing the kitchen from the living room rang.

Ross handed the deck across the table. "Don't cheat," he said. He came up out of his chair and walked toward the counter. Behind him, McLaurin studied the backs of the cards carefully.

The telephone rang again as Ross pushed its speaker button. "Hello."

"Mr. Channing, this is Bailey Williams. If you recall, I asked you to keep me informed nightly."

"I haven't done anything yet."

"You haven't done anything?"

"I telephoned my source in Mexico. He had heard the same story you have. He's going to find out what he can about it."

"That's not something I should be aware of?"

"Yes, ma'am, that's why I just told you."

"When will you hear from him again?"

"I don't know—soon, I expect."

"Am I on a speakerphone?"

"Yes, ma'am."

"That's the second time you've addressed me as ma'am. I am not your mother or gray-haired next-door neighbor—*Miss* will be sufficient. And I don't like speakerphones."

Ross lifted the receiver to his ear. "The ma'am's an old Southern habit that comes back from time to time. I'll call you as soon as I learn anything."

"Thank you." Bailey Williams hung up without saying anything more. Ross replaced the receiver.

McLaurin was standing now. He stuck his hand behind him and fanned his buttocks. "Whew."

The telephone rang again.

"What is this," McLaurin asked, "*Larry King Live*?"

Ross punched the speaker button.

"Yes?"

"Ross, Manuel called and said to tell you what he has learned so far."

Then Estelita began to repeat what she had been told.

Bailey Williams still had her hand on the telephone receiver. Meg walked into the bedroom, all five-foot-eight and one hundred and forty pounds of her shaped in oversized curves and bound in a tight blue dress. "From the expression on your face, it's either real good news or real bad news," she said.

Bailey lifted her hand from the receiver. "Neither."

Meg waited a moment. "Don't be so informative," she said.

"You're just nosy."

"Aren't I always?" Meg stopped in front of the dresser and fluffed her hair. She looked down at the tubes of lipstick on a silver tray, and chose a shade of red near the same bright color of her hair.

As she moved the lipstick toward her mouth, she stared at Bailey's reflection in the mirror and said, "Well?"

"Nothing, Meg—only business."

"So I don't have the brains to understand business? When I finished with my last husband, he would have disagreed with you on that. Prenuptial agreements, a bunch of bull—if you felt sufficiently threatened at the time you signed it." Meg smiled, not so much at Bailey, but at the satisfaction she felt within herself. She adjusted her shoulder straps and straightened her back more, swelling her ample bust under the tight material of her dress. "A deep breath is worth a thousand pictures," she said, staring at herself admiringly.

"Mommy," came a small voice from outside the bedroom.

"In here, Tommy," Meg answered.

A small red-haired child of nearly four years of age walked into the bedroom. He wore white slacks, a blue jacket, and a red bow tie. He carried a Power Ranger action figure in one hand and a plastic slingshot in the other. "I'm hungry," he said, looking up at Meg.

"We're going to dinner in a few minutes."

The boy frowned and walked toward the open balcony door.

"Watch it, Bailey," Meg said. "He'll be taking a nosedive off the rail and my lawyer will be preparing a liability suit." Meg blotted her lips with a tissue and brought the lipstick back to her mouth to touch up a spot. "You don't keep any eyeliner for your friends?"

"In the drawer."

The boy had stopped at the center of the balcony and stared up at a large spider beginning to weave a web in the glow of a balcony light. The outer circle was complete and a dozen glistening strands ran through it. The spider, its legs moving rapidly, scurried in a curve as it started a second thread close to the outer edge of the circle. The boy reached into his pants pocket for a small Nerf ball the size of a Ping-Pong ball and fitted it into the strap of the slingshot.

"Oh, no, don't shoot him, Tommy," Bailey said.

"I don't like spiders."

"Big spiders are harmless," she explained. "They eat flies and mosquitos for us. See how hard he's working—you wouldn't want to shoot him while he's doing that."

"Okay," the boy said, lowering his slingshot. "I'll shoot him when he's finished."

Bailey couldn't help but smile.

Meg stepped from the bedroom. "No, you won't, Tommy. I told you I was going to whip your little butt if you killed any more bugs."

The boy looked at his mother and walked past her back into the bedroom. Meg stared after him. "I caught him running around our swimming pool stomping on ants like he was doing a Mexican hat dance. I'm afraid I have a serial killer on my hands."

Bailey smiled and walked to the balcony rail, rested her hands at its top and stared across a panoramic view of the bright lights of Los Angeles from the ocean to Century City to downtown.

Meg looked back at her son, now attacking the dressing-table mirror with swoops of the Power Ranger. "You ought to try for one," she said to Bailey. "The little monsters grow on you."

Bailey nodded.

Meg shook her head in exasperation. "Every time I tell you that, you agree. When are you going to suck it up and get pregnant? What's your real age—twenty-eight, twenty-nine? You don't have forever, you know. God didn't design our plumbing to work indefinitely. You know ancient people had children in their preteens. I don't even remember if I was having my period that young." Meg rested her hands against the balcony. "Of course they died in their twenties, too."

The telephone in the bedroom rang. Tommy hurried to answer it.

"It's for you," he said, holding the receiver out as Bailey walked toward him.

In his kitchen, Ross held the telephone receiver to his ear, waiting for Bailey to answer.

When she did, he said, "I just heard from Mexico. Evidently there's a basis to your story that's been exaggerated over time. There was an American doctor, a Dr. Sebastian Post, who operated a charity clinic in the mountains between Mexico City and Acapulco, close to a town named Taxco. The Indians became convinced the doctor was growing babies."

"What do you mean *became convinced*?" Bailey asked.

"There was a spate of birth deformities. The Indians evidently wanted someone to blame. This grew into a legend that the doctor was growing demon children. My contact is going to try to find out more."

"Mr. Channing, you have said *evidently* twice. What have you learned for certain?"

"I just told you what I know." Ross's words came out more sharply than he intended, and he found himself listening to silence on the other end of the line.

McLaurin was shaking his head. "Scratch the fifty thousand dollars," he mouthed.

Then Bailey said in a low tone, "Mr. Channing, you said a Dr. Post. Without my once again bruising your pride sufficiently to push you into another outburst, might I ask why your contact didn't simply speak with him?"

"Because the doctor might be dead. Or left the country."

"Again, Mr. Channing, is there any way to verify that one way or the other? Or whatever it is your contact *can* verify."

"He's doing that now. The doctor might have graduated from Tulane Medical School. If so, it will be a simple matter to track him down—if he is in this country."

"Tulane's in New Orleans."

"Yes."

"Then would it be too much to ask of you to fly there tonight—so you can get an early start in the morning?"

"I'm sorry, but I already have something scheduled here in the morning."

"Mr. Channing, again, without bruising your pride, I'm paying you, aren't I?"

When Ross frowned before he answered, McLaurin held up his hands in prayer against his chest and mouthed, "Please don't blow it, Ross."

"Miss Williams, when I take on an investigation personally, my expenses are added to my fee—and I charge an extra three hundred dollars a day."

McLaurin grinned.

"That will be fine," Bailey said, "so long as you leave tonight."

"I'll see when the next flight leaves."

"Thank you," Bailey said. "One more thing. If this doctor is alive, that's who I want you to speak to—the horse's mouth, so to speak. You manage that, and whether he did or didn't experiment with out-of-womb birth, there will be another ten-thousand-dollar bonus in it for you. The horse's mouth, Mr. Channing."

And Bailey Williams hung up without saying anything else.

"What?" McLaurin asked.

"She wants me to fly into New Orleans tonight. She said another ten thousand dollars if I can find the doctor."

McLaurin grinned again. "Damn, we're prostitutes, aren't we? Isn't it great?" Then his face took on a serious expression. "What is it that you had to do here tomorrow?"

"The vet's going to cut a cyst out of Cooper's hip."

McLaurin's eyes narrowed. "That's it?"

"I can catch the noon flight."

"You told Bailey you were going to take the first one out."

"Yeah, I did, didn't I?"

"Damn, Ross." McLaurin shook his head again. "Fifty thousand dollars," he mumbled.

Meg stared at Bailey, still sitting on the bed after replacing the telephone receiver. Meg had an incredulous, one-sided smile across her face.

"I can't believe you're serious, Bailey. The story was fun to talk about, but it's only a crazy cocktail party story. Damn, Bailey, what's wrong with having a baby the old-fashioned way? You get a stretch mark, they'll airbrush it out."

Bailey stared now. "I am twenty-nine. An old woman in this business. I don't want to lose a day of whatever time I have left."

"Damn, Bailey, I didn't know you were so stuck on yourself as to—"

"But that's not the reason, Meg. I can't have a child."

"What do you mean?"

"You knew my parents were killed when I was a child."

Meg nodded.

"It was in a car accident. I was with them. I didn't look like I was injured. It was all internal. My uterus was torn. It was left scarred. If I have a child, doctors say it will likely rupture—I could bleed to death."

Meg was silent for a long moment. "I'm sorry, Bailey, but there are other ways. I mean real ways."

"You mean a test-tube baby I can have another woman carry for me—and she'd change her mind when the tabloids start convincing her how much money the baby will be worth to her if she keeps it."

"You could adopt."

"I want *my* child. I'm sorry, I'm a selfish bitch."

"You won't get a lot of disagreement on that, Bailey. But you can be reasonable. Damn, you've had your own way for so long you don't listen to anybody."

"Meg, the model from Mexico—her father was a burn specialist in Mexico City. He treated Dr. Post when they flew him in."

"Who?"

"Dr. Sebastian Post. The Mexican military flew him in from Taxco after his clinic was burned. He's the doctor who Channing was talking about. Dr. Post was nearly dead, talking crazy, hallucinating, her father thought. He was yelling about the children he had grown—in artificial wombs. He *did* it."

"Bailey, he was hallucinating."

"He did it, Meg, and he survived his burns and left for the United States—said he was going home—and then he disappeared."

"I don't believe it, Bailey. Still, if you do believe it, why didn't you tell . . . what the hell is his name— Ross? He's a good-looking bastard, but poor. Sadly that tends to eliminate a man's name from my mind. Why didn't you tell him what you heard? You even knew the place."

"Because I wanted to see if he was good enough to find out on his own, Meg. If I was going to hire somebody to try to find Dr. Post, I wanted to know he was good. He's going to have to be good. There's not a doctor practicing in the United States named Sebastian Post—at least not one that would be close to seventy and confined to a wheelchair from his burns. Not a man in the United States using his social security number— not on a tax return, not for disability payments, or welfare, or anything else."

"Damn, Bailey—his tax return? You used your invitation to the White House to good advantage. I told Phyllis the lecherous old bastard had a crush on you." Meg's eyes narrowed in thought. "Hey, you don't think you might find out if my last husband's making more income than he's telling me, do you? I can't believe with all his films he's still stuck at a couple of mil a year. You help me to get more alimony, I'll give you a cut." Meg smiled broadly.

Then the smile went away. "I am sorry, Bailey."

MOUNTAINS OUTSIDE TAXCO

Tony's mother, walking slowly, coughing almost continually, having to stop often to catch her breath, then forcing her short steps forward again, came up the middle of the narrow dirt road, only dimly lit by the cloud-covered moon above.

She had done this from where she had started from her house, six long, painful miles away, after Tony had been dragged away by the two men. Coughing, her thin blouse soaked with perspiration despite the cool night temperature, she forced herself on.

Ahead of her, on a plateau mostly cleared of trees, Captain Enrique Bandez's small adobe house loomed as a low square in the darkness.

The two men she had seen earlier stood outside the door.

She gathered her shawl closer around her shoulders and moved off the road and across the soft dirt toward the house.

The men started toward her.

She stopped. "*Mi Capitán Bández,*" she shouted as loudly as she could.

The men increased their pace toward her.

Behind them, the door to the small house swung open.

Captain Bandez stepped into the doorway. He wore a loose sleeping gown that hung above his thick calves. He ran his hand through his dark, mussed hair and stared at the woman.

She slowly fell to her knees, clasping her hands out in a pleading motion before her as she did.

"*Te ruego, mi capitán.*"

At her begging him to help her, Bandez's face took on a quizzical expression, as if he didn't know what she wanted.

She shook her head in her anguish. "*Por favor,*" she pleaded.

She began to cough, moving her clasped hands to cover her mouth as the coughs came deeper and deeper.

Bandez frowned at the coughing, turned his head to the side and signaled with a flip of his hand toward her for her to leave. The men stepped forward and pulled her to her feet. They pushed her toward the road.

"*Por favor,*" she cried again over her shoulder, and then she called her son's name loudly, "*Mi Tonito.*"

"*Mi Tonitooo!*"

The men gave a final shove and she fell forward onto her hands and knees in the road.

Crying, she struggled to her feet. She looked back at the house. Bandez had closed the door. The two men stared at her from the side of the road.

Still crying softly, she started slowly back in the direction of her home, her short steps obviously painful.

In the distance a faint flicker of lightning illuminated the sky. Overhead, the clouds had grown thicker.

The two men returned to their position outside Bandez's door.

In a moment, the first cold raindrops began to fall.

CHAPTER 5

Your flight leaves at noon," Dorothy said, handing Ross his ticket confirmation number. "Don't worry about Cooper; he likes staying at my house."

McLaurin shook his head and said, "You should have been on the six A.M. flight." McLaurin looked at Dorothy. "If Bailey Williams calls, say he's already gone."

Dorothy smiled.

McLaurin looked down at Cooper, staring up at them from beside the reception desk. There was a gauze pad taped on his hip above the place where the veterinarian had removed the cyst. "Damn," McLaurin mumbled, "Fifty thousand dollars."

Ross smiled as he walked from the office.

Dorothy waited until the door closed behind him. "I almost wonder if Cooper was just an excuse to put off going to New Orleans as long as he can?"

"What do you mean?" McLaurin asked.

"You realize it's been almost three years since he's been there, Mac. His father has never visited out here. It's not that they don't care about each other. Ross has a couple of photographs of him in his living room, and his father has called to tell me if Ross ever needs anything to let him know. But it's something. I'm a mother. I know."

MOUNTAINS OUTSIDE TAXCO

The pickup's bed was wrapped partially around a thick pine trunk. The cab was nearly torn loose and its windows had shattered at the force of the crash. A thick limb, broken off and splintered at its end, protruded through the windshield above the steering wheel. Manuel's body lay under a tarpaulin a few feet from the cab. Large green flies buzzed around the tarp and disappeared underneath it.

Captain Bandez, dressed in his dark blue uniform, his shirt open across his chest, stood at the edge of the road, in front of two Jeeps. He held an unlit cigar between his forefinger and thumb and had his other hand slid casually inside a pocket of his trousers.

A fat, sweating photographer in police uniform took another shot of the wreckage and looked toward the road.

Bandez pointed with his cigar and the photographer moved the length of the truck and raised his camera to take shots from a different angle.

Up the steeply inclined road leading back toward the crest of the mountain, an old Indian man leading a donkey laden with a pair of large wooden kegs strapped across the animal's back, stopped at the sight of the wreck and the uniformed police officers working around it. He saw the large man with long black hair hanging down past his shoulders step out of the trees behind the Jeeps. The old man quickly ran his hand up and down and across his chest in the sign of the cross, then tugged on the donkey's bridle, pulling the animal off the side of the road into the undergrowth, where they disappeared from sight.

At the wreck, Bandez looked across his shoulder as the large man came past the Jeeps toward the side of the road. He had the facial features of a Caucasian, but the straight black hair of an Indian. Around forty years of age, he was tanned a dark brown, wearing sandals, baggy trousers, and a leather vest open across his wide chest. A scarf was wrapped across his head and under his chin, with the last couple feet of the material draped back across his shoulder. Underneath the scarf, a side of his face was swollen from his head to his chin. A glazed, unseeing eye stared blankly from that side of his face. He walked to Bandez's side.

"Mi Aurondo," Bandez said.

Aurondo didn't return the greeting, but only stared toward the wreck as a pair of officers caught the tarpaulin at its ends, lifted Manuel's body off the ground and carried it toward the Jeeps.

Aurondo brought his eye back from the tarpaulin to the wide, chalky-blue stone he had slammed down through Manuel's raised hands the night before. He spoke in Spanish to Bandez. Bandez called to the photographer and pointed at the stone.

The photographer turned his face in the direction Bandez pointed, set his camera down and moved to the stone. He leaned and caught it by its jagged ends, strained as he lifted it from the ground, then walked to the edge of a deep gully running behind the trees.

He lifted the heavy weight above his head and, with an effort causing him to grunt, heaved it in an arching trajectory out over the edge of the gully.

The stone made a low thud as it hit against the side of the steeply inclined slope, then bounced, bounced once more, and rolled out of sight into the thick weeds at the bottom of the gully.

The photographer looked back at Bandez and Aurondo, stared a moment at the bulging scarf, but lowered his gaze when he saw Aurondo's eye staring back at him.

A few miles away, a door creaked in the wind.

It swung partially open from a solitary door frame that stood in stark contrast to the fallen, charred blocks that had once been a wall of the Post Medical Clinic.

Inside the ruins of the clinic, another doorway still contained by the building's original interior walls, now blackened and covered with vines, led to a room lit dimly by sunlight pouring in through a jagged hole in the tin roof.

A shaft of light shined down on six silver crosses arranged in a circle atop a small cabinet. In the center of the circle, the surgical instruments were heaped in a small pile again.

Underneath them lay the charred bundle of envelopes, tied again with a piece of twine, back in their resting place once more.

The return address on the top envelope said simply, MARY.

CHAPTER 6

Ross stepped from the airline terminal into the humidity of the Deep South in August. The feeling was not unfamiliar. On the flight from Los Angeles, he had thought about how he should be pleased he had a reason to return to New Orleans, that he should be looking forward to it—but he wasn't.

He took a cab to the Tulane University Hospital and Clinic and was let out at the La Salle Street entrance. After asking directions from a half dozen nurses, being questioned by a security guard, and riding up and down elevators, he found his father outside the surgical wing on the building's third floor. His tall frame was dressed in the green scrubs Ross pictured him in every time he thought of him—in fact, he couldn't visualize the man who had raised him alone since he was seven in anything else.

His father glanced down the hallway and saw him then. The nurse looked down the hall, too. But she saw only a dark-haired young man she hadn't seen before, and she started speaking to Dr. Benjamin Channing again.

And Dr. Benjamin Channing turned back to listen.

He hadn't seen his son in three years, and still he turned back to the nurse. Of course Ross knew they had to be speaking about something important. It always was important. For, after all, his father was one of the premier neurosurgeons in the country. Ross had even seen his photograph in the *Los Angeles Times* once, displayed over an article about a new technique for treating certain aneurysms. Ross walked toward them.

His father turned to meet him as the nurse walked away. "Son," his father said in a friendly voice. Friendly, polite, very important—his father.

"You must have business in town," his father said. Ross shook his hand. His father's grasp was firm, manly, proper. They hadn't seen each other in three years and the greeting was "You must have business in town."

His father glanced at his watch. "If you're staying the night, I'll try to arrange it so I can take you out to dinner."

Try to arrange it, Ross thought. Never a total commitment—something important might come up. *Damn, why do I always do this to myself?* Ross thought. "That would be nice, Dad."

"What are you here for?"

"I'm trying to find some information on a doctor that possibly graduated from the medical school."

"I'm certain Alumni Relations will have anything you wish to know. In fact, I have a few minutes for lunch. Let me take you over to records and see if I can help."

"No, that's okay. It will only take me a little while. One thing you might do is call over there and pave the way for me."

"Certainly."

"I'll be staying at the Monteleone, and if you're able to get free for dinner—"

"Oh, I will," his father said before Ross could finish. "Anywhere in particular you would like to go?"

"I haven't been here in years. You pick it for us."

"Fine, son—I'll leave word."

His father extended his arm again, and again they shook hands. Dr. Benjamin Channing even reached out and clasped his son's elbow warmly as they shook hands. And then, looking back over his shoulder, giving a last polite smile, his father walked away, his pace growing faster with each step he took down the hall. Soon there was a nurse on each side of his tall frame, all of them talking earnestly, rapidly—it was bound to be something important.

Ross knew his father had taken time to call Alumni Relations when the director greeted him at the door to the department. Dr. Benjamin Channing *was* an important name at Tulane. All the records were on computer and it was a simple matter to find Dr. Sebastian Post's student record. He had graduated forty-eight years before. His birth date showed him to be seventy now. He was—or had been—a genius, graduating from high school at sixteen and from the Tulane undergraduate program at eighteen. He had taken the full four years for medical school and spent four years in residency, a practicing gynecologist at twenty-six. Ross pulled a memo pad over and copied Post's social security number as the director watched with an expression that approached an unapproving look across his round face. But nobody connected with the medical center was going to object to anything Ross did, or even ask him a question; not the son of Dr. Benjamin Channing. Not after Dr. Channing himself had called to pave the way.

Ross thanked the director and asked where he might use a telephone. The short little man offered his own personal line in his office, and stood politely outside the door as Ross pushed in the numbers.

The call was to Los Angeles, to a longtime friend in the IRS's Problem Resolution Office there.

"Ted, I need a little help."

And he gave his friend Dr. Sebastian Post's name, date of birth, and social security number.

It only took a few minutes for Ted to run the information through the IRS's computer database. "Ross, I can't find him anywhere. He's not filing tax returns, receiving social security payments or disability checks, or on welfare. Last known address is a long time back, forty-four years ago—New Orleans. Will that help?"

Ross knew it wouldn't. Estelita had said Manuel told her Post arrived in Mexico forty years before. Based on what Ted had said, forty-four years must have been when Post actually left for there, or for somewhere on his way there—as soon as he had finished his residency.

And nothing of record showing him back in the United States since. Did that mean he hadn't survived his burns, or had, but hadn't returned to his home country?

As a last bit of work, Ross used the director's small Sharp Z-57II copier to copy Dr. Post's photograph from a yearbook in the office's collection, and walked toward the door. He would check into the Monteleone and give Manuel another few hours to call. If the doctor had died of his burns, there was no need to search further. There would be no "horse's mouth" to talk to.

MOUNTAINS OUTSIDE TAXCO

It was still bright daylight when the Jeep drove off the narrow dirt road and nearly up to the wooden door of the small dwelling with its mud-block walls. A tarpaulin wrapped into a thick roll and bound with cord was pushed out of the Jeep to thud against the dry ground.

The wooden door flew open. Tony's mother saw the two Indians driving off—and the rolled tarpaulin lying in the dirt a few feet in front of her.

Her hands came to her mouth. She stared wide-eyed at the tarpaulin—then ran to it.

She yanked at the cord around one end. It pulled loose. She threw a loop of the tarpaulin back.

The blackened, shriveled face of her son stared with empty eye sockets toward the sky, his teeth burned a yellow brown against the charred black skin of his face.

"*Tonnnnito!*"

NEW ORLEANS

Ross rested his head against the pillow doubled up against the headboard in his hotel room. His father hadn't called about dinner yet. He doubted he would. *Something important came up.*

That's how it had been ever since his mother died. His father keeping the hours a neurosurgeon must in his residency, there were literally weeks at a time when he didn't see him. A series of baby-sitters had become both his father and mother, except for an occasional quick call from the hospital. The residency had eventually ended, but Ross remembered not being able to tell it by the hours his father was home. Dr. Benjamin Channing was already developing his reputation then— a man never too tired to assist when he had no case of his own, no matter how many hours he had already spent in surgery. And what neurosurgeon with a particularly difficult case wouldn't want Dr. Channing by his side during surgery?

Maybe I wouldn't be so bitter, Ross thought, if his father had just said, *No, I'm sorry, son, but I won't have time to do that with you.* But he never did. He always promised. *Yes, we'll go fishing this weekend, son. Yes, duck season starts next week. Yes, I would like to see that movie, too.* But he never did. Always another important case.

The summers were easiest, Ross remembered, his father simply putting him on a plane to another summer camp. At least that way there were no expectations for eight to ten weeks at a time. He had turned one summer camp stay in Mexico into a year's additional residence as an exchange student at a high school in Durango. That's where he had met Manuel. He remembered thinking at the time what reason did he have to go back to New Orleans? He didn't.

Now he closed his eyes and tried to force the negative thoughts from his mind. In a way, they weren't fair. His dad had provided him with everything a father was supposed to provide, and more—except for his time. And how could Ross condemn him for that?—there were no doubt dozens of people alive now who wouldn't be except for the highly dedicated Dr. Channing. How could Ross even think about endangering even one of those lives for time with his father—even when he was a little boy, scared because his mother was dead, and lonely, wanting to be loved?

"Damn!" Ross mumbled aloud, and sat up. What a pansy ass, he thought, whining like a baby. It was done now anyway, and something done couldn't be undone. And he *wouldn't* change a single thing his father had done for his patients. Ross only hoped that if anything happened to him he would be cared for by a doctor equally as dedicated. The telephone rang. He lifted the receiver to his ear. "Yes?"

"Ross, it's Estelita. I still haven't heard from Manuel. I'm starting to worry."

"He has his cellular phone with him?"

"He doesn't answer it."

"There are a lot of hospitals there, Estelita, he just hasn't found the right one yet."

MOUNTAINS OUTSIDE TAXCO

Tony's mother leaned forward from her knees, digging alternately with the blade of a hoe and her hands, digging in the soft dirt next to the creek Tony loved to hear running, coughing and digging and crying. Tony's body, now wrapped in the best blanket they owned, lay

CHAPTER 7

M_r. Channing, you have a message from Dr. Benjamin Channing. He said he would meet you for dinner at Emeril's at nine."

Even though Ross arrived at the famed restaurant fifteen minutes early, his father was already seated at a table. That surprised Ross. That his father was actually there, whether late or early, surprised him even more. A bottle of Caymus cabernet sauvignon had already been ordered. That was surprising, too. His father almost never drank—in those infrequent times he was away from the hospital he could be called back at any moment. The wine was a thought-out gesture to the homecoming, Ross knew. Maybe a gesture of a lonely man. His father had to be lonely, twenty-five years with his wife gone, and over ten years since his son had lived close by.

"I'm going to have the red snapper," his father said.

Ross ordered a steak.

"How did your search go?"

"Not very well."

"What were you looking for?"

"I'm trying to locate a Dr. Sebastian Post. He graduated from here nearly fifty years ago, before anyone on the present faculty was here."

"But not before Jerome was here."

"Who?"

"Jerome Pettus, a maintenance man—a janitor."

His father explained as they drove toward Jerome T. Pettus's home, "He showed up at the medical school as a fifteen-year-old kid needing a job to keep from starving. He was there for the next sixty years. Totally uneducated, I don't know if he even finished grade school. Yet I doubt very few students passed through the medical school with any more innate intelligence—I never believed in a photographic memory until I met Jerome. He slept in a boiler room on campus to save paying rent; kept every penny close by. Invested in small parcels of woodlands here and there. Makes his living now from a mixture of timber sales and oil and gas royalties from wells that ended up being drilled on the property."

They turned into a driveway laid out in a wide, half-moon-shaped circle fronting a two-story modern Colonial. Gas lights flared to each side of an arched antique door at the front of the mansion. Jerome, his thin body clad in a soft blue robe over bright red silk pajamas, opened the door a moment after they rang the doorbell.

He had thick white eyebrows highlighting a lean, smooth face and a head covered with equally thick white hair.

"Dr. Channing," he said in a pleasant voice. He looked at Ross.

"This is my son, Ross Channing."

"Pleased to meet you, boy," Jerome said, extending his hand.

Ross clasped it. The old man's grip was firm, but

gentle at the same time. His hands were permanently callused from his decades of work.

"You're here because somebody needs to know where a line runs," Pettus said and smiled. "Happens all the time, always someone coming over from the school wanting to know where a line runs. I knows where 'em all runs in every building—plumbing, electrical, all of it. Was there as they installed most of 'em. I'm older'n about anything they haves there 'ceptin' the original buildings."

"And remembers every student who ever graduated," Ross's father said.

"Keeps 'em right here," Jerome said, touching his forefinger to a side of his head, "and in my heart—most of 'ems."

"Ross is trying to find information on a Dr. Sebastian Post who graduated from here nearly fifty years ago."

Ross saw his father's eyes come around to his. "Son, did he do his residency here?"

"Did," Pettus said.

Ross's eyes went back to Pettus's. "You remember him?"

"Couldn't hardly keep from it. Was a genius. I mean not like those students who just could memorize things and make an A, but a man who could sure enough think as well as top'n his class."

"I'm trying to locate him."

"Can't say I can help you none there, boy. You all come on in—mosquitos coming in the door."

Inside the house the marble tile of the entry corridor spread back toward a large main living area furnished with a mixture of overstuffed furniture and fine antiques.

Jerome waited for them to seat themselves on a long couch, then settled into a leather recliner across from them. He kicked off his houseshoes and leaned back in the chair, crossing his ankles as his feet were lifted into the air. "Nary was another student come through the school I'd pick with such smarts," he said, nodding his head, obviously impressed with his memory of Dr. Post. "Specifically remember him because he was 'bout as poor as I was. Dr. Branch took a shining to him is 'bout the only way he graduated. Ran out of money for tuition after'n he had been here awhile, was 'bout to head back home. Dr. Branch gives him a job teaching in the lab to students a year behind him. 'Stead of paying him, they let the teachin' pay his tuition. Couldn't do that now what with all them government rules and unions, but could then. Did. And he was good at teachin'. Bet them students learned more 'bout lab under him than any been taught by any of the professors been here. That is 'ceptin' you, of course, Dr. Channing."

Ross's father smiled politely. "Probably me, too."

"Dr. Sebastian Post," Jerome said, "remember him well. Now to where he's practicing at the moment—iffen he is, he'd be in his sixties now—no, right near seventy. Time goes by, don't it? Went to Mexico right after his residency, you know—gonna treat those Indians free. That's another thing he was, too—a man always thinking 'bout helping others, he was. Didn't have no money, but he had a doctor's license then. That's where he went."

"There was a fire at his clinic there years ago," Ross said. "He was badly burned. I'm trying to find where in the States he came back to—if he survived."

"Oh, he survived, Mr. Channing."

Ross was taken aback at the certain tone in Jerome's voice. "How do you know?"

" 'Causin' I seen Mary a few years back—and she didn't have nary a word about him being gone. Mary Alexander Walker—she worshipped Dr. Post. Fact she was going to follow him down there to Mexico when she graduated. She was a couple of years behind him in school. But weren't behind him none in how she thought. Like two peas in a pod, they was, when it came to wanting to help people. When you'd see her, that's all she would go on about—helping them poor Indians that nobody else gave a care to. If Dr. Post was dead she would have said something 'bout it, if he was, and if she known 'bout it, that is. And she would've known 'bout it, if you known Mary like I does."

"Where did you see her?"

"Biloxi. I was driving out of Boomtown Casino. Little gambling to keep my mind sharp. Had to stop to keep from running over her crossing the street. Mary, she looked right at me without recognizing me. Says she did when I told her who'n I was, but she didn't—I could tell. Now I don't mean she weren't smart, too, she was. Smart as any of the doctors graduatin' from the school, though she attended nursing school rather than medical."

"She was a nurse?"

"Still is, Mr. Channing. Just like being a doctor. Once you is, you always is—'ceptin' maybe a couple over the years got in drug trouble and lost out. Only thing is, she looked kinda worse for wear, not like a nurse or a doctor's wife dresses—that is, if she married Dr. Post— and I wouldn't be at all surprised if she ended up marrying him. Worshipped him, she did. 'Course I didn't think to ask her if she had, before she told me she had to run on—about marrying him that is—so I don't—"

As Pettus paused, his white eyebrows knitted. He shook his head at whatever passed through his mind. "Here I am going on like I'm some kind of smart myself, and that don't even occur to me—she said she was visiting when I asked her. She and Dr. Post were both from the Biloxi, Gulfport area come originally. Iffen she was visiting, then whoever she was visiting would know where she's visiting from, wouldn't they?"

CHAPTER 8

Ross awoke early and took a cab from the Monteleone to the LSU School of Nursing, where Jerome said Mary's records would be. It took only a few minutes on the computer to find Mary Alexander Walker. She had graduated two years after Dr. Post had finished his residency at the medical center. Her birth date showed she would be sixty-four. Ross copied her social security number and used a pay telephone in a hallway at the school to call Ted at the Problem Resolution office in Los Angeles.

"No tax return, no social security checks, nothing," Ted said. "Last known address is Gulfport, Mississippi—but it's forty-two years old."

The length of time since she had graduated from the nursing school. So she had wasted no time in leaving for Mexico to join Post. And no record—at least that the IRS had—showing she had ever come back to the States. No record Post had come back—if he had died of his burns the lack of records would be understandable. But Jerome had seen Mary.

Ross wrote down her last address in Gulfport.

Then he found a worn yearbook containing her photograph.

He stared at her distinguishing facial characteristic, a prominent nose jutting out from a thin face—then made a copy of the photograph.

He rented a brown Ford Taurus. The trip to Gulfport took less than an hour and a half via the interstate. The first casino he saw was the Gulfport Grand, rising high into the air on the beach in front of the dark waters of the Mississippi Sound. He had heard the Mississippi Gulf Coast was now third only to Las Vegas and Atlantic City in gaming, with one after another of the multimillion-dollar casinos rising along the white sand beaches fronting the Sound. But he hadn't been in the area since he was a boy, when the coast as he remembered it had been little more than a series of small towns, fish-processing factories, and sleepy fishing marinas. Mary's last known address was now occupied by an older couple. They had purchased the house from a younger couple who had lived there three or four years after buying it from a retired Air Force colonel who had lived there for more than a decade. The couple didn't have the slightest idea who had owned the house before the colonel—and had never heard of a Mary Alexander Walker or a Dr. Sebastian Post. Ross drove to the Holiday Inn on the beach and went to the bank of pay phones past the lobby.

The telephone directory included the entire Mississippi coastal area. It didn't contain a listing for a Mary Walker or a Mary Post or a Sebastian Post, doctor or otherwise. In all there were about a dozen Walkers and Posts combined and he tried them in turn, but none were relatives of a Mary Walker or a Dr. Post, nor had they ever heard of either one of them.

The information operator told him she didn't have an unlisted number for either a Post or a Walker.

His next stop was at the Gulfport Public Works Department. The list of water and sewer connections listed to either a Walker or Post matched the names he had already seen in the telephone directory.

At the Biloxi Public Works Department in Gulfport's neighboring city, there was a new name, a water and sewer connection to the home of a Mary Post who hadn't been listed in the telephone directory.

A city street map he purchased at a service station lying in his lap, he found the address down a side road close to Keesler Air Force Base. A young woman dressed in sweatpants and a T-shirt watered the shrubbery at the front of a small brick house. She turned toward him as he parked at the curb and walked across the freshly mowed lawn.

"Ma'am."

She smiled a greeting.

"I'm looking for the residence of a Mary Post or a Sebastian Post?"

"I'm Mary Post."

"There wouldn't happen to be another Mary Post here—your mother or your grandmother, maybe?"

"My mother is Mona Post, and she lives in San Francisco. My grandmother's been dead for over fifteen years."

MEXICO CITY, MEXICO

Estelita had become concerned that Manuel still hadn't telephoned. Now she feared she had reason for concern. She stared at Police Captain Bandez's identification card. He stood in front of her desk. Dressed in jeans, western boots, and a loose white shirt open at the neck, he had one hand slipped casually inside his trouser pocket. She handed the card back to him.

He asked her again who sent Manuel to the Taxco area.

Manuel under arrest, she thought, that must be what's happened with a member of the Federal Police from the rural area outside of Taxco questioning me. But under arrest for what?

"*Señorita*," Bandez said, growing impatient.

She shook her head and told him she didn't know who had hired Manuel.

Bandez's expression tightened.

Manuel in a jail cell, she thought, waiting for me to do something. Manuel had friends in the government. She reached for the telephone at a side of her desk.

Bandez's hand came out of his pocket and covered her hand on the receiver.

Her eyes widening, she stared at the hand, swollen and misshapen with fingers as bloated as thick sausages.

Behind Bandez, a large man with long black hair hanging down across his shoulders stepped through the doorway into the office. She stared at the scarf, at the bulge on one side of his face.

She came up out of her chair. Bandez held her wrist. She tried to pull loose from him, but couldn't. He jerked her to him. Her scream was cut off by the meaty softness of his hand clamping across her mouth.

The tall man came around the desk. He stopped in front of her. She looked into his face and felt stark terror.

"His name is Aurondo," Bandez whispered in Spanish into her ear.

Aurondo's hand came up to her throat. He dug his forefinger and thumb into her skin and jammed them upward, nearly lifting her off of her feet, causing an excruciating pain under her jaw. Bandez's mouth whispered against her ear again. She would tell them who hired Manuel, or die.

She whimpered, tried to shake her head. But Aurondo's grip was like that of a granite statue. The fingers dug deeper. Her shoes barely touched the floor. And then they didn't as he lifted her into the air. The pain shot down her spine as her neck tried to stretch.

She couldn't breathe. She kicked. Her feet hit harmlessly against Aurondo's thick legs. His face began to spin through her blurring vision. Her shoe came off. Aurondo released his pressure.

Her feet touched the floor. Her breath returned with a whistling sound through her constricted windpipe. Aurondo's face was close to hers, his glazed eye, fixed and unmoving, dead on the swollen side of his face, directly in front of one of her eyes, his seeing eye staring into her other eye.

He didn't say anything, but she knew that the next time he tightened his fingers he wouldn't stop until her body was lifeless. Tears ran down her cheeks. She pointed with her finger toward the Rolodex on her desk. Bandez came around from behind her and took it into his hand. He looked back at her.

She didn't want to, but she was scared. Her throat hurt, the eye stared into hers. "Ross Channing," she whimpered.

She felt Aurondo's hand tighten. Her eyes widened as he began to lift her off the floor. She threw her hands at his face, tried to dig her fingernails into his eyes.

Bandez pulled the card from the Rolodex and stared at it.

ROSS CHANNING
McLaurin/Channing—Bail Bonds/Process Servers
Los Angeles, California

To Bandez's side, Aurondo slammed Estelita into the wall, pulled her back toward him, and slammed her into the wall again.

BILOXI

Ross stopped the Taurus against the curb in front of a house two streets over from Boomtown Casino, the casino Jerome Pettus had been leaving when he saw Mary. All the narrow streets in the area were similar, lined with small houses occupied by a multiracial community; whites, blacks, Vietnamese, and an occasional Hispanic. No one he had asked had ever heard of a Mary Alexander Walker or a Sebastian Post. He opened the Taurus's door and stepped outside. An older woman trimming the bushes at the front of her narrow house looked at him as he walked toward her.

"I'm an attorney representing the estate of a Richard Post in California," he said, repeating the same words he had voiced to everyone he had spoken with along the streets.

"There's been a rather substantial inheritance bequeathed to a Mary Post and a Sebastian Post." He showed the woman the copies of the yearbook photographs.

"All I have are these old photographs—they were taken over forty years ago and the parties could look quite different now. But there are distinguishing characteristics, especially the woman—note her prominent nose. There's a five-hundred-dollar reward for anyone who can help us locate either of them."

MEXICO CITY

The squat, old cleaning woman hummed as she came down the third-floor hallway. Through the wide windows at the end of the corridor she could see black clouds forming over the city. She hoped her nephew remembered to bring his car for her when she finished work—she had told him it was going to rain. There hadn't been any clouds then, and she hadn't even looked at the weather forecast on TV, but she had a feeling about things like the weather. She smiled at how she could sense things like that, stopped at the suite containing the offices of Detectives y Seguridad Alvarez, and used her key to open the door.

She flicked on the light switch—and her mouth dropped open in shock.

The wall behind the desk at the rear of the reception area was covered with blood splatters. Narrow streaks of the thick liquid had run down toward the floor. Estelita's hosiery-clad, slim legs extended out past a side of the desk. A red high-heeled shoe lay a few feet away. A puddle of blood, turning black as it dried, had run out from under the desk.

HOLIDAY INN BEACHFRONT, GULFPORT, MISSISSIPPI

Ross stepped inside his room, set his suitcase on the floor, and closed the door behind him. He looked out toward the Mississippi Sound's waters sparkling in the moonlight as he pulled the curtains at the front of the room closed.

The telephone rang.

He had just checked in.

He walked to the night table past the bed and lifted the receiver.

"Hello."

"You the one wanting to know about the old lady with the big nose?"

CHAPTER 9

The gray-haired black man pointed his finger out the Taurus's passenger window toward the house. It was an aging, narrow, wood-frame setting in a line of similar houses built close together, two streets over from Boomtown Casino. Past the small front porch, the house's door stood open, and Ross slowed the Taurus as he drove slowly by the shallow yard. He glimpsed a person inside the shadowy interior, but couldn't make out whether it was a man or a woman.

"You can let me out on the corner," the man said. His name was Anderson. He went by his first initials, A.C. He had worked the last forty years at an icehouse a few blocks from the home. He had told Ross that he had seen the old white woman with the prominent nose when she had come to buy ice after the power company turned her electricity off. Ross didn't know how the man found her home—he just hoped his luck was about to change.

He turned the Taurus around at the street's intersection with Bayview Avenue to start back down the line of houses. A.C. reached for the handle to his door—and held out his other hand for the reward money.

"I'm going to have to see if she's who I'm looking for first," Ross said.

A.C. moved his hand from the door handle. "Now, boy, how am I going to know if she's not the one or you just say she's not?"

"If I go inside to talk to her, you'll know she is, A.C."

As Ross approached the house again, he guided the Taurus toward the curb. No movement could be seen through the open door now.

It suddenly closed.

"Don't count against me none if she won't talk to you," A.C. said. "If she is the right one."

Ross stopped the Taurus and stepped outside. As he started across the lawn, the smell of salt from the nearby Gulf filled his nostrils. From the porch of a similar house only a few feet from the one he approached, an old Vietnamese woman in a rocking chair stared at him. He nodded a greeting toward her, and she turned her face away.

He came up the steps in front of him and knocked on the door.

After a moment with no response, he knocked again. He could see by the raised windows to the sides of the porch that the house was now completely darkened inside.

He knocked again.

The woman on the porch next door was looking at him again.

He turned the doorknob, felt the door begin to open. Whoever had closed it, hadn't thought to use the lock. He stepped to the side of the door and inched it open.

"Excuse me, I need to speak with you, please."

Still no response. He moved farther to the side, where he wouldn't be in plain view of the doorway—possibly a target. He pushed the door gently open.

His gaze swept across a small living room illuminated only by the moonlight filtering into the house through the raised windows. Then he saw them. From the shadowy entrance of a hall at the rear of the room, a heavy-set woman in a loose dress hanging below her knees stared back at him. A thin man wearing a robe sat in a wheelchair beside her.

"Dr. Post? Mrs. Post?"

With his eyes beginning to adjust to the darkness, Ross could make them out better. The man had white hair hanging down across his forehead. They didn't move.

"Dr. Post?"

"Go away, please," the woman said in a voice so low he could barely hear it.

Ross ran his hand up the wall inside the doorway, found a light switch, and flicked it on. A bare overhead bulb in the living room ceiling flashed to life, framing the couple in its sudden light as if it were a flashbulb.

Ross didn't need to reach into his pocket and pull out the copies of the yearbook photographs to be certain. There was no doubt—the ages were what they should be, the man in his seventies, the woman in her mid-sixties, her prominent nose, the brown hair she had in her photograph still obvious, though now heavily streaked with gray. A side of Dr. Post's face was matted with scar tissue that appeared a dead, dull gray against his pale complexion—he had been burned, and burned badly. They kept staring at him—waiting for him to do something. He had pushed the door open silently like a thief—or worse.

"I apologize, but the door came open when I touched it. I've been sent here to ask you about your experiments in Mexico, Dr. Post."

Post, who had been partially bent forward in the wheelchair, staring blankly, his mouth gaping slightly, as if unable to comprehend what was going on, narrowed his eyes. Mary laid her hand on his shoulder.

"Sent by whom?" she said. Her voice was still so low Ross could barely hear it.

"A person in Los Angeles is interested in what you did." Ross looked at the shabby surroundings in front of him—a worn couch, an easy chair that tilted to the side, a straight-back chair in front of a card table set up as a dining table next to a kitchen the size of a walk-in closet. The heat inside the house was stifling. There was obviously no air-conditioning, not even a window unit he could see. Mary was a nurse. Even with Dr. Post too disabled to work, she could make more than an adequate living for the both of them. At least enough where they wouldn't have to live like this.

"A person in Los Angeles?" Mary questioned.

"Yes." Ross looked at the shabby furnishings again. "And I think there will be some money in it for you if—"

Post's sudden loud voice was almost startling. "Stories. Crazy stories. Cra—" He had to take a deep breath. He shook his head, gasped, took another deep breath, the sound audible as the air slipped down his throat. "Crazy," he said in a much lower voice. "Leave here now."

"Doctor, I, uh—"

"Leave here now," Mary said. Her voice was still low. But now she took a step forward. She hesitated a moment, then walked slowly but determinedly across the worn carpet toward Ross.

He backed up as she raised her hand as if she were going to push against his chest.

"We operated a child-care clinic in Mexico," she said, "nothing more. Leave us alone."

Her voice had dropped even lower now that she was close to him. He could barely hear it.

She still held her palm up, pressuring him backward. He saw her wedding band, silver and imprinted with small squares. She caught the edge of the door and pushed it shut in his face.

The light inside the house went off, its glow disappearing from the windows. Ross heard a cough come from the old man, then his low moan, in a raspy tone.

Anderson waited on the sidewalk with his hand held out.

Ten minutes later, Ross talked on a telephone at a service station off Highway 90. He told Bailey about finding Dr. Post, that the man had a wife who had been at the clinic with him, and that they were living in virtual poverty.

"She's wearing a design of wedding band I've seen in Mexico," he added. "I'm going back there in the morning to try again. I don't think it's going to do any good. But if I get them to say anything I want to know exactly what you want to know."

"No, you don't go back," Bailey said. "*I'll* talk to them. I'm taking the first flight out of here."

CHAPTER 10

The first flight out of Los Angeles wasn't quick enough, and any commercial airliner would have had to land in New Orleans, with Bailey having to drive the rest of the way to Biloxi. So she came in a private aircraft. Ross watched the blinking lights on the sleek Learjet LR-25 as it made its approach from over the Mississippi Sound. He wondered what the trip from California cost. A hundred times the price of a commercial airline ticket? He didn't guess that really mattered to a woman who had ranked thirty-second on the *Forbes* celebrity top earners list the year before. He remembered reading she had made thirty million in the previous twelve months the magazine article had covered. As the jet taxied across the tarmac, he walked to meet the craft. The pilot held the door open for Bailey. She stepped outside, dressed in jeans and a loose red blouse.

"Let's go," she said, walking past him.

He turned and looked after her, but didn't move.

She stopped. "Well?"

"It's still an hour until dawn. I don't think they'd be happy to see us right now."

* * *

* * *

They ate breakfast at the Waffle House on the beach in Biloxi. Between bites of pancake, Ross said, "What's so important you had to come in here during the night?"

"I don't waste time," Bailey said, not answering his question. She sipped her coffee.

"Is it because you're trying to get to him before someone else does?" he asked.

Bailey looked at him strangely. "What?"

"You wanted to know about the legend," he said. "You wanted it from the horse's mouth. I found him and now you want to talk to him yourself. I was wondering if this has anything to do with movie rights."

Bailey frowned and shook her head. "I was just starting to think you had some brains."

He stared at her. She took another sip of coffee, then raised her eyes back to his. "Why aren't you an MD?"

When he didn't respond immediately, she said, "Your grades were tops in college."

This time he couldn't help but smile a little. "What did that information cost you?"

She sipped from her cup again—and waited for an answer.

"When I started college I told my father I didn't want to be a doctor. He said it was because the years of studying seemed like an unending time to me at that age. He said if I would go ahead and keep a grade point average high enough to be admitted to medical school, he would accept whatever decision I made at that time. I was accepted at Tulane. I told him I still didn't want to go."

Bailey nodded. "And so you became the black sheep of the family—your grandfather and your father were both doctors."

He smiled again. "On which side?"

"Your grandfather? On your mother's side. Your other grandfather was a professor. Why didn't you go on?"

The waitress leaned to refresh their coffee. He nodded his thanks. Bailey said, "No, thank you."

The waitress nodded, stared a brief moment at Bailey, and then walked away from the table. After a few steps, she looked back across her shoulder.

"I asked you why you didn't go on to medical school," Bailey said.

"Because I didn't want to do what doctors do."

She didn't have the faintest idea what he meant, but she didn't ask him to explain, instead simply said, "And so you ended up a bail bondsman?"

"That's how I paid my way through law school."

"What did you do before that?"

"I had a friend in Mexico—Manuel, the one who found the information for you—his father was the police chief in Durango. I worked for him part-time. I went to Los Angeles for him and ended up staying there."

"And you didn't make it as a movie star."

"That wasn't one of the options I was considering."

"So now you're a lawyer."

"If I passed the bar exam. You don't happen to know my score on that?"

"Why that option?"

"Because I can be my own boss, I guess, plan my schedule around anything I want to do—whenever I want."

"Mr. Independent, huh? Why aren't you married?"

"This conversation is getting a little one-sided," he said. He noticed that the waitress who had refreshed their coffee was now standing by the cash register with a magazine open in her hands. The cashier looked at a page the waitress pointed to, then raised her eyes toward their table, nodded, and said something to the waitress. They both grinned, then the waitress carried the magazine toward another waitress a few feet away.

"You ever cared about anybody?" Bailey asked.

"A couple of times, sort of."

"Sort of?"

"Yeah, sort of." He saw the two waitresses now coming toward the table. Each held a ballpoint pen in one hand and a glamour magazine in the other.

"Autograph time," he said.

Bailey was surprisingly gracious, not only autographing her photograph in the magazines, but inscribing a short personal note across the top of the page for each of the women.

They waited until shortly after eight A.M.

Bailey stepped from the Taurus and he came around to join her as they walked toward the small porch. From the house next door there was the sound of a baby crying, and the soft accent of a woman speaking in Vietnamese to the child.

Bailey sprang lightly up the steps in front of her and started to knock on the door as it opened.

Mary, wearing the same loose dress she had the night before, stepped back from the doorway. Bailey stepped inside and Ross followed her.

Dr. Post had his wheelchair at a vantage point beside the window. He had seen them coming. He pulled the collar of his robe tighter around his thin neck. His gray hair hung down nearly to his eyebrows.

Bailey said, "I'm sorry to disturb you unannounced, but I didn't know any other—"

Mary didn't let her finish. Speaking in the same low voice she had the night before, her words barely perceptible even in the deep silence inside the house, she said, "We did perform in vitro fertilizations on Indian women who weren't able to conceive children. There were some deformities at birth, quite apart from the in vitro fertilization, but these were superstitious people we were dealing with. They became convinced that the children came from demons."

A wheezing sound came from Dr. Post. He had fitted an oxygen mask over his mouth and was breathing deeply into it. Ross hadn't noticed the mask last night. Two oxygen tanks were strapped to the rear of the wheelchair.

Bailey spoke now, looking directly at Dr. Post as she did. "I've communicated with Dr. Gerardo Samora who treated you for your burns in Mexico City, doctor. He said you told him you had mastered the process of out-of-womb birth. He said he didn't think such a procedure possible yet, but that you made a strong case for the technique you said you used."

Mary now stared at Bailey. Dr. Post moved the oxygen mask from his mouth. His thin, gnarled hands worked in his lap, opening a small bottle. It was an aspirin bottle. He shook several of the white tablets into his palm and moved them into his mouth, his narrow jaw moving up and down as he swallowed them.

Bailey said, "I've also spoken to a researcher in California. He said if there was a proper blood supply, nutrients, some way to contain the placenta in a weightless state, that such a procedure would be feasible. In fact he said it *will* be feasible—soon. He said there is animal experimentation on such a procedure taking place at the moment. You're dying of emphysema from the fire scarring your lungs . . ." At Bailey's sudden cold statement, Ross looked at her.

"Where did you get money for your oxygen tanks?" she continued, still looking at Dr. Post. "Brought your life savings with you from Mexico?"

As Bailey paused, she glanced around the small room at the shabby furnishings. "Not much money left, is there?" she said. "Not much—if any."

Now she looked at Mary, but continued addressing Dr. Post. "Your wife's going to take care of you until the last moment. Then when you're gone she's going to go off and starve. I'll pay you *one hundred thousand dollars* to fertilize one of my eggs and bring a child to term outside my body."

Ross stared at her.

Dr. Post glanced up at Mary. Her expression hadn't changed.

"And if it's a successful birth," Bailey said, looking back at Dr. Post, "I'll purchase an annuity that will pay her fifty thousand dollars a year every year for the rest of her life. By doing what I ask, you can pay her back for taking care of you. By doing something I *know* you can do."

Post raised his eyes toward Mary again, this time holding his stare. She shook her head no. Post breathed deeply from the oxygen mask. His hand trembled. He lowered the mask.

"Yes," he said.

"No," Mary said.

A tired expression crossed Post's face as he stared up at her. "What difference does it make if I die tomorrow?"

Mary shook her head. "No, Sebastian."

"I want to help you, Mary—please."

Mary continued to stare down at him for a long moment, then, slowly, she raised her face. Her voice was still low, so low it was hard to hear, but her words were clear. "I want fifty thousand dollars for Sebastian, too, each year he's alive." She looked down at Post, and then raised her face again.

"It will be a successful birth."

CHAPTER 11

Ross and Bailey stepped out onto the small porch of Dr. Post and Mary's home and the door closed behind them. The couple had asked to be alone to talk something over. Ross looked at Bailey walking toward the far side of the porch. She gazed over the houses across the street in the direction of the bright lights above Boomtown Casino while she pulled a pack of cigarettes from her purse. Not a movie idea, Ross thought, but something she actually believed possible. Something the old woman said was possible, said they would do.

"Bailey."

As he walked toward her, she turned in his direction, used a silver lighter from her purse to light her cigarette, took a puff from it, and held it up by her shoulder.

"Bailey, something like they're talking about . . ." He shook his head. "Can you imagine if such a breakthrough ever was possible the amount of research there would have to be behind it, dozens of scientists, millions of dollars, the most modern state-of-the-art medical facility? Post had a small clinic in the mountains. The electricity probably had to come from a generator—if the place even had electricity. They might even had to have their water carried in."

Bailey shook her head in disagreement. "The basic concept is simple."

"Simple? Lady, you have to be out of your mind."

Her voice stayed level. "The concept, Ross. I met Dr. Presnell at a party—Rollin Presnell, the researcher I mentioned to Dr. Post. I thought the story was as crazy as you do. But Dr. Presnell said that everything that's needed for a successful pregnancy, whether you're talking about a pregnancy formed inside the body or outside of it, is contained in the fertilized egg. The fetus ends up with its own circulatory system and the placenta is formed from the egg material as a reaction after the fertilization. All that's needed for the fetus to grow outside the body is a way to give it nutrients, oxygen, and a manner of waste removal. He said scientists have known all the requirements for artificial birth for decades."

"You going to hang the embryo from a tree?"

"The placenta will be contained in fluid, to cushion it, where it can be kept at the proper temperature—I suspect something akin to the composition of salt water from what Dr. Samora in Mexico City said Post told him."

Salt water? He now felt he was looking at one of those celebrities talking about their past lives as kings and queens. There was about as much likelihood of that being possible as what she was discussing. And what could all of this be for? Narcissism—she didn't want to chance stretch marks, or think of her body swollen with child? The irritation he had felt with her manner since he had first met her was now mounting.

"Ross," she said. Her voice was softer. There was a different look in her eyes. "Ross, really, it's not as crazy as you think. The idea of growing artificial skin is crazy; wouldn't you agree with that? Yet, did you know that scientists now take a tiny piece of skin and have it multiply into a sheet the size of a blanket in a few days, skin that stretches, breathes, absorbs, does everything else skin does—it is skin. It is being used on diabetic patients and others with hard-to-heal wounds. I mean right now. And there's research aimed at shaping this same artificial skin into human organs complete with their own circulatory system. With these organs there will be no rejection problems like there are in organ transplants now. The tissue used to grow the organs will be from the body of the same patient who's going to receive the transplant. Dr. Presnell says it's just around the corner. He says you wouldn't have to shape a complete womb, though. Scientists would only need a section of womb tissue, grown in a medium like they do with artificial skin; a place for the egg cluster to attach. Ten years ago doctors would have said *all* this was impossible, not only the idea of an artificial womb or artificial organs, but even growing skin."

"Bailey, we're talking about thirty or forty years ago when Post would have had to be doing what he claims."

"No, Ross, twenty years ago when they burned his clinic because he produced a demon child. A demon child, Ross. To the Indians in a rural area living much like they did a hundred years ago, a child produced in an artificial womb could seem to be a demon child—it wasn't natural. And as for whether it was twenty or thirty or even fifty years ago when he developed the process, that doesn't make it any less likely he did. How many breakthroughs in science have been made, and it was found out later that scientists years before, even decades before, were on the same course to the same results, but made a wrong turn? If they had made the correct turn we would have had scientific break-throughs years before they were actually made. How can you say that Dr. Post didn't make that correct turn?"

"Bailey, the process of an artificial womb is too com-plicated for someone to simply happen to make the correct turn. It's not where you add chemical A instead of chemical B and get it to work right. You would have to come up with something that could mimic a woman's body."

Bailey took a puff of her cigarette and blew the smoke out to the side. "Or the fertilized egg wouldn't implant, Ross? Is that what you're saying? Okay, why does it implant in a normal pregnancy inside a woman's body? It shouldn't, you know. It's a foreign object. Dr. Presnell talked about that. He said the fertilized egg and the resultant egg cluster contains half of the male's chromosomes, his DNA. Everything the male contributes is foreign to the woman's system. Short of a woman taking anti-rejection drugs like she would have to do if she had a heart or liver or kidney transplant, all pregnancies should be rejected by her body. So if doctors didn't know how pregnancies were formed and somebody asked them if an egg with this foreign male matter in it could coexist within a woman, they'd say no. You're a doctor's son, you know medical science doesn't have all the answers. How many things do doctors warn their patients against one generation and decide those same things are beneficial the next? And why couldn't Dr. Post have made the correct . . ."

Bailey suddenly stopped talking.

She continued to look into his eyes for a moment, then turned her back to him and stared toward the lights of the casino.

"It doesn't matter whether you think it possible or not," she said in a low voice. "It doesn't really matter whether *it is* possible or not. What chance am I taking if it turns out Dr. Post is not capable—we're only talking about an egg—and he can either do it or he can't."

The door opened behind them.

Mary, clutching a thick Bible under her arm, rolled Dr. Post's wheelchair out onto the porch. His thin arms circled a pair of paper grocery sacks stuffed with clothes in his lap. A worn briefcase the size of a small suitcase pressed against his chest. His oxygen mask was in place and Bailey quickly stubbed out her cigarette.

"If we are going to help you, we must leave now," Mary said.

Ross looked at Bailey. She nodded toward the wheel-chair.

Seconds later, he was managing one side of it down the steps while Bailey and Mary struggled to control the other side.

There was some difficulty in getting Dr. Post into the Taurus's passenger seat. His oxygen tanks went beside him. The wheelchair was a foldup kind, and fit into the trunk. Mary and Bailey slipped into the backseat. Mary held Dr. Post's large briefcase across her legs.

As Ross started the car, Dr. Post held a stack of stapled, yellowed sheets of paper toward him.

"We need everything on this list," he said in his breathless voice.

It was a list of medical equipment, and a long list of medicines and chemicals.

Bailey handed Ross a platinum American Express card across the back of the seat.

They were all crazy.

CHAPTER 12

Ross checked Dr. Post and Mary into the Holiday Inn in Biloxi under his name. The first thing Mary did when inside the room was pull the curtains. Dr. Post stared at her until she did. A crazed, reclusive old couple who suffered from agoraphobia, among other things. But, worse, Bailey believed in them.

He tried to talk sense to her one more time when they stepped from the room and started down the walkway toward their rooms. "For the sake of argument," he said, "let's stipulate for the moment that Post can do what he says. If so, why did he jump at your hundred-thousand-dollar offer? A hundred thousand dollars would be nothing to what he could have already made. Think of how many women are unable to bear a child because of diabetes, women with hypertension who can't take the chance, lots of reasons. After the clinic fire, Post might have been too physically disabled to perform such procedures himself, but he could have taught others; there would have been a way for him to have earned a great deal of money in licensing the procedures, maybe even patenting the process. Don't you think something's wrong here that he didn't—that this is a con job?"

"I'm not paying him anything until the baby is born," Bailey said.

"They're going to eat better."

"So if I'm wrong, I donated food to someone who needed it. That's not all that bad. But I'm not wrong," she added. "And, by the way, they're not hiding out from some con they pulled on anybody else, either. Mary said Dr. Post suffers anxiety if she doesn't keep the house dark. He can be set off by noise, almost anything."

Ross's first thought had been of a con being perpetrated by the couple. Bailey had stumbled unexpectedly into their house like an insect tumbling down into a ground spider's pit and they had jumped at the chance. But he thought of something worse, too.

"Bailey, what if Post really can do what he says— halfway?"

"What do you mean?"

"What if, as crazy as it seems, he did come up with a way to perform an out-of-womb birth, but the procedure was only partially perfected—and couldn't be perfected any further. That would be a reason he wouldn't have licensed it. You remember what I said Manuel told Estelita—the whole story could be traced to a rash of children born with deformities from Indian women under Dr. Post's care."

Bailey shook her head. "Didn't you listen at all to me talking to Mary on the way over here?" she asked.

He had heard them, but Mary's low voice was hard to understand even when you were looking at her lips. Bailey had done little but sit in the backseat and listen.

"Mary said Dr. Post only performed one birth," Bailey said. "It bothered him religiously. He wondered if he was playing God. He was about to perform a second birth when the clinic burned. He thought he was being punished. He wasn't going to help anybody perform another one."

"Why is he suddenly going to help you now?"

"Look at how Mary lives—she's lived that way the entire time they've been back here. He's going to try to leave her better off—whatever happens to him now."

She stopped in front of her room. "And he didn't perform the procedure on Indians anyway," she added. She lifted her purse in front of her and reached inside it.

"He performed it on a woman from here who was an old family friend and couldn't bear children." She tugged an eight-inch reel of sixteen-millimeter film from the purse. Ross remembered his grandfather having some family vacation scenes from the fifties on similar film.

"Mary gave me this," Bailey said. "It shows the child."

LOS ANGELES

The Los Angeles International Airport handled a larger number of Hispanic passengers flying in and out of the country each day than did many of the largest Latin American airports. Absolutely no attention would have been paid to Enrique Bandez debarking from a flight from Mexico City and walking toward the terminal's exits, except for the tall man with shoulder-length black hair walking beside him with a scarf wrapped across his head and under his chin, covering a face swollen out to one side.

BILOXI

The old projector Ross had rented from an antique store gave off a high-pitched whine as it ran. The scene flickered against Ross's motel room wall, the images grainy and in gray-and-white more than black-and-white. The newborn child cried and moved her hands up and down as Mary held her toward the camera and smiled. Mary was surprisingly attractive at forty, her prominent nose somehow being downplayed a bit by the beauty of her deep, dark eyes. In the background, Dr. Post showed his satisfaction by nodding. Based on the date written in ink on the film leader, he had been forty-six at the time the scene had been filmed, still handsome, slim, with a pencil-thin mustache and thick, shiny blond hair hanging casually across his forehead. He was in his surgical scrubs, just as he would have been after delivering a child. But he hadn't delivered this little girl in the conventional sense. He had pulled her from an artificial placenta—according to Mary. The sequence ended and the sixteen-millimeter bulb cast a bright light on the wall. Ross turned on the table lamp.

"Wasn't she beautiful?" Bailey exclaimed.

Ross continued to stare at the glaring bright image the projector cast against the wall. Not that he thought any other images were to follow. It was evident from the transparent, light-gray color of the remaining film on the reel that none of it had ever contained an image.

"A perfect child," Bailey said in a low, thoughtful voice. "Mary said everything in an artificial placenta can be controlled, the amount of nutrients, oxygen. An artificial placenta doesn't smoke, or drink, or take drugs, or lift something too heavy."

Ross turned off the projector.

"We're going to start ordering the items on the list right now," Bailey said. "We're going to stay here as long as it takes to get everything in."

She quickly added, "I'm sorry, Ross. I know you might have other things to do. If you could do this for me, please . . . I'll double what I'm paying you."

There was an almost pleading expression on her face. It was the first time he had seen her when she didn't look like she thought she was in charge. "Please," she repeated.

"You're paying me enough. I don't have anything

scheduled for a few days in Los Angeles. But I can tell you now there's going to be some things on that list that medical supply houses don't simply send out to just anybody."

"We'll divide the pages and each of us call half," Bailey said. "If you run into a problem on your end, let me know—I have connections."

She smiled back at him as she stepped from his room and closed the door. He looked at the projector sitting quietly now. Was the film another part of some kind of elaborate con Dr. Post had committed in the past, or an actual recording of a real event? If it was real, the baby certainly showed no sign of deformity. She wasn't Indian, either, but a Caucasian child, as Mary had told Bailey. In fact it was a child from a family from the Biloxi area, a childless family Dr. Post had known. Ross had thought about asking if Post would take them to see the child. But if it was a scheme, Post could certainly claim the child no longer lived in the area. And whether it was an old con being perpetrated again or a real case of artificial birth, what business was it of his? Ross thought. He had found Dr. Post. What he had been paid to do. Bailey was aware of the possibility of a con. He had reminded her of the tale of deformities in the Indian babies. Now he was being paid to make phone calls— not to give advice. He stepped to the bed, reached to the bedspread and lifted the pages Bailey had left behind for him. Some of the items listed were typed, others displayed in Post's scribbly handwriting. The pages were yellowed, obviously old. Maybe forty years old. At least twenty years old. He wondered if the medical equipment listed on them even existed anymore. Even twenty years passing was long enough to make much medical equipment obsolete. He recognized some of the simpler items listed—petri dishes, flasks, a couple of the chemicals—by name, though he had no idea what their use would be. If there was a legitimate use. The list could be a bunch of items Post had made up to impress those who wanted to believe in him. Ross looked at an item termed a laparoscope. What in hell was a laparoscope? He reached to the telephone on the bedside table.

A few seconds later, he had his father's receptionist on the line. Amazingly, his father was actually in his office rather than in surgery.

"Dad, what's a laparoscope?"

"Basically it's an endoscope designed to permit visual examination of the peritoneal cavity."

Examination inside the body. "That wouldn't have anything to do with an artificial . . ." His father was going to think him crazy.

"Excuse me, Ross?"

"What would a laparoscope have to do with a pregnancy? Especially twenty or thirty years ago?"

"You said artificial, Ross. If you're speaking of artificial fertilization, a laparoscope would have been used in connection with piercing ovarian egg cysts and removing the eggs that were to be fertilized. A small incision would be made in the area of the belly button and the laparoscope inserted there. That's no longer the case. A non-surgically invasive procedure using a vaginal ultrasound is the choice now. What kind of case are you on?"

"Not a case, more something I'm debating with a friend. This might sound a little far out, but do you think an artificial placenta will ever be developed where a child can be grown outside a woman's body?"

"Outside of . . ." his father started, then was silent a moment. "Ross, you're out of my area of expertise now. I don't know if the placenta itself will actually be artificial, but, yes, scientists are on the verge of being able to clone or grow anything. I don't see the growing of a placentalike tissue or the womb itself presenting any more problem than growing any other specific organs or tissues. The primary difficulty in producing an actual birth would be in supplying the embryo with what the mother's body affords it, the actual connections that supply the nutrients and oxygen and afford waste removal—"

His father was repeating almost verbatim what Bailey had said.

"Overall, though," his father continued, "to answer your question directly, yes, it is inevitable that this will happen, maybe even in my lifetime—if not, then almost certainly in yours."

CHAPTER 13

Ross spent the next few days ordering and receiving overnight packages from medical supply houses, occasionally conversing over the telephone with McLaurin about business. Twice he went to the casinos and won; one morning he chartered a fishing boat for a trip beyond the barrier islands and caught a near-record lemon fish over a sunken liberty ship off Dog Keys Pass. But the best day was when Dorothy called him. He had passed the bar exam.

Manuel still hadn't called, though. Ross tried Manuel's office, as Dorothy had already, and Estelita didn't answer either, only the recording of her young, pleasant voice asking for any messages to be left and promising she would return the call as soon as she could.

At the answering machine's beep, Ross left word that they had found Dr. Post and Mary, and that Dorothy had already mailed Manuel's check to him. He reminded her that she should send Manuel's bill for expenses to Dorothy.

Then he added to his message: "I might be down there to see you in a few days."

He had been thinking about that for some time. Estelita was one of the women who had passed through his mind when Bailey asked him if he ever cared for a woman. He had met her a little over two years before, when he had visited Manuel shortly after she had come to work for him. He had already made three trips down there. Manuel had grinned and said he didn't know he had suddenly become such a good friend. Estelita had made two trips to Los Angeles in the past few months. So far all they had was a lot of fun together—but he had started thinking about her more and more often lately. There was something in her smile that reminded him of his mother's photograph. Maybe he was a lot more like his father than he thought.

After a week of living in the motel, Ross found the kind of house Mary had specified for the place where she and Dr. Post would live while the fetus developed—a secluded house where Post would feel at ease, one with a room at least thirty feet wide by twenty feet deep that could be transformed into the laboratory where the birth itself would take place, and a connecting room where they could sleep and Post could move easily back and forth in his wheelchair. She had suggested a house with a basement. There were few homes with basements in the low-lying coastal area. He had found the next best thing.

It was in Ocean Springs, an older waterfront community across the long bridge spanning the bay east of Biloxi. A three-story antebellum house beginning to fall prey to dry-rot, it was owned by a family that had made their fortune from vast timber holdings along the coast in the 1950s, but who now lived in Boston. It sat in complete isolation, surrounded by marshland and huge oaks draped in Spanish moss, on a sliver of land jutting out into the bay.

The first floor consisted of four big, brick-floored rooms with a small bathroom off one of the rooms. That level could be entered only by French doors leading into the house from the rear, or by a narrow, spiral staircase coming down from the house's second level.

The second floor, consisting of a big dining room, a sitting room, and a wide living room looking out over the bay, was built fifteen feet above the ground in the original occupants' attempt to protect the home's main living area from tidal surges that might be forced against the house by a hurricane. Wide, steeply inclining entry steps passing between tall, white columns rose up to this level.

The third story contained three large bedrooms.

Ross leased the house in his name and paid for the first three months in advance with a check from Bailey.

The next day Mary rolled Dr. Post through the French doors at the rear of the house into its ground level. He looked around him at the spacious room that would be the laboratory. To its far sides, doorways led to two smaller rooms. A door twenty feet in front of him led into a moderate-sized room and bathroom that would serve as his and Mary's sleeping and bathing areas. He nodded his satisfaction, pointed to the doorway leading to the bedroom, and Mary pushed him forward in his chair. Bailey carried an armful of cleaning chemicals, a mop, a bucket, and a broom inside from the Taurus. Ross carried the heavier boxes, then departed to rent a U-Haul trailer to pick up the beds, mattresses, and other furnishings Bailey had ordered.

A couple of hours later, Ross once again parked at the rear of the house and began unloading the trailer. Mary had nailed sheets over all the windows on the lower level.

"You know they're serial killers," he said to Bailey, only half kidding. And yet Bailey had already let Post administer her menotropin and gonadotropin, medication meant to stimulate a woman's ovaries into increas-

ing their egg production, his father had said. Post did
that the second day they had been at the motel. Ross
couldn't believe Bailey had taken the medication simply
on Post's saying it was okay, or that she would eventually take any of the other medicines he had ordered.
At least the man still had a valid license to write prescriptions and order the medications.

The medical supply house had filled the orders in any
case.

Bailey had obtained the blank prescriptions with
Post's name neatly lettered at their top—no telling what
she had to pay for them. Or do. Ross didn't want to
know.

An hour later Ross received almost as big a shock as
he had when he had first heard Mary say Dr. Post could
indeed produce an out-of-womb birth. Bailey, her hair
tied back with a rubber band into a ponytail, her slacks
rolled up her calves, and barefooted, worked a mop
back and forth across the brick floor of the wide room
that would be the laboratory.

Ross continued carrying heavy boxes inside under
Dr. Post's gasping orders. There was very little to set
up—an examining table of the kind seen in any gynecologist's office, complete with metal stirrups, a small
instrument cabinet, and an autoclave for sterilization of
instruments. One heavy item was a portable generator,
and Ross borrowed a dolly from a furniture store to
move that. As Dr. Post wheeled himself out of one of
the smaller rooms he had selected as a storage area,
Ross stacked medicines and chemicals on a line of
shelves already built into the wall. The examining table
sat to his side. He stared for a moment at a two-foot-
tall by three-foot-long fish aquarium Dr. Post had ordered. *Something akin to salt water,* was what Bailey
had said she suspected would cushion the fetus as it
grew. He stared at the tank, trying to imagine a baby

floating inside it. Everybody was crazy, with Bailey the leader of the lot, and him not far behind—as he was going along with everything that had to be done. At least he had the excuse that he was being paid.

He stepped from the storage room back into the central room that would be the laboratory. Maybe the ones who *weren't* crazy were Dr. Post and Mary. They certainly weren't doing badly for themselves in agreeing to help Bailey. He had assembled a pair of queen-size beds for them in the room just beyond the laboratory. The last room to the far side of the laboratory was now equipped as a lounging area with a couch, a chair, and a TV still in its box. Bailey had already bought the couple new clothes. They had to be living better now than they had in a long time, if ever. The question kept coming back to him: A monumental con job perpetrated by a couple of con artists who had done it before? Despite Mary telling Bailey what she had about Dr. Post's anxieties, was the real reason they were huddling behind covered windows like fugitives because they *were* fugitives?

Ross looked inside the doorway to the room that now contained the couch, easy chair, and TV.

On the brick floor against the far wall sat the worn suitcase-size briefcase Post had clutched against his chest the day he had been wheeled from his small home.

Ross looked back across his shoulder. Post was in the bedroom. Mary was preparing his bath. Bailey had gone up the spiral staircase to the main level of the house.

Ross stepped into the room and walked toward the briefcase.

CHAPTER 14

Ross knelt on one knee, laid the worn briefcase down on the brick floor and opened it.

It was stuffed with old notebooks and pads and folders as yellowed and browned with age as the pages Dr. Post had given them to order the equipment and chemicals he needed.

He opened the first folder.

It was filled with copied pages from gynecological manuals, and some of the actual pages themselves, torn loose and stapled together.

He moved the folder aside, lifted a notebook into his hands and opened it.

Its first page was filled with the names of chemicals, some listed by their generic names, some by their brand names, and many by their symbols. There were some formulations. He recognized one from a chemistry class he had taken—H_2O_2, hydrogen peroxide, a simple antiseptic solution. The rest, he had no idea—CHI_3, $C_{17}H_{22}N_3Cl$, H_3BO_3 . . . they continued down the page.

The next two pages contained similar information.

Ross removed another notebook from the briefcase. A date on its cover went back twenty years, about the time Dr. Post was burned out of his clinic.

The first page contained a column of letters Ross didn't recognize as chemical symbols.

UAV-AL
SL-MA
GR-LM
LX-MZ
CW-BZ
EO-GP
DC-NR
SL-LM
SL-CA
SL-EA
SL-CE

The remainder of the pages were empty.

He lifted a folder from the briefcase. It was filled with loose papers, again stapled together like those in the first folder. There was another date printed in faded ink at the top left-hand corner of the first page. Thirty-seven years ago—seven years after Post arrived in Mexico.

The notations running down the page were in script this time, and resembled the type of near-illegible writings that doctors scribbled across their prescriptions. But there were places where what was being recorded could be understood. Much of the writing was in the form of diarylike notations:

Implantation: Day 1.

Ross quickly ran his gaze down the page. Day 2 through Day 5, deeper implantation was discussed. The placenta was mentioned in Post's scribbly hand . . . He used the term *synthetic* in the sentence.

Day 6 through Day 8 the notes still focused on implantation, with particular notations on *multiplying* and *forming of cells* and the *exocoelomic* and *amniotic cavities.*

Day 9 through Day 15: continued detailed observations, with notations mostly concerning the *yolk sac*, the *neural plate*, the *chorionic villi branch*.

The days continued; a notation made every day, sometimes observations made hourly. Ross's eyes stopped on four words at the end of a line mentioning that the embryo's eyes and ears were forming as they should—*alkaline mixture working perfectly*.

The next page started with the notation *Eyes showing pigmentation*. There was a long paragraph about the hands and legs taking shape.

Dr. Post meticulously recording what he was seeing. How could he see something so clearly and in such detail that was contained in a womb? Thinking this, Ross felt his pulse increase. He turned to the next page. It started out with a paragraph describing the placenta, again in technical terms.

Halfway down the page the typing ended and the rest of the paper was filled with what closely resembled a balloon with an embryo floating inside it. The embryo's large eye cavities were shaded in with pencil. Beneath the sketch, the words *artificial womb* were underlined.

Off to the side and circled was a brief note. *Energy intake . . . male . . . 0.0–0.5 . . . 4 kg . . . x36'*

A hand came around Ross's shoulder.

He flinched and whirled around, coming to his feet.

Mary stared into his eyes and reached for the folder, pulling it from his hand. Still staring at him, she leaned to close the briefcase and lifted it from the floor.

A moment later, without ever speaking, the heavy briefcase swinging at her side, she walked toward the door to the laboratory.

Ross felt embarrassed and stupid. He had been concentrating so hard on the material contained in the folders he had never heard her come up behind him.

And then he noticed that, even now, as he watched her walk away, he still couldn't hear her steps.

* * *

A couple of minutes later he found Bailey in the small bathroom off the foyer on the main level of the house. She was leaning over the lavatory, cleaning it out with a soapy rag.

He said simply, "I'm beginning to believe there might be something to this—maybe I'm as crazy as you are."

Bailey pushed a lock of hair back off her forehead with her knuckle and smiled. Then she held out the rag. "You finish here, I'm going to start on Post and Mary's bedroom."

Two more days of hard work had the lower level as Mary wanted it and as clean as Bailey could get it. It wasn't sterile; it was a long way from that. But Dr. Post had told Bailey that wasn't necessary. "You ever thought of how unsterile the inside of a woman's body is?" Post had asked her. "The placenta will create its own little sterile area for the embryo. That's all that's needed."

Other than to offer those kinds of explanations to Bailey's questions, Dr. Post had done little else but sit in his wheelchair in his robe, breathing hard and taking handfuls of aspirin at a time. He wasn't able to do much more than that, constantly in pain from the matted scar tissue that covered the backs of his hands and arms and one side of his face, and from the nerve endings that had been left supersensitive from the burns he had suffered. Ross understood now why Mary hadn't used her nursing degree to make her and Post a better living—it took all she could do to take care of him. To hire someone in her place would have probably cost as much as she would have made at a job.

And it was doubtful that Dr. Post would have accepted anyone else anyway. He was continually calling out for her when she was out of sight for more than a few minutes at a time. His dependence on her was enormous, and, quietly, seldom speaking except in short, two- and three-word responses to Post's questions, she answered his every need.

On the last day before Ross was to accompany Bailey back to Los Angeles, he wandered through the house. He looked through the rear windows of the living room across the bay toward the tall silhouettes of the casinos and their accompanying hotels in Biloxi. A large white heron, its wings spread out to its sides, glided through the air between the rear of the house and the water. Off to the left, the marsh grass swayed in the breeze coming in off the Gulf. He walked to the narrow, spiral staircase circling down to the ground level.

In the laboratory, curtains were up now instead of the sheets Mary had first nailed across the windows. Bailey had chosen light blue and pink curtains—as if she were decorating a nursery. The brick floors and walls were now clean and glowing. Around the walls, a long counter and a set of factory-made cabinets such as those found in a kitchen were in place. On top of the counter, the generator now sat next to a stainless-steel-and-glass container about the size and shape of a ten-gallon gasoline can. Dr. Post hadn't added any of the chemicals to the container yet, but Ross believed he was looking at what was going to serve as the artificial womb.

He walked out of the laboratory into the room made into the lounging area, now neat and tidy with the couch, easy chair, and TV arranged close together. There was now also a two-eye hotplate, a microwave, and a large refrigerator set against the wall to his left. The refrigerator was crammed with everything Bailey could possibly think of when she had gone shopping for the couple. Part of her shopping zest had come after she had peered into the refrigerator in the little house where Post and Mary had lived. It had held only a mostly empty half-gallon carton of milk, a jar of peanut butter, a half-pack of bacon beginning to turn moldy, a sack of generic brand coffee, evidently stored there to keep it away from the cockroaches that swarmed the house, and a plastic container a quarter full of cooked several-days-old white beans.

Ross looked back at the closed door leading to the room now serving as Post and Mary's bedroom. Their beds sat against the room's back wall. He looked at the aquarium on the chest of drawers to a side of the room. His earlier thought that the aquarium might have something to do with the birthing process had been proven wrong when several two- to three-inch brightly striped marine fish had been delivered by overnight courier to the house. Bailey had ordered them after Post had spoken to her about how an aquarium relaxed him. *A pleasant distraction for a man who can't enjoy much*, she had said. Post had spent a great deal of time in the bed, staring at the fish and reading from old notebooks out of his briefcase, repeatedly lifting the oxygen mask to his face and gulping aspirins and other medicines he now prescribed for himself to hold back the pain caused by his burns and the resultant scar tissue. Ross walked by the bedroom door.

Ahead of him was the closed door to the room that had been turned into a storage area. It was also where he had erected the examining table and where Post now checked Bailey to see if the gonadotropin had worked. Ross remembered cringing when Bailey had explained what she would have to endure to see if cysts full of eggs had formed properly in her ovaries. Her stomach would be blown up with CO_2 gas to the point it was distended, and then, as his father had mentioned, there would be a tiny curved slit cut next to her belly button—a little smile, Bailey had called it. The laparoscope would be inserted through the incision for Dr. Post to examine her ovaries and then used to penetrate the cysts and extract eggs.

Here though, Post had displayed more initiative than Ross would have guessed possible in the old man. He had asked for several modern gynecological texts and had spent hours in the bedroom going through them and comparing them to his old notes. Ross had stood at the door once and watched Post, seemingly only skimming the pages of the texts, turning them rapidly, one after the other, but obviously absorbing what they said as, from time to time, he furiously scribbled something on a notepad at his side. A moment later Post had turned toward the doorway and called for Mary.

He wanted a vaginal ultrasound ordered. It was expensive—Ross had found one for fifty thousand dollars in a medical supply house catalogue. But expensive or not, it was a cost he himself would have endured if he were having the same process run on him that Bailey would. With the more modern ultrasound technique, there was now no longer the need to make the "smiling face" incision—the ultrasound probe was simply inserted up through the vaginal sheath into the womb to locate and retrieve the eggs without the need for any invasive surgical procedure. The door to the room opened.

Bailey had a smile on her face.

"We have several eggs," she said.

She was staring at him. She kept staring. "What?" he asked.

"The eggs are ready. Ross, this means a lot to me. Your father's a genius. You're not a dummy yourself. I want my baby to have the best genes he can."

He realized why she had taken the time to learn so much about him and his parents, even his grandparents.

"Ross?"

"You can forget that."

"The eggs have to be fertilized."

"Use Dr. Post."

"He's too old."

"Call one of your boyfriends."

She frowned. "How much?" she asked.

"You don't have enough money."

"For a sperm sample?"

"To *own* a kid that's mine."

Bailey stared at him, her lips tightening.

Dr. Post rolled his wheelchair out from the storage room. Behind him in the room, a sheet lay half off the examining table. He held a small notepad with a red cover.

"What is your whole name?" he asked, looking up at Bailey.

"Bailey Leigh Williams."

"The same as mine," Dr. Post said. "L-E-E. Is yours spelled the same way?"

"L-E-I-G-H," Bailey said.

"And your date of birth?" Post asked.

Bailey told him and he scribbled the information on the pad, and then Ross saw Post's eyes come up toward his. "And you?" Post asked. "As the sperm donor."

"Actually, it's Douglas Ross Channing. But you have the wrong person, doctor."

Post looked at Bailey.

The doorbell sounded.

Mary looked toward the opening at the top of the spiral staircase. Post did, too.

The doorbell sounded again, its loud ring reverberating through the rooms above them.

Ross walked toward the staircase.

Outside the beveled glass door at the top of the steps leading up to the second level of the house, a young man with closely cropped dark hair glanced at his watch. He used one hand to tighten his necktie and pull his coat straighter around his slight frame. In his other hand he held a briefcase.

Ross opened the door.

The young man smiled his greetings.

"Are you the manager of this business?" he asked.

"Business?" Bailey asked.

The young man smiled politely toward her. "A friend of mine with UPS said you've been having office supplies delivered here. I'm Bo Button. I represent Southern Office Supplies. I was wondering if you might have a minute to let me show you our prices?"

"No, thank you. We have everything we need now."

"I think you'll find our prices lower than the company you buy from," Button said.

"I own the company I buy from," Bailey said.

She probably did, Ross thought. He guessed he knew now where the printed prescriptions had come from.

The man nodded reluctantly, glanced back over his shoulder at his red Toyota sitting in the dirt drive at the front of the house, and turned and walked down the wide steps toward the car.

Ross closed the door. "Small town," Bailey said, looking through the beveled glass at the man. "I wonder if somebody is going to be a friend of the driver who delivered the medical equipment? All I need now is the media out here."

She turned from the door toward him. Her voice was soft. "Now, Ross, I don't understand why your giving a sperm sample would—"

"No."

LOS ANGELES

Maybe I can help you," McLaurin said.

Bandez, his hand slipped inside his jeans pocket and his shoulder slumped, as if he had something troubling him deeply, turned slowly from Dorothy's desk.

"I need to speak to Mr. Channing with great urgency."

"I'm his partner."

"Yes, I know, sir," Bandez said. "Your secretary told me. But I need to speak with Mr. Channing."

"He's expected in tonight or early in the morning," McLaurin said. "If you'll leave a number, I'll see that he gets it."

"He's out of town?" Bandez questioned. The Hispanic's eyes narrowed at that.

McLaurin waited a moment. "If you leave your number, I'll give it to him when I see him."

"My business is with Mr. Channing personally. If you'll pardon me, perhaps I can come back later?"

"Certainly," McLaurin said.

CHAPTER 15

I can fly someone in who will donate the sperm," Bailey said as Ross parked the Taurus in front of their motel rooms.

"I'm certain you can," he said.

"Ross, there won't be a child that's ever been loved more. Why am I going to all this trouble if I didn't care so much? The doctors say I can't have a child the usual way or I would."

"No," he said, and switched off the car's ignition and opened his door.

"Ross, I believe in environmental influences, but I believe in heredity, too. You're intelligent. You're nice-looking. Your grandparents all lived into their seventies, your grandmother on your father's side is still alive—in her nineties. My mother and father are in their seventies. My mother was still fertile enough to conceive me in her forties. A child couldn't choose a better genetic heritage for its intelligence, for its health, for a long life."

He stared at her. "You couldn't have had this planned when you first came to see me. You didn't know I would find Post."

"All I had was a background check run on you to get as much of an idea as I could of whether I could trust you not to run to the tabloids. After I received the report I saw where your father was a neurosurgeon and about your grandparents. When I was in your office and saw the law books . . ."

Bailey nodded her head as she paused. "Yes, I started thinking about you then . . . if you found Post. I want my baby to have the best chance possible." Bailey looked directly into his eyes. "I wish you would reconsider."

He didn't answer her, and stepped from the car and walked toward his room. Behind him he heard the Taurus's passenger door slam.

Inside his room, he sat on the bed. Bailey was thinking about his genes, her genes, as if the child was something she was ordering from assembly line parts.

He leaned back against the headboard of the bed. But whether the way she spoke sounded coldly calculated or not, he couldn't blame her for wanting her child to have the best possible chance. And there was no doubting how badly she wanted a child. He believed her when she said no child would be loved more.

Her child, he thought again. He thought about *his* child now—for if he did what Bailey wanted it would also be his. A child of his could have it worse than to be born into the kind of world Bailey could afford. If he ever even had a child, he thought. He was thirty-three, and had yet to find a woman he cared deeply enough about that he had even remotely considered marriage. Was it the women or him? Was he, in the final analysis, really the same as his father, too busy with his life for anything else? And, again, if he was the unborn child, with a chance to be born into the conditions that Bailey offered, the wealth and the expressed love, what choice would he make?

Biloxi, Mississippi," Bandez told the information operator and asked for the residence of Gerald Trehern. Aurondo waited in the van.

Apache Trehern answered the telephone. Her tone was light and pleasant at first, then she said "Yes" in a lower, more serious voice, and listened silently as Bandez told her to check on Sebastian and see if anyone had contacted him.

It had been nearly an hour. Ross used the extra key to Bailey's room without knocking. Still dressed in her jeans and blouse, she was lying back against the headboard of the bed, its pillows bunched behind her shoulders. She stared at him.

He walked to the bed and pitched the yellow pad that contained three sheets of his writing onto her lap.

His first legal contract as an attorney.

Bailey picked it up and looked at the first page without rising from the pillows.

As she continued to read, a smile spread across her face. She raised her eyes toward his. He repeated the terms he had spelled out. "One million dollars put in trust for the child—with me as trustee to make certain it goes to the child. I'll decide when. I want to be able to see him whenever I wish. I want him to know where he came from."

"I want you to see him," Bailey said. "He deserves to know where he comes from. The only thing, I want a chance for him to love me first. You can see him— but I don't want him to know you're his father until after he's in school."

Until he's been with her long enough she can buy his love, Ross thought. But the child would eventually become old enough to know that with a million dollars from a trust fund he wouldn't have to stay where he wasn't shown love. *I'll be around*, he thought, *to remind him of that if it comes to it.*

Bailey was looking at the last paragraph of the agreement. "If something happens to you the child gets the corpus of the trust immediately?"

He nodded. "And if I live, when I say he does."

"*He?*" Bailey asked. "Do you realize how much trouble a teenage boy with a million dollars could be?"

She held her hand out for a pen.

Apache parked her Maxima at the curb in front of a line of aging houses with narrow fronts and stepped outside. The full moon reflected brightly off her pale skin and blonde hair. She showed nothing of the racial coloring that her name might suggest. In fact there was no Indian blood of any kind in her heritage. The name had only come to the nurses when she continued to squeal and turned a deep red after she had been cleaned up and placed in the bassinet. The name they had originally planned was dropped. She became Apache, and with a daring personality and lively spirit since the beginning, a name that all who knew her said she had been destined to have. Now, at twenty-four, she was in the full bloom of her youthful beauty. But there was a serious expression on her face as she hurried up the steps to the front door of the small home, used the key from her purse to turn the lock, and stepped inside.

The moonlight flowing into the house through the raised windows showed all the furniture was still there. But Dr. Post and Mary were not in any room. Their few clothes were gone, with the closet door standing open and a drawer not fully closed in the small dresser in their bedroom.

As Apache exited the house, her lips were tight and her eyes narrowed. She saw the old Vietnamese woman who had come out on the porch of the small home to the side. The woman sat in a chair, gently rocking a small baby. Apache came across the narrow strip of lawn between the houses to the porch and looked up at the woman. The baby gurgled and clapped his hands. Apache smiled sweetly.

The old woman quickly warmed to her, but simply was unable to tell her where Dr. Post and Mary had gone. She knew the day that they had left, however, and had a strong description of the two strangers who had driven them away.

"A handsome man. Thirty-one, thirty-two, thirty-three, maybe. Dark hair. Strong body, but not heavy. Six feet, six-feet-one. The woman was very beautiful. Long dark hair. Slim body. Younger than man. Three, four years. The man drove a new Taurus. Louisiana license."

Ten minutes later Apache used a pay telephone inside a lounge off Highway 90 to call the number Captain Bandez had given her.

When he answered, she spoke in a low voice. "They are gone."

CHAPTER 16

Apache finished her conversation with Bandez and replaced the telephone receiver. She felt the presence of the man standing next to her. He was forty to forty-five years old, at least fifteen years her senior. He was overweight and wore a white shirt unbuttoned halfway down his chest and hanging out over a pair of knee-length shorts. His thick sideburns made his face seem wider than it was. He leaned his elbow against the wall next to the telephone and held a bottle of Bud Light up before her.

"My pleasure," he said. "If you'd like."

She started to move past him, but he pushed off the wall, blocking her way. She moved farther to the side and stepped around him. One of his friends, a man of similar build and age, grinned from his bar stool. Apache walked toward the exit.

The man looked toward his friend at the bar, then hurried after her. Coming up close behind her, he began walking slowly, but with long strides, theatrically exaggerating the swing of his hips, holding his beer out to the side. His buddy at the bar laughed and ordered another drink.

Outside the lounge, Apache stepped off the sidewalk

toward the parking lot. The man behind her walked normally now. He stayed a few feet behind her.

When he pitched his beer bottle into a trash can off to the side, Apache looked over her shoulder. He increased his pace toward her.

She stopped and turned to face him. He stopped, keeping a respectable distance away.

"Just making conversation," he said.

She didn't speak.

He stared into her eyes, then ran his gaze down her blouse, then down her skirt to where it stopped a few inches above her knees. The skirt was red. Her blouse was white. Her shoes were blue.

"Red, white, and blue," he said with a smile, "a regular all-American. I like that." He grinned at his joke.

Apache turned in the direction of her car.

The man stepped forward quickly, coming up beside her. He spoke in a softer tone now. "I do come on like a fool, don't I? But you just blew me away when I saw you." He smiled at her, as if his explanation made everything okay.

She only shifted her path slightly away from him as she continued toward her car, and increased her pace.

He stepped up his strides, too. "That was a compliment, in case you didn't catch it," he said.

She stopped beside her Maxima and ran her keys forward to the door lock.

"Nice-looking piece of machinery," the man observed.

She suddenly turned toward him, her back against the car. "Go away, or you're going to be sorry," she said.

"Sorry, maybe," the man came back, "if you just drive away after this long walk out here to talk to you. But, sorry for being in trouble, no way. I'm not going to touch you unless you ask. And in case you do, my name's Wesley. What's yours?"

He thought of what his buddy inside the lounge had

just told him. *Ask every babe you see that turns you on if she would like to put out. You'll get your face slapped a lot, but you'll be surprised how much nooky you'll get, too.*

He wasn't ready to go that far, but he did slide his hand across his groin. Apache didn't seem to notice as she turned back toward her door.

He touched her shoulder.

"Get your hands off me!"

He jumped back from her as she whirled toward him.

"Damn, woman," he muttered, taken aback by her sudden movement. "What do you think, you're so hot-looking you're gonna get raped or something?" He stuck out his hand and flicked his fingers against her shoulder. "Well, you're not so hot-looking."

"Don't touch me again," Apache said.

Wesley stared at her a moment, then reached his hand out and flicked her shoulder again.

"Damn you," she yelled and slapped at his hand.

He grabbed her shoulders.

She tried to jerk backward. *"Let me go!"*

He yanked her against him.

She tried to knee him, but he caught her blow on his thigh. He grabbed the back of her head and pulled her face to him and ground his teeth into her cheek. He pushed her backward.

His saliva glistened on her skin.

"Should have bit you," he said, and then added, "You're not nuthin'."

He laughed and turned back toward the bar. "Not nuthin' but nuthin'," he repeated to himself.

"Wait a moment," Apache said in a soft voice.

He stopped and looked back at her.

She smiled at him.

Slowly, a smile came to Wesley's face.

"Come here," she said.

You want to give me a hand?"

It was a lame joke by Ross meant to cover up his embarrassment. A grown man of thirty-three, a man who more than once in his past had participated in parties that would catch Hugh Hefner's attention, and yet he did feel embarrassment—Bailey standing there in front of him, Dr. Post looking up from his wheelchair, Mary standing inside the bedroom by the bathroom door holding a small sterile flask in her hand. Waiting for him to do what he was supposed to do.

"I think you can manage by yourself," Bailey said.

Ross took a step forward and, feeling like he was walking awkwardly, moved into the bedroom. Mary opened the bathroom door before he got there.

Dr. Post had used the vaginal ultrasound and a long pipette to retrieve eggs from Bailey's uterus. Though not a surgical procedure, it was at least a medical process. The collecting of the sperm was a simpler matter. "Should be routine for you," Bailey had said with a slight smile. Ross had stared at her.

He stepped inside the bathroom, turned on the light, and shut the door behind him.

Wesley guided his Thunderbird into the tree-lined area off the highway and parked. Apache had insisted on bringing her own car. The Maxima drove up into the trees behind him and stopped. Its headlights went off.

He sat there in the dark.

Back across the highway behind him, the gentle white surf of the Sound, kicked up by a strong wind coming in off the Gulf, broke softly against the beach. The foam created by the waves' movement glistened in the moonlight.

The interior light still hadn't come on in the Maxima.

Wesley kept looking in his rearview mirror. She had told him to wait in his own car. She had stared directly into his eyes with those soft brown eyes of hers and said, "I don't want to make a mess in my car."

He hadn't even asked her for any, like his buddy had advised; hadn't taken a chance on being slapped, hadn't taken a chance on anything, and yet here he was, waiting for a girl with a face and figure to rival any he had seen in his buddy's collection of porno films.

Waiting.

She still hadn't opened the Maxima door.

Suddenly she was standing right beside his window.

There must not have been any interior lights in the Maxima. Burned out. Or she had taken the bulb out, he thought. He grinned—taking the bulb out for times like this, with privacy in mind in case she needed to crack the door to get her feet outside or something when she was doing it.

He opened his door.

She leaned forward and slipped her head in between the front and rear seat. He reached behind him, pulling the seat forward. As she slid into the rear of the Thunderbird, he got out and slipped in behind her.

She waited for him in the middle of the seat. He moved his arms around her and started to press her backward.

"*No*," she said, knocking his arms away from her.

She hadn't been gentle.

Taken aback, he stared at her.

"*No*," she said again, this time in that incredibly soft, sexy voice. "I don't like to be held."

Before he could respond, she slipped to the side and pressed him down on his back by pushing against his chest, and came up over him.

She smiled down at him.

He raised his hands toward her.

"*No*," she said, "let me do everything."

She shifted her weight, moving her legs to the outside of his. He felt the pressure of her ankles lock tight behind his calves, and the pressure of her abdomen locking forward against his.

Damn, he thought, wondering how long he could last.

She pulled at his arms, and he allowed her to move them up over his head, so she could slip his shirt up over his shoulders rather than unbutton it.

He waited for her to begin.

But she didn't take his shirt off. Instead, she slipped her arm between the back of his neck and his arms, raised out past his head. Her hand tightened against his arm that was nearest the front of the seat, pulling it toward his other arm. His hands up against the car door, touched together. It was uncomfortable. He started to move one of his arms to lessen the strain.

She tightened her arm, preventing him from moving his.

"Babe, this isn't exactly the most comfortable—"

She had used her free hand to reach down to her purse on the floorboard. She held a razor blade in her hand. He tried to move his arms. "What in the—"

He pulled harder now to jerk his arms loose. But he couldn't. It was like he was in the grip of a man.

"What in the—"

She slipped the razor blade inside her mouth. It disappeared, then appeared again, gleaming between her white teeth. She smiled, coming down, toward him.

He bucked. She rode him like a horse, her legs locked under his like a vise holding them together.

She leaned her face into his neck.

"What in the—stop! Stop! Arrrgh. *Arrrrrgh*. *Ar*—" A gurgling sound now. Then a softer sound, almost like the gentle bubbling of water coming up through thick mud.

Even after Wesley quit moving, Apache kept nuzzling her face against his neck, up one side to his ear, down across his throat, up the other side to his ear and back to his throat.

When she finally raised her face, it was smeared red, red even into her hair, where it stuck the blonde strands together, and red smearing her eyebrows, a red brighter than the brightest skin of those from whom she got her namesake.

CHAPTER 17

As Ross climbed from the taxi he noticed that Mc-
Laurin had already received permission to hang an additional sign below the one advertising their bail-bond
and process-serving business. It read ROSS CHANNING—
ATTORNEY-AT-LAW. The sign had a noticeably large
space left blank above the lettering—where McLaurin
would add his own name and title in a few months.

Above mine, of course, Ross thought.

Smiling to himself, he hurried inside the building and
up the steps.

When Ross entered the office, McLaurin stood at one
side of Dorothy's desk with a big grin across his face.
Dorothy smiled as she came to her feet. She held the
letter saying he had passed the California Bar Exam up
for him to see.

"Ta-da," she trumpeted.

Ross walked to the desk, took the letter in his hands,
and looked at the words he had waited to see. Then his
gaze came up from the letter. "Did Manuel or Estelita
ever call?"

"All I get at the office is the answering machine, and
nothing at their homes."

He shook his head. "It wouldn't be unusual for her to be helping him on a case, but one of them should have called here after he checked the hospitals."

"I could call that police captain you know—Alberto."

"Manuel will laugh at us," he said. "But, yeah, do that if you don't mind."

McLaurin pulled a small tube of breath freshener from his pocket and held it out. "Your first case as an attorney," he said.

Ross took the tube.

"Friend of mine named Henry Ford," McLaurin said. "He got his fourth DUI. But he had just pulled out of a restaurant after having a couple of drinks with his dinner. Alcohol could have still been in his mouth. That would have thrown the test off—made it look like he had more alcohol in his system than he really did. Then he used that freshener to try to cover up his breath just before the cop gave him the test. Look on its side—one of its ingredients is alcohol. That would have thrown the test off even worse. I quoted him a fee of ten thousand."

Ross raised his gaze from the tube back to McLaurin. "And he wants me to represent him when I haven't ever set foot in a courtroom before? I don't know about that."

"I told him Perry Mason didn't have nothing on you," McLaurin said. "What's the big deal, anyway? Ninety percent of cases are settled on a plea bargain—why not a DUI? It's all political—you rub the DA's back, he rubs yours. Besides, Assistant DA handling the case is Edgar Coleman. You've known him for years." McLaurin grinned and rubbed his hands together. "Ten thousand dollars. Piece of cake."

Bailey's face had a smile across it as she held the telephone receiver to her ear.

Dr. Post's voice, often interrupted as he wheezed and gasped down a breath, droned on. Once he was suddenly silent, and Bailey heard him breathing deeply into his oxygen mask, but the smile never left her face.

"Thank you, doctor. Thank you."

She replaced the receiver. Meg stared from the balcony.

"Oh, Meg, it took. The egg cluster implanted—it's growing."

Meg swatted at Tommy pulling her hip. He dodged and made a swoop at her with his Power Ranger.

"I'm hungry, mother."

"I'll buy you a prime rib, Tommy," Bailey said. "A lobster—whatever you want. You can help me celebrate."

"Four-year-olds don't eat steak, Bailey. They might choke. And they could have an allergic reaction to seafood. Lady, have you got a lot to learn about kids."

Meg ignored Tommy's thumping her hip with his slingshot now as she looked directly into Bailey's eyes.

"You mean it's really working?"

BILOXI

Dr. Post had kept the oxygen mask pressed against his mouth for a full minute after he had finished his conversation with Bailey. Now he lowered the mask and looked across the laboratory at the artificial womb sitting on the counter. Barrel-shaped, the size of a ten-gallon gasoline can with its front half made of rounded Plexiglas, it was filled with a clear liquid. Inside the glass against the flat rear of the container, a mass resembling a pink sponge a few inches in diameter slowly emitted tiny bubbles of gas.

Mary walked to the counter and opened the cabinet above the container. A series of small tubes not much larger than drinking straws snaked up from the artificial womb through a hole cut in the bottom of the cabinet.

The tubes divided in the cabinet. One ran to a compact, softball-size air compressor which, in turn, was connected by a hose to an oxygen bottle. One ran to a sealed glass container two-thirds full of a creamy liquid. One ran off to the right into the next cabinet, where it was connected to a plastic box the size of a portable sewing machine. A low hum came from the box. The box was clear and filled with a pink liquid—a mixture of a sterile solution, chemicals and some of the blood platelets Dr. Post had taken from Bailey before she left for Los Angeles. Mary opened the hinged side of the box, looked at the slowly moving plungers and valves, and the pink liquid, slowly swirling around and around. She checked the temperature gauge, closed the box, and moved a few feet down the counter to the standby generator, silent and unmoving now. It had an electrical splice wrapped with black tape running into a fuse box in the wall to its rear. She pushed the generator's starting button. Its motor caught and started running. The exhaust fumes traveled into a thick black hose taped to the motor. The hose ran along the counter and turned up the wall to pass out a slightly raised window and through the screen. Mary turned off the motor.

At the sound of a speedboat passing on the bay waters behind the house, Dr. Post stared toward the French doors.

Mary looked out the window.

CHAPTER 18

Ross carried two books on DUI defenses from his Jeep Cherokee toward the small house he rented in West L.A. After he opened the door, he waited on Cooper as the bulldog balanced his thick body on three legs and relieved himself against the base of a bush to one side of the door. Seconds later Cooper came past Ross's feet into the home's small living room and stalked stiff-legged toward a stuffed, two-foot-tall dinosaur lying on its side on the floor next to the kitchen table.

Ross walked to a rectangular-shaped aquarium on a stand to the side of the door. He looked at the inch-long, brightly colored tropical fish moving in the warm water. The temperature gauge registered a perfect seventy-five. He tapped the feed distributor with the tip of his finger. A tiny shower of dry flakes sprinkled the top of the water and the fish swarmed as one to the surface and began attacking the food. As he watched them, he thought about the aquarium Dr. Post had ordered, and about Bailey thinking that something similar to salt water would cushion the embryo in the artificial womb. He stared at the aquarium a moment longer, and turned toward the kitchen.

Cooper had rolled the stuffed dinosaur over onto its back and now stood straddling it, growling down at its neck.

"Get him," Ross said.

Cooper growled louder.

Ross walked around the counter separating the living room from the kitchen and opened the refrigerator. His choices included the Wendy's cheeseburger he had bought on his way home from the airport the night before, a wiener from a half-empty pack of twelve that had been opened before he left for Mississippi, or one of the TV dinners in the freezer.

He selected the cheeseburger.

The bun felt wet and he slid the meat, cheese, lettuce, and tomato off onto a slice of bread from a loaf on top of the microwave. He finished repacking the sandwich by applying a second slice of bread to its top, slipped a bottle of Heineken from the refrigerator, and walked to the telephone on the counter. He rang the District Attorney's office. He had called twice from the office and Edgar Coleman wasn't in.

This time he was. "Afternoon, Ross," Coleman said in his slow voice. "Heard you passed the bar."

"Yeah, and you're prosecuting my first client—felony DUI. Name is Henry Ford."

"Okay, hang on a minute while I look him up."

It was nearer five minutes, and Ross had begun to wonder if he had been cut off when Coleman came back on the line.

"Yeah," Coleman said. "Has two prior public drunks in addition to his DUIs."

"Don't think he deserves this one though, Edgar."

"Don't, huh?"

"Listen to me for a minute," Ross said, and then quickly laid out his argument: Breathalyzers could be highly inaccurate, mainly because the instrument came up with its reading by measuring the amount of alcohol in a driver's breath and multiplying that amount by a factor of over two thousand times to establish the alcohol content of the blood. If a driver had taken a drink a short time before a test was administered there could still be alcohol in his mouth rather than only in the mist in his lungs, and this would cause the machine to wildly overstate his blood-alcohol content. Henry had not only been pulled over and given the test immediately upon leaving the restaurant, but he had been using a spray breath freshener containing alcohol right up to the moment he had been administered the tests.

"Well, maybe you got a point there, Ross," Coleman said, "and this is your first case."

Ross smiled.

"So I'll give you a deal, Ross. You plead him to public drunkenness and we'll think up something else to add to that, where the judge can sentence him to five years, all of it suspended, plus five years probation, a maximum fine, driving privileges revoked for six months, and have the judge enter an order that he not take a drink for a year. If he does and gets caught, he goes in for the full five years."

"My God, Edgar, for a public drunk? People convicted of manslaughter serve less time than that."

"People with manslaughter don't have three prior DUIs. That would have been enough warning to anyone but an alcoholic. As far as I'm concerned it's time he kicks the habit before he runs over somebody. Maybe he wasn't drunk this time—and I have so damn many cases I don't have time to prosecute them all—so I'm giving him a break. Bottom line, can he stop drinking or not?"

Ross was quiet for a couple of seconds.

"You can take a chance with a jury," Coleman said.

"I'll see if Mr. Ford wants to accept your offer."

"Pleasure being the first one to do business with you, Ross."

Ross said, "Thanks," and replaced the receiver. He lifted the cheeseburger, looked at it a moment, then laid it back on the counter.

The telephone rang.

He pushed its speaker button. "Yes."

"Ross?" Bailey said.

He quickly lifted the receiver. "You're not on the speakerphone," he said.

"I didn't say I was," Bailey said. "Ross, it implanted. Dr. Post said that was the hardest part, fooling the cluster into implanting. And it worked on the first try."

All he could think of to say was, "Congratulations."

"Ross, I'm going to throw a party to celebrate. But I still don't want anyone to know. Except Meg—she's the one who told me about you, remember?"

Before he could answer, she added, "I want you to come to the party. I want somebody here that can celebrate with me—who understands how I feel. Isn't that crazy?"

Again, before he could speak, she said, "I don't care if it's crazy or not."

Her voice was full of excitement, genuinely expressing her feelings, something he wasn't certain he had ever heard her do before.

"The only thing, Ross, I have to leave for Bermuda in the morning. With the time I spent in Mississippi, I have three photo shoots stacked up back-to-back. I'm going to be gone for three weeks. But it's going to be a *big* party when I get back. I wanted to make sure you knew so you wouldn't have anything else planned."

She finally stopped talking, but only for a moment. "Well, are you going to say anything, Ross?" There was still the excited tone to her voice. A happy tone.

"I'll be there," he said.

"You know, Paulie—that's the name I selected—he's going to be part of you, too."

"You already know it's a boy?"

"It's a child, Ross, not an *it*. A boy, a girl, who cares? Paul if he's a boy. Pauline if she's a girl. Paulie is going to be my nickname for whatever it is. *It*, did you hear me say *it*, too?" She giggled. Actually giggled aloud.

He was smiling himself when he replaced the receiver.

And the telephone immediately rang again.

"Hello."

There was no response.

"Hello."

"Ross."

It was Dorothy.

"Ross, I . . ." There was a moment of silence. "Ross, Alberto called back. Manuel was killed in a car accident."

Ross felt his stomach twist.

"Ross," Dorothy started again. "Estelita's dead, too."

Ross suddenly was sick.

"She was murdered in the office," Dorothy said. "Alberto thinks it must have been a thief. The desk drawers and the files were rifled. I . . . I'm sorry, Ross."

He took a deep breath to steel himself. "Do you know when the funerals are?"

"They've already had them. They took Manuel back to Durango. They buried Estelita in her family's plot."

Ross felt his lip tremble. "I don't know her family's telephone number."

"I'll get it for you, Ross. Why don't you wait until morning to call?"

CHAPTER 19

Estelita's parents were small. Her mother had light-brown skin. Her father's coloring was more the pale complexion of nearly pure Spanish heritage. His hair had a red tint to it. Estelita's hair had featured auburn highlights. They hugged Ross, then stepped back from the door and he walked inside their small home.

A portrait of Estelita smiled down from above the mantel over the fireplace.

"She was very beautiful," her father said.

Ross nodded.

"How is Manuel's father?" her mother asked.

Ross held out the small stack of photographs Manuel's father had given him. "He said he wanted you to have these."

The photos were of Manuel and him and Estelita at a nightclub in Mexico City. They were all smiling. Estelita had her arms around both of their necks and Manuel toasted the camera with a raised glass of wine. Estelita's mother looked slowly through them, then raised her gaze to Ross.

"Don't you want to keep them?" she asked.

"He made a set for me, too."

The small woman nodded and passed the photographs to her husband. "Do you want us to go with you?" she asked.

He shook his head.

"We're happy you came by," she said. "Estelita will be, too."

Thirty minutes later, Ross stood among the gravestones and crosses and crypts inscribed in Spanish. Estelita's final resting place was in a grave next to that of her grandmother in a family plot surrounded by a short wrought-iron fence.

Ross opened the small gate, walked between the graves, and knelt on one knee next to hers.

He touched the ground gently with his fingers above where her face would be. The sod was still soft. He laid a small bundle of roses at the foot of the cross above her head. It had Jesus's form on it, His outline depicted with His arms spread out along each wing of the cross.

Ross's eyes moistened.

He didn't say anything.

She knew how he felt.

CHAPTER 20

Bailey's party was a big one, even if nobody in Los Angeles knew why she was giving it. In the city all that was needed for a celebration was an invitation. Especially from Bailey Williams. The street in front of her house was lined with cars along both sides of the pavement as far as Ross could see. Off-duty policemen and Los Angeles County Sheriff's deputies, still in their uniforms, directed traffic. Ross turned his Jeep into the circular drive in front of the house and parked next to the wide steps leading up to the two-story mansion's front door. A smiling young muscular male valet with shoulder-length blond hair opened the Jeep's door and took Ross's keys as he stepped outside into the warm night air.

As Ross came up the wide steps at the front of the house, a short, older butler with nearly white hair opened the front door. The man scrutinized him closely. "Are you Mr. Ross Channing, sir?"

Ross nodded.

"Good, sir. If I had missed your arrival, Miss Williams would have had my tail."

The man nodded toward a wide hall running to the

right off the spacious, marble-tiled foyer inside the doorway.

"This way, please."

The soft sound of music coming from beyond the foyer faded as Ross followed the butler down the hall. But soon the sound started to rise again, and the hallway curved back into the same oversized living room he would have reached if they had gone straight ahead from the door. He saw why he had been directed this way. A good forty feet wide at its narrowest point in any direction, the living room looked like the inside of a sardine can stuffed with milling guests. Bailey stood under the wide arched doorway leading into that side of the room. Though NO BUSINESS TO BE CONDUCTED had been lightheartedly printed on the invitations, Ross recognized one of the biggest directors in Hollywood making points to her by jabbing his finger into his palm as he spoke. She was shaking her head no.

The butler stopped beside her, whispered something, and Ross watched her face turn toward his—a brightly radiant face highlighted by a stronger use of makeup than he had seen her wear before. Her hair was up at the back of her head. She wore a low-cut dress that fit her small waist tightly and flowed down toward her feet. A sparkling diamond necklace hung above the swell of her breasts. She smiled in his direction, said something back across her shoulder to the director, and came across the floor.

"Happy anniversary," she said as she stopped in front of him. "Paulie's six weeks and five days since he implanted."

"Happy anniversary," he said.

"So how is practicing law?"

"Well, I managed to get my first client hit with the most severe public drunk sanction in history."

"Don't brag," Bailey said, and smiled. "You'll have your bad days, too." She caught his hand and pulled him down the hallway in the direction of the rear of the house.

Moments later, they stepped outside into the sprawling grounds behind the mansion. She kept leading him until they reached the side of a giant, circular swimming pool. The illumination from its underwater lights reflected off the back wall of the home, sending gently rippling waves of light-blue color across the shrubbery, casting her face in dim relief. She leaned forward and kissed his cheek softly.

"What's that for?"

"Because I wanted to do it," she said. "I owe you so much."

"Don't let Mac hear that."

"Who?"

"My partner—he'll bill you if you give him a chance."

"The short little man?"

"Don't let him hear that either—he wears elevator boots."

"He was cute, bringing me an ashtray. I do owe you, though. I had already tried to find Dr. Post. For all the time and money it cost me, all I found out was basically what I already knew—a doctor named Post in the mountains around Taxco. He had been burned out and evidently left the hospital for this country. That was the end of the trail."

"If you knew Post had come back here, why didn't you tell me?"

"Because there was no trace of where he came back to—or if he even did, actually. I wanted you to start from the beginning. To see if the detective agency I used missed something at the very beginning. It worked." She caught his hand again. "I want to go to Mississippi and see Paulie."

He smiled. "I doubt if there is much to see in six weeks."

"Six weeks and five days, Ross. I want us both to go see him. I can always use a bodyguard along. I'll pay you if I have to."

It was a little before lunch when Ross reached the airport the next day. Bailey waited for him with their tickets in her hand. She had a small frown on her face.

"Well, do I pay you now or later?" she asked.

"A check to the office will be sufficient when we get back," he said.

She frowned again. Then it went away. "Well, I guess you have to make a living," she said.

"Mac would be happy to explain that to you," he said.

They waited by a wide picture window, watching the airplanes come in. It was a full fifteen minutes before their flight boarded. They were among the first passengers to walk onto the aircraft. Settled in their seats, they didn't notice any of the other passengers that came on after them. Even if they had, they wouldn't have known who Bandez was. Only McLaurin and Dorothy had seen him.

He settled into a seat five rows behind them.

CHAPTER 21

Bailey had rented a Lincoln Town Car when they landed in New Orleans. Now Ross guided it off onto the rutted gravel road that led to the old house sitting on the sliver of land jutting into the bay. Bailey had telephoned Dr. Post and told him they were coming. He let them in the French doors, backed his wheelchair away, removed the oxygen mask and let it dangle by the strap around his neck as he stared up at them.

"There's nothing much to observe," he wheezed, "to a layman. If you were a man of science you would realize what an advance you were witnessing." There was a note of pride in his tone.

He wheeled himself around and rolled his chair toward the portable cabinets down the wall. Ross saw the barrel-shaped container with the Plexiglas front sitting on top of the counter. It was indeed what Post had used for the artificial womb. The placenta wasn't artificial. Glowing a dark pink, now grown to about the size of a softball, but opening up like a big flower, it displayed its many folds and ridged projections. It floated seemingly weightless in the clear liquid inside the container.

As Ross drew closer, he noted that the flowerlike,

overlapping petals were moving gently, like a crimson-pink living animal projecting from an ocean reef. It was rooted against the flat back of the container.

Dr. Post rolled his wheelchair next to the counter and leaned forward close to the container, nearly pressing his narrow, scarred face against the Plexiglas. He canted his head to the side and seemed to be staring with one eye into the liquid while he motioned with a crooked, bony finger for them to come closer.

Bailey leaned nearly as close to the glass as Post.

He flicked a switch at the edge of the counter. A blue-green glow filled the tank, turning the placenta translucent.

"See," he said. "In the center."

"Oh," Bailey gasped. "I do. Ross, look."

He leaned toward the glass. At the center of the shifting living mass, he saw the form now. Not much of a form, so small it would fit into a walnut, but distinctly shaped in the outline of a partial C among the undifferentiated matter of the placenta.

"It's Paulie," she said. "Is he . . . she . . . ?"

Dr. Post shook his head. "We won't know for another month."

"Isn't Paulie cute, Ross?"

If a caterpillar larva is cute, Ross thought.

Bailey kissed Post's head. Startled, he looked up at her. She smiled. Slowly, the first smile Ross had seen on the face of a man constantly racked with pain, formed across the scarred lips.

Bailey's face pressed closer to the glass.

Ross looked at the tubes that ran up from behind the container and disappeared through a hole at the bottom of the closed cabinet above the container. He wanted to open the cabinet to see what it contained, but didn't know what Post would consider private.

A slim book with the color photograph of a fetus on its cover lay next to the artificial womb. Beside the book was the small notepad with the red cover that Ross recognized as the one where his full name and Bailey's had been written on the first page. The pad was open halfway through its pages now. The page he stared at was full of Post's scribbled handwriting. Ross wouldn't have minded turning the pages back to the beginning to see what Post had written about the development of the fetus—and maybe some clue as to what took place to make the process work.

"Where's Mary?" Bailey asked.

Post had fitted his oxygen mask back in place. He held it to the side of his mouth as he spoke. "I ran out of coffee. I have to have my coffee. That's something I can still enjoy."

A gentle smile crossed Bailey's face as she looked at him. "I'll buy you a ton of coffee, if you want. Any kind. From anyplace. Anything you want."

Mary clutched the sack of Folgers coffee against her chest as she stepped from the small quick-stop food mart. She glanced nervously up and down the sidewalk, then walked as rapidly as her hurried short steps could carry her to the taxi waiting at the curb.

The driver used his tongue to push a wad of chewing tobacco to the side of his mouth and looked back over the seat.

"Where to now, lady?"

"Back to where you picked me up," Mary said.

It had been at the very front of the old house, where she had waited in the dark under the thick limbs of an oak stretching over her head. She would have preferred to have had the taxi pick her up somewhere else, but the long walk from the house out to the nearest paved road would have been much farther than she would have been able to walk at her age.

She glanced back across her shoulder through the rear windshield of the taxi, and sunk lower in the seat.

CHAPTER 22

After Mary stepped out onto the ground at the front of the old house, she waited until the taxi's taillights disappeared down the gravel road between the tall oaks. Then, clutching the small bag of Folgers to her chest, she walked around the house to its rear, unlocked the French doors, and hurried inside.

Dr. Post sat in his wheelchair next to the counter.

"They came back today," he said.

Her eye ticked with her nervous reaction—she couldn't help it—and she tightened her arms around the bag of coffee.

Dr. Post realized how his words had sounded. "No, no, no, Mary. Ross Channing and Bailey Williams came by." He lifted his oxygen mask to his mouth and took a few breaths. "They called after you left, from a telephone somewhere close. They didn't want to drive up and scare us—they know how we are."

At the explanation, Mary closed her eyes a moment, then walked toward the wheelchair and held the coffee out. Dr. Post smiled through his mask and took the bag into his arms, cradling it like a baby. She turned his chair around and pushed it toward their bedroom.

"They were excited about the embryo," Post said

without looking back at her. There was the same pride that Mary had heard in his voice more than once in the distant past. She shook her head in sorrow.

Paulie is cute," Bailey said.

"If you say so," Ross said.

"I wish you would have come without me having to pay you a daily rate," she said. "I wish you had wanted to come."

"I'm glad I came. But I have a partner that's not wild about wasting time—and not getting paid for it."

"Didn't you feel anything when you saw Paulie?"

He had. When he looked through the Plexiglas at the brightly colored tissue . . . it was at the same time both artificial and living, and he had felt something. Felt a strange sensation. Though Bailey wouldn't like it expressed that way. What he really would have liked to do was read the scribbled notes contained in Post's notepad.

"Aren't you curious about why this can happen?" he asked.

"What do you mean?"

"That pad where Post wrote our names is half full of his scribbling now. I imagine they're his observations on what is taking place."

Bailey shook her head. "At the risk of sounding unintellectual—if there is such a word—I could care less, so long as Paulie's satisfied. Now I asked you, didn't you feel anything when you saw him?"

"It's the start of a life."

"It's part of you. It's going to be a child. Our child. You're the father."

"I know."

"You know?" she questioned. "Mr. Straight Face. Don't you ever just mellow out and enjoy life?"

Knowing the sharp tongue she had, he smiled at her talking about him mellowing out. Though she *did* seem more laid back than he had ever seen her. The child . . . the fetus . . . was making her happy.

But now she frowned.

"I thought you said you wanted to enjoy life," he said.

"*Me*? I'm having a good time."

"What are you frowning about?"

"Oh, it just passed through my mind that I have to be back working again in a couple of days. I'd rather stay here. I like it all. Paulie. The atmosphere. The food." She pointed her fork toward her plate. "This is absolutely the best thing I ever put in my mouth."

They sat on the glassed-in porch at Mary Mahoney's, an old French home converted into a restaurant. He had ordered for both of them: the oyster soup, the lobster and shrimp mingled in a cream sauce, the Caymus cabernet sauvignon. He had immediately acquired a taste for the wine when he had sampled it at Emeril's with his father.

"This is simply a beautiful place." She looked over her shoulder at the restored two-hundred-year-old hotel and shops a hundred feet away. Only a few feet away was a two-thousand-year-old oak with branches thicker than some tree trunks.

"You know what I want to do when we get through eating?" she said.

He put his hand across his mouth to keep from yawning.

She frowned across the table. "Ross, if I asked some people if they knew what I wanted to do, they might be interested in knowing."

"I'm sorry, you talked all the way here on the airplane. I couldn't get any sleep. I told you I didn't get any last night."

"I want to go back and see Paulie before we check into a motel."

Before we check into a motel, he thought, and smiled

at the idea of going to bed with her. He didn't normally read sexual content into innocent remarks, but neither had he ever sat across from such a beautiful woman in so romantic a setting. Of course, he also hadn't had any sleep in twenty-four hours and he had drunk half a bottle of wine. He grinned a little.

She saw his expression. "You don't mind?"

Don't mind? He looked at her deep eyes, the way her hair framed her oval face. Her lips. "No, I wouldn't mind at all. Not at all." He remembered McLaurin bringing her an ashtray to get her attention. He hadn't sunk to that level at least . . . yet.

Bailey was looking at his face now. "I don't know if you need any more wine," she said.

Dr. Post leaned forward in his wheelchair, his elbows resting on its arms, his face only a couple of inches from the Plexiglas of the artificial womb. His bony finger flicked on the switch at the counter's edge. The liquid glowed blue-green. The placenta weaved slowly in a translucent, crimson-pink fluid, the white pupa-like capsule at its center barely big enough to see. He slipped a magnifying glass out of his robe pocket, brushed his thin gray hair back from his forehead, and placed the magnifying glass between his eye and the Plexiglas. Behind his oxygen mask, his lips formed into a smile for the second time that night.

He heard the footsteps on the spiral staircase. He looked across his shoulder.

Aurondo's large frame nearly filled the narrow passageway coming down between the curving steel rails. Dressed in heavy boots, jeans, and a white shirt open across his wide chest, he had a scarf wrapped over the top of his head and under his chin, the deformity Dr. Post remembered so well causing the material of the scarf to bulge out to the side of his face.

Aurondo stepped down onto the floor and walked forward.

Post turned his wheelchair toward the stairs and waited. He showed no fear. His only thought was of Mary.

Aurondo stopped at the wheelchair. He reached past Post's shoulder, caught the back of the chair and whirled it around where Post's eyes faced into the Plexiglas of the artificial womb. Aurondo's hands came down past Post's head and grasped his neck.

With a tightening of his thick forearms, he lifted Post bodily up out of his seat and pressed the scarred face forward into the Plexiglas.

Gasping, Post's bony fingers came up to pull at Aurondo's hands. Aurondo tightened his grip. Post's hands clawed a moment more, trembled, and fell back to his sides.

Aurondo ground Post's face harder into the Plexiglas. Post's eyelids fluttered, his gasping barely audible. Blood began to seep from his nose, smearing against the Plexiglas.

He convulsed, and quit moving.

Aurondo continued to press Post's face against the artificial womb. Then for the first time since entering the laboratory, Aurondo spoke. "No more," he said.

Dr. Post was unable to hear the words, unable to ever hear any words again. Aurondo, his hands still tightly clasped around the doctor's neck, raised his arms. Post's head hung to the side, his arms limp at his hips, his knees bent where his feet touched the floor.

Aurondo turned, pulling Post's body past the wheelchair, and let him collapse in a heap to the floor, where his arms splayed and his robe, come open, spread out to his sides. His bare legs were bent and lay sideways against the bricks.

Aurondo turned back to the artificial womb. He pushed the wheelchair aside, causing it to roll in the direction of the far wall. The hose from the oxygen mask dangled behind the back of the wheelchair and swung back and forth.

"*Nooo!*"

Mary stared at Post's body from the door of the bedroom.

"*Nooo!*" she cried again.

Aurondo turned to face her.

Tears started down Mary's cheeks. She shook her head back and forth. "No," she cried again, "No. No. No. No." Still shaking her head, she walked slowly, as if in a daze, toward Post's limp body.

Aurondo turned toward the artificial womb.

"*Nooooooo!*" Mary screamed.

She suddenly lunged forward, stumbled across Post's body and slammed her hands into Aurondo's back. She tore into his shirt with her fingernails.

He turned. She tried to claw his face. He raised his forearms in front of him to stop her. She kicked at him and screamed. He backed away.

She moved between him and the artificial womb, holding her arms out wide to her sides as if to protect it.

"*Nooo!*" she screamed, leaning her face forward toward him, shaking her head. She looked down at Post's body. She shook her head more slowly this time. "No."

She looked up at Aurondo. He was staring past her toward the artificial womb. "No," she repeated. "It's not the same. No, for God's sake, no."

She looked at Post's body and shook her head again. "There was no reason," she said.

Aurondo stared at her now, his one good eye searching her anguished face, his other staring blankly ahead.

Then he looked down at Post's body, and turned and walked toward the French doors.

"No, Aurondo," Mary said. "There was no reason."

CHAPTER 23

Ross had let Bailey drive. "An attorney doesn't need to be driving drunk," he said.

"So I do?" she questioned.

"You can afford a chauffeur if you lose your license."

She turned too sharply and a rear wheel of the Lincoln bounced through the edge of the roadside ditch as they moved onto the dirt drive leading to the old house.

"You definitely need a chauffeur," Ross said.

"I didn't do that from drinking," she said. "It's dark." She giggled.

Ross leaned forward and peered through the windshield.

"What?" she asked.

"Nothing."

"What?"

"I thought I saw somebody by the marsh."

Bailey cut the steering wheel sharply, guiding the Lincoln toward the thick oaks at the side of the drive and bouncing between them. "Damn, Bailey!"

The headlights shined all the way to the tall water grass.

Nothing moved beside the marsh.

"So who's drunk?" she said and giggled again, then

gunned the Lincoln in a sharp circle back into the drive.

She pressed hard on the brakes at the front of the house, and the Lincoln slid a few feet before it stopped and rocked back and forth.

"We're back to see you, Paulie," she shouted.

Ross opened his door and met her as she came around the hood of the Lincoln. "We're definitely calling a cab when we leave here," he said. He started around the side of the house toward its rear, but Bailey hurried up the inclined steps toward the beveled glass door on the second level.

"Where are you going?"

"I want to see the view from the deck. Paulie doesn't mind waiting a minute."

Ross shook his head and followed her up the steps to the porch. As he felt in his pocket for the key, Bailey reached for the doorknob. The door was already cracked open. "The reclusives forget to lock the door?" she said. And then she smiled. "Maybe it wasn't coffee Mary went after for Dr. Post."

She stepped inside the house and Ross closed the door behind them.

As they walked toward the living room at the rear of the house, he could hear the faint crying coming up the spiral staircase.

Bailey had a sudden concerned expression on her face. "Mary," she called. Ross hurried for the staircase.

He spun down the steps into the laboratory. Bailey rushed down behind him, and stopped as she saw Post's body sprawled on the floor, his limp arms outstretched, his face smeared with blood and Mary crying, holding his head in her lap.

"*He* killed him," she wailed, looking at them.

Ross remembered the figure he thought he had seen. He sprinted across the floor to the French doors, threw them open, and dashed outside.

Twenty feet from the edge of the house he stopped

and stared between the oaks toward the marsh. He couldn't see anything in the dim moonlight but the trees and the tall grass fading in the distance into darkness.

Inside the house, Bailey reached for the telephone on the laboratory cabinet to dial 911. As she lifted the receiver Mary caught it and, with surprising strength, forced the receiver back down to the counter.

Bailey stared at her.

"You want your baby brought to term?" Mary asked.

Bailey looked at the artificial womb. When she had come down the staircase and saw Dr. Post's body, she had brought her hand to her mouth in horror. Then she had raised her gaze to the artificial womb and felt her heart break. But she couldn't think of herself or her baby that wasn't a baby yet, not with a human being lying dead before her. She was ashamed even of her momentary thought for herself, and at the same time her heart was still breaking. Mary's eyes bored into hers.

"I can bring it to term for you," Mary said.

Bailey stared at her, then down at Dr. Post lying crumpled on the brick floor, and then back at Mary again.

Mary could bring it to term?

"Yes, I want the baby."

"I will see that it is born," Mary said. She was speaking in a low voice again. The emotion she had displayed when they had come into the laboratory was totally gone. Only where tears had dried down Mary's cheeks was her stoic expression betrayed.

Bailey looked at the crimson-pink bloom, translucent in the blue-green light and slowly moving. From where she stood she couldn't see the tiny white embryo, not much bigger than her fingernail, but she knew it was moving, too.

"Yes, please, Mary."

"We can't call the police until we've hidden the womb," Mary said.

Bailey looked at Post's body.

Ross knelt in the moonlight beside the wide boot prints pressed into the moist ground next to the edge of the marsh. They were made by a large man with a long stride. *But not a man in a hurry,* Ross thought. The depressions showed the heel and toe portions of the boot sunk nearly equally into the ground, not with the heels barely touching or not touching at all and the toes digging in as would have been the case with someone running.

Ross came to his feet and looked in the direction the prints headed, toward the gravel road leading away from the entrance to the dirt drive.

A moment later, keeping his gaze moving from side to side through the thick oak trunks in front of him, he moved toward the road.

Mary showed surprising strength in her arms as she slid the large, rectangular-shaped aquarium to the edge of the chest of drawers in the bedroom. She began dipping the water out with a sauce pan in order to make the aquarium light enough to carry. The three- and four-inch-long, brightly banded saltwater fish swam wildly back and forth, dodging her sweeps. "We'll set it in the lab next to the womb," she said. "The fish, the aquarium, sitting next to the womb—the placenta behind the Plexiglas—it will look like it's some kind of marine growth."

Bailey glanced back over her shoulder through the doorway at the womb. Water splashed out of the pan and soaked the floor as Mary continued to dump it into the two-gallon pot she had gotten from the cabinet under the hotplate in the lounging area.

Bailey glanced toward the French doors and then looked back at Mary.

The fish continued to flash back and forth and tried to jump over the side of the aquarium. The water splashed. Mary bailed rapidly.

"Mary, did you see who it was?"

Mary kept dumping pans of water into the boiler pot.

"You said *he*," Bailey said.

Mary kept bailing.

Ross stopped at the thick line of undergrowth bordering the side of the gravel road. He ran his eyes left and right and back again across the shadowy shapes of bushes and tall weeds and the thick trunks of willows growing along the roadside ditch. The boot prints had disappeared a hundred feet behind him, when he had reached the more solid, dry ground.

He heard what sounded like a car door closing.

He pushed his way though the undergrowth out onto the road.

A hundred yards in the distance, a small van sat in the darkness along a line of tall oaks. Now the van moved into the center of the road and, slowly picking up speed, drove in the direction of the highway. It passed through a bright patch of moonlight and he could see that the van was dark-colored, a dark red or dark brown, maybe, and a newer model, maybe a Nissan; but from the distance there was no way to see who sat inside it. He watched the van until it disappeared from sight. Then he turned back toward the house.

As he reached the spot where the boot prints had begun near the marsh, he stopped. A couple of hundred feet away, the moonlight sparkled off the waters of the bay. He noticed a glint of light reflecting off something near the shoreline and walked toward it.

It was an empty beer can.

There was another one lying a few feet away. And

then he saw a third, a fourth, and a fifth can. The remains from a small campfire lay directly in front of him. The ashes were melted where water had been poured on them to douse the fire. Neither the ashes nor the cans had been there before he left for Los Angeles. He looked out across the bay.

A few minutes later, Bailey, coming out of Mary's bedroom carrying a two-gallon pot in front of her, was startled at the French doors suddenly swinging open, and she stopped abruptly. Water sloshed from the pot and splashed against the floor.

A questioning look on his face, Ross walked toward her.

The pot contained the fish from Dr. Post's aquarium.

CHAPTER 24

Blue flashing lights from the police cars reflected against the rear of the old house as the stretcher bearing Dr. Post's sheet-covered body was wheeled out the French doors toward an ambulance. Inside the laboratory, Ocean Springs Police Lieutenant Ron Browning jotted something on a notepad. Tall, in his late fifties, with light-brown skin and closely cropped black hair, he wore slacks and a sport coat with his shirt collar unbuttoned and his tie loosened. He looked at the police photographer walking toward him.

"I shot everything," the man said.

Browning nodded.

The photographer walked toward the French doors. Browning slipped the notepad inside his coat, pulled out a pack of Wrigley's Spearmint gum, and looked down at the thin smear of blood on the brick floor in front of his shoes.

It was the only blood still present in the room, except for a small splatter on an arm of the wheelchair. Mary had carefully wiped the red streaks from the Plexiglas so as not to draw attention to the artificial womb. Ross was concerned she might also have accidentally wiped away the killer's fingerprints, but she had finished the task before he had noticed what she was doing.

Inside the barrel-shaped container, the placenta glowed a light pinkish-red, its folds moving slowly, almost imperceptibly, in the clear liquid illuminated with blue-green light. Similar lighting from the aquarium's interior bulb illuminated the two- and three-inch, brightly banded fish hovering in the clear, warm salt water.

Ross knew, as far as Browning was concerned, the containers were only aquariums, one displaying salt-water fish, the other seemingly a type of colorful reef growth. Not that the lieutenant had been told that. Mary had quite truthfully said that Dr. Post was conducting research on fetal growth. Since Browning could see nothing of the research displayed, nor any of the tools of the work, except for the sonogram and examining table, he must have assumed that Post hadn't progressed very far into the project yet. Ross could see his license to practice law being revoked for being a party to withholding information in a murder investigation. But, on the other hand, whatever kind of research they were doing wasn't material to the investigation, and Bailey had pleaded with him. She didn't want the manner in which her child was going to be born to become a source of attention for the whole nation and the child hounded the rest of his life. Lieutenant Browning held a stick of the Wrigley's out toward Bailey.

She shook her head.

"And you are financing the research?" he asked.

"Yes."

"Might I ask why the Mississippi Coast—in a house like this instead of a regular laboratory?"

"The research is not cumbersome," Bailey answered. "And this area has been Dr. Post's home for years."

Again, the truth. No lies.

Unless Mary had lied.

Ross looked at her. When he had asked her if she had seen the killer, she had said no. It was the same answer she had already given to Bailey while he was outside the house following the prints left pressed into the ground. But they had heard her use the words "he killed him" when they had rushed down the spiral staircase at the sound of her wailing and she looked up from the floor, cradling Post's dead body.

When pressed, Mary had finally retreated into saying it was possible she had used the word "he" in her emotion, but that she could have easily as said "they killed him." *He* was only a manner of expression. All she had known for certain when she found Post crumpled on the brick floor was that he had been murdered.

But somehow she had seemed even more nervous explaining away her use of *he* than she was from the murder itself.

And that made no sense. Not if she had seen anyone murdered, and had seen who did it, but especially not if she had seen Post's attacker, the murderer of the man she had worshipped for over forty years.

Ross studied her face now. Stoic once again. Had she realized yet how much of her life had ended with Post's death? What would her purpose in life be now that her primary focus was gone?

Or had she already thought of her future? He saw her glance toward the barrel-shaped container, the womb from which would come Bailey's child if Mary could indeed continue Post's work. Had she thought of that as something of Post she could hang on to for a while longer—a part of him maybe? Showing the same devotion to him after his death that she had while he was alive? Or had she suddenly, shockingly, realized that she had nothing—and at her age very few options left? Except that she could have a hundred thousand dollars and fifty thousand dollars a year to follow if the baby was born. Ross stared at her, and simply had no idea what drove her now. The lieutenant had held a stick of gum out toward her, and when she declined had said, "You still can't think of any possible enemies Dr. Post might have had?" She had shaken her head no.

"And nothing valuable in here?" the lieutenant added, looking around him at the few petri dishes, beakers, flasks, and other small items of medical research spread out across the counter. He had already asked that question twice.

Mary shook her head once more.

"And where were you?"

Browning had asked that three times.

"Asleep," Mary said.

"Yes, you told me that," Browning said, and looked toward the bedroom door. It wasn't more than thirty feet from where the murder took place—and yet Mary had said she heard no sound of the attack. But he didn't say anything about that. Instead he glanced around the laboratory.

"The killer could have been attracted by somebody using the house again," he said. "Thought there might be something they could steal. Yet with the lights on he must have known someone was present at the time. Why did he just walk in here? Twenty, thirty years ago I would say we're missing something. But with the coke-heads now—they're so spaced out they don't know what they're doing."

As the lieutenant paused, he looked slowly around the lab once again, obviously trying to make certain he wasn't missing something. "The killer came in through the French doors," he said, voicing his thoughts aloud as much as speaking to them. "Confined to a wheel-chair, Dr. Post would have been easy prey—but why kill a man for the sake of killing him?"

As Browning stopped his words, he shook his head in exasperation. "Hell, it happens all the time now. I'm planning on retiring in eight years. Had that pegged for years so I'd still be young enough to get in a little fishing. But if it gets much worse I'm not going to wait around that long."

When he quit speaking, the lab was full of silence, no one volunteering anything—as it had been since he had arrived.

"Well," he said, "I guess that's all there is here in the house. If you don't mind, I'd appreciate your not walking around outside before we go over the grounds again in the daylight. If there are more prints outside we haven't found yet, I don't want one of you walking over them. I'm going to leave an officer out here, so don't get spooked if you hear him moving around."

Browning walked to the doorway leading into the bedroom. He had already looked inside it a half dozen times. He stared again at the queen-size beds. The one farthest from the door was where Mary said she had been taking a nap. Its cover was rumpled and its pillow was out from underneath the cover. Her Bible lay next to the pillow. Browning walked inside the room, moved around the beds to the Bible, picked it up, opened its cover, stared idly at a page and closed the cover again. He looked around the room, held his gaze on the open bathroom door for a moment, then walked from the room and started toward the French doors.

"Mr. Channing, will you come with me, please?"

A few minutes later, outside the house close to the marsh, Browning looked down at the places where plaster casts had been made of the boot prints. The residue remained, ridges of a white substance, now hardened. In each place that the plaster had been used, chunks of it had been thrown to the side as a technician had smoothed the excess material from the molds.

Browning gazed at the lines of Ross's prints following alongside the boot prints as he had traced them toward the road. "All you can tell me is you heard a door slam and you saw a van, a dark one, maybe a Nissan, you think, but nothing for certain, not who was inside it?"

"It was too far away," Ross said.

"There's prints out in the road beside where it was parked," Browning said. "But not boot prints. Two sets of tennis shoe prints. One set's either a small man, a child, or a woman. So maybe it was a couple of kids out parking. It was a coincidence they happened to leave when you reached the road. Maybe." Browning held out the same stick of gum he had offered Mary and Bailey. Ross shook his head.

A young officer stepped up beside them. "What about the beer cans?" he asked.

Browning stripped the gum of its wrapper as he looked in the direction where the cans and the ashes of the campfire lay close to the shoreline of the bay. Then his eyes came back to Ross's. "You're certain they weren't there before you left for Los Angeles?"

"I'm certain."

"Teenagers," Browning said. "The house has been vacant for so long, and with Post and his assistant not having a car here while you were gone, I doubt the kids had any idea anyone lived here now."

Browning turned his face back to the young officer's. "But we'll take a couple of the cans with us for prints— just so we'll have them on file."

The officer nodded and walked toward the shoreline.

"Guess that's all, Mr. Channing," Browning said. "If you think of something else about the van, I'd appreciate your calling me. Now, if you don't mind, I think it's time for you to go back inside the house."

Browning folded the stick of gum into his mouth as he walked away.

A couple of minutes later, inside the laboratory, Ross watched the police cars driving off as he closed the door. Bailey and Mary walked toward the artificial womb. Mary lifted Dr. Post's small notepad from next to the womb, showed something on one of its pages to Bailey, then laid the pad back on the counter and walked toward her bedroom.

When she stepped inside the door, she closed it behind her. Ross stared at the door for a moment. She couldn't have slept through the murder if Dr. Post had cried out. Why wouldn't he cry out? It couldn't have been because the killer struck too quickly. No one could have come through the French doors without him seeing them, or down the spiral staircase for that matter.

Ross looked toward the room used for a lounging area. It was possible Post could have been in there and not seen the intruder enter the laboratory from outside. When he came back out through the door, he could have been grabbed before he could cry out.

But the actual murder was carried out in front of the artificial womb—at least that was where the blood had been. Why would anybody drag him over there before killing him?

Ross looked back at Bailey. She had placed her palm against the plastic covering the artificial womb's front. She traced her fingers along the metal seams where the Plexiglas joined the solid walls of the container at its sides. Her hand came back to her chest. She looked at her fingers as she rubbed them together, then looked at him as he walked toward her.

As he stopped in front of her, she said, "Mary's going to be so lonely."

He glanced toward the bedroom. "I don't see how she failed to hear something. Him crying out—something."

"Maybe he kept quiet on purpose," Bailey said. "So they wouldn't know she was here."

Ross had thought about that. But it would also be logical that Post would have thought the intruder would discover Mary anyway. If he had cried out he would have at least warned her.

But who was to know how a mind reacted?

Bailey lifted the notepad Mary had left on the counter.

"She says she can do it, Ross. She says anybody can bring Paulie to term now."

Ross took the notepad from her. Its first page contained his and Bailey's names, scribbled there the day the sperm was taken to fertilize the egg. The next page contained a checklist of things to monitor. Not a very long list—temperature, liquid heights, nutrition levels, oxygen pressure, waste accumulation.

There were some notations in Post's scribbly handwriting out to the side of the checklist. The notations were short, appearing to be notes Post had made to himself. *In place of the bathing in maternal blood and lymph,* he had written with no further explanation. An arrow was drawn from the sentence to a note about the nutrient and liquid levels.

On the next page there was a note about a tube enclosing several smaller tubes taking the place of the umbilical cord. The two words, *Key exception* stood alone by themselves, again without any explanation. The longest notation read, *Nutrients, antibodies, and oxygen to fetal blood—waste from fetal blood to artificial membrane.*

"She said that the fetus takes care of itself," Bailey commented, "as long as the pressures are kept where there is a proper exchange back and forth through the membranes."

Bailey's hesitant tone made her statement sound like more of a question.

"She has been with him since the beginning," he said. "I doubt there's anything he knew that she doesn't."

"I hope so," Bailey said, her tone still unsure. She glanced toward the bedroom. "I don't want to go back to Los Angeles right away, Ross. I want to stay here for a while."

He nodded.

"In the house, Ross. I want to stay in Mary's room, if she'll let me. I want to have time to talk to her— about this. Do you mind?"

"You're paying the bill, lady."

She smiled. "Thank you."

"I'll get our clothes," he said. He walked to the French doors and opened them. The officer standing by a patrol car looked in his direction.

"I need to get some things out of my car trunk."

"Sure, man," the officer answered. "Go through the house and come out the front door rather than walking out here, if you don't mind."

Minutes later, out at the Lincoln, Ross looked through the trees toward the road leading away from the head of the drive. The killer didn't just stumble upon the house. He came up the road in a van. Whoever he was he knew where he was going and why.

But that was all Ross was certain of.

He opened the Lincoln's trunk. Minutes later, carrying his suitcase, his hanging clothes, and Bailey's large suitcase and leather folding bag, he had to walk awkwardly sideways down the narrow spiral staircase to come back down into the laboratory. He placed Bailey's things against the wall next to the bedroom, and stared at its closed door.

Mary had said *he*. Ross kept remembering how her face had looked as she cradled Post's body and stared up the stairs at them. There wasn't just grief on her face, but a look as if she had seen a ghost.

And how nervous she had seemed as she had explained her using the word *he* was only a figure of speech.

And yet, again, it couldn't be possible that she had seen the killer and not say so.

Certainly not with Dr. Post the victim.

Bandez drove the van. Aurondo stared straight ahead through the windshield from the passenger seat. He had removed his scarf and his straight black hair hung down around his shoulders. Apache sat in the rear seat. As the van stopped at the side of the street in front of her house, she opened the door and stepped out onto the grassy strip between the pavement and the sidewalk. She stared back inside the passenger window.

Aurondo's face came around toward hers, his good eye staring directly into hers, his fixed eye, pale-gray and glazed over, unmoving.

"I will finish it," she said.

Ross used the blankets Bailey had brought him to make a bed out of the couch in the room used for a lounging area. She had gone back inside Mary's room. Mary was in the laboratory. He had left the door to the lab open where he could see the French doors. He opened his suitcase, slipped his holstered automatic out from among his socks and underwear and laid it on the coffee table next to the couch.

He killed him still kept coursing through his mind.

He stared through the doorway at Mary for the longest time.

Lieutenant Browning sat in his office chair with his feet on his desk.

"The old woman didn't hear squat," he said as he unwrapped a stick of gum in his lap. "And yet the bedroom is so close to where he was killed she could have heard him rattle a beaker."

"I don't know, Lieutenant." The officer replying wore sergeant's stripes and sat in a chair on the other side of the desk. He was about the same age as Browning, in his late fifties, but with a much heavier build.

"What is it you don't know?" Browning asked.

"Kitchen at my house is right next to our bedroom," the sergeant said. "My wife's in there rattling dishes around and I'm yelling at her that I couldn't get any sleep if my life depended on it. But when I've worked a double shift, I don't even hear it. The old woman out at the house might have had a hard day. She was out cold."

Browning was silent for a moment. "Why in hell would a model from Los Angeles—got more to do than she's got time to do it—and she makes a trip down here to check on some kind of research on fetal development that hasn't even started yet from the looks of that place they call a lab. And why there, anyway?"

"Lieutenant, you're thinking that somebody like that model would be involved in something like this? I mean, murder?"

"Don't know what I'm thinking, Ed. I just know that I'm thinking. What do you think?"

The sergeant shrugged.

"Tell you what, Ed. You run along home and get yourself some sleep. Tell your wife not to rattle the dishes. Then, tomorrow, when you're all bright-eyed and bushy-tailed I want you to run all the checks you can on everybody out there. I mean all of them—from date of birth to what they eat for breakfast."

CHAPTER 25

The reporters appeared at the entrance to the dirt drive before dawn. They stayed there all morning, taking photos of the house and the officers who had come to search among the oaks for additional shoe or boot prints. They found none. By lunch a satellite truck from a New Orleans station arrived. Its occupants joined the cameramen already present from a newspaper and a pair of Mississippi TV stations.

The murder wasn't the main interest now.

"I need to get it over with and maybe they'll go away," Bailey said.

As she stepped from the front door of the house out onto the porch, someone in the group at the head of the drive saw her and a half dozen cameras focused in her direction. The cameras followed her as she moved down the wide steps.

As she went around the front of the Lincoln toward the passenger side, Ross walked to the driver's door.

Seconds later, he drove the Lincoln slowly up to the entrance of the drive and stopped. Lenses focused past his face, through the windshield, and through the passenger window, all of them aimed at Bailey.

She lowered her window. Mikes were thrust toward

her. Behind them, a variety of shoulders and faces seemed glued together in one mass as reporters jostled for the same spot.

"Miss Williams, were you frightened?"

"Miss Williams, what research are you funding?"

"Miss Williams, is it true you used your car to chase the killer—is this the car?"

A cameraman backed up and panned his camera along the Lincoln's side.

"I arrived after the murder," Bailey said in a soft voice. "I didn't see anyone." The reporters pressed closer together.

"Where were you coming from?" a woman with a square face and thick neck yelled. She stood at the back of the crowd. She had a tape recorder in her hand and held it up above the others' heads.

"We were returning from dinner."

"Who's *we*?" a tall, skinny man with a narrow face and slicked-back black hair shouted.

"Don't yell in my ear," a short male reporter with thick glasses growled.

He was pushed to the side by a larger man in a sweatshirt with a video camera perched atop his shoulder.

"I was having dinner with Mr. Channing," Bailey said, and looked toward him.

Ross noticed a couple of the camera lenses swing his way. In front of the Lincoln, a man with a 35-mm camera was snapping shot after shot through the windshield.

"Who are you?" a woman asked in Ross's ear. It was the one with the square face. How she had gotten to his side of the car so quickly he had no idea.

"He's just her bodyguard," a man's voice said.

The cameras swung away from him back to Bailey. The woman with the square face kept her attention focused. She leaned close to his shoulder and pushed the tape recorder forward. "Mr. Channing, did *you* see the killer?"

"No."

"Lieutenant Browning said you might have," she said.

"I saw a van drive away."

"You couldn't tell anything about it?"

"Only that it was a dark color."

Bailey stepped outside the Lincoln and was instantly encircled. Even the square-faced woman rushed that way now. Ross was left alone.

A hundred feet up the road, a white Maxima pulled to the far shoulder and stopped. Apache pushed her shiny blonde hair back from the side of her face and stared at the group at the head of the drive. She focused her gaze on Bailey. Then she stared inside the Lincoln at Ross, clearly visible in the bright sunlight shining through the windshield. She studied his face, too.

A moment later, she touched the Maxima's accelerator lightly and began to back down the road. She glanced forward only once to see Ross's face again, then backed onto a dry area off the side of the road, turned the Maxima around and drove in the direction of the highway.

As Bailey stepped back inside the Lincoln and shut her door, Ross started the car slowly forward. The cameramen parted reluctantly, moving out of the way just before they were bumped. The woman with the square face stuck a fashion magazine and a pen inside the car through Bailey's window. Bailey quickly scribbled her name on the cover, handed the magazine and pen back to the woman, and raised the window.

Ross turned out of the drive onto the narrow road and increased their speed.

"They don't care about Dr. Post anymore," Bailey said.

Ross looked back through the rearview mirror.

Nobody was following him.

It was fifteen minutes to the Bradford–O'Keefe Funeral Home in Ocean Springs. It was where Post, after seeing a picture of the beautiful, old antebellum-like structure on television, and having had a particularly bad night with his breathing, had told Mary he wanted to go at the end.

She had done everything Post had asked since first meeting him over forty years before, Ross thought as he walked between a pair of tall, white columns to the funeral home's front door. She was still honoring his wishes to that moment.

As Ross stepped inside the funeral home, a lightly tanned man dressed in a dark suit came came toward him. The arrangements took about thirty minutes to finalize. Ross paid in advance with Bailey's credit card. She had remained in the car staring through the windshield in thought. When he came back outside and opened the Lincoln's door she looked across the seat at him.

"The laboratory felt lonely," she said. Her tone was reflective. "The Plexiglas was warm when I touched it but not . . ." She searched for a word. ". . . Homey warm. I read where a baby inside the mother can hear her voice. The article said part of a child's later language recognition comes from this. I listened, and the only thing I could hear was the hum of that little motor in the cabinet."

Bailey said no more on the way back to the old house. She didn't smile when they drove past the half dozen reporters grouped at the entrance to the drive. Ross parked the Lincoln at the rear of the house to be out of sight of the cameras. Bailey remained silent as she walked inside the laboratory.

Mary sat in Post's wheelchair in front of the artificial womb. Her gaze came around toward them. She came to her feet as Bailey walked toward the counter.

Bailey stopped in front of the Plexiglas, stared through it, and then, turning her face toward Mary's, said, "I want to see the child Dr. Post produced—the little girl. She would be in her twenties now. You said her family was from here."

Mary didn't respond.

"It's important to me," Bailey said. "I want to see how she turned out—how she is now."

When Mary still didn't speak, Bailey said, "I want to know how she bonded with her mother, Mary." She looked through the Plexiglas. "I want to know how she bonded," she repeated.

Mary stood a moment longer in front of the wheelchair, looked at Bailey, then walked slowly toward the bedroom.

Inside the room, she leaned into the closet. When she straightened, she held a sheet of paper in her hand.

As she walked back toward the doorway, Ross saw that she was actually carrying three sheets of paper, stapled together.

She held them out toward Bailey. They were old and yellowed, like the notebooks and pads he had gone through in Post's briefcase. He hadn't seen the briefcase since Mary had carried it from the lounging area.

A soft smile crept across Bailey's face as she studied the top sheet. She flipped it over to the next sheet.

A moment later her smile went away to be followed by a questioning look crossing her face. She looked at Mary and flipped the second sheet over to stare at the last one.

Now Ross watched her eyes come around to his.

"There were three," she said.

Ross took the pages into his hands. Each was about a separate child. A separate birth.

"You said one," Bailey said.

"One was enough for you to know it succeeded," Mary said.

Ross looked at the pages. All the information was there. The date of the birth. The names of the parents, their addresses at the time, and the names of the children. Bailey was smiling softly again as she looked past his shoulder at the name of the child at the bottom of the first sheet.

"Apache," she said.

CHAPTER 26

The three children born to Dr. Post's experiments had been given the names Apache, Justin, and Billy. From the birth dates on the sheets of paper, Apache would be the oldest at twenty-four, Justin would be twenty-three, and Billy, twenty-two.

Ross opened the telephone directory to the J's. There were over three pages of Johnsons, the name of Billy's parents, Richard Paul Johnson and Cheryl Ellen Johnson. There was a Billy listed with a Biloxi address. He punched the number into the telephone. It rang three times, then an answering machine clicked on. He replaced the receiver.

Justin's parents were named Barnes, Jonathan Jay Barnes and Elizabeth Alberta Barnes. There were more Barneses listed in the directory than there had been Johnsons, but none of them with the names he looked for. He turned to the T's, looking for Apache's parents, Carl Cash Trehern and Carol Ann Trehern.

There were only a few of this more unusual last name listed, and none listed as Carl or Carol or Apache. But any one of the names could be a relative who would know how to locate the young woman, the same as the long lists of Johnsons and Barneses could contain the name of a relative of Justin or Billy. Ross decided to start with the fewer Trehern names first. As he punched in the first number, Bailey sat down on the couch next to him.

A female voice answered the telephone ring and he said, "I'm calling to see if you might know a Miss Apache Trehern or her parents, Carl and Carol Trehern?"

She didn't, and Bailey read aloud the second number. He punched it in and leaned back in the couch. He sat forward again when, in response to his question, the man who answered the call said, "Yes, Apache's not in at the moment, but I expect her back at any time."

Three cars driven by reporters followed the Lincoln after Ross drove out of the drive. "I don't want them to be there when we meet Apache," Bailey said.

At the first traffic signal he waited until the light turned from amber to red, and ran it. Only one of the cars followed him through. He lost that one by whipping the Lincoln around a blocking line of large trucks carrying cement to a casino under construction.

After looking through the rear window to see that no other cars trailed them, Bailey faced back to the windshield and was silent as Ross turned the Lincoln onto Highway 90 and drove west toward the address the man had given him over the telephone. His name was Gerald, Apache's uncle. He lived in Pass Christian, only a few miles down the beach west of Gulfport.

Bailey looked through the passenger window as Ross slowed to turn into the driveway leading to the house. It was a two-story, Colonial-style brick home, thirty to forty years old, but perfectly maintained, with a wide, manicured yard bordered by tall bushes and a giant magnolia shading its western side.

Gerald Trehern waited for them on the shallow porch

between a pair of tall columns rising up to the over-hanging roof.

He greeted them by shaking their hands in turn. The door behind him opened and a beautiful young woman with long, shiny blonde hair stepped outside onto the porch. She smiled politely. "Mr. Channing. Miss Williams."

Bailey smiled as she shook Apache's hand. When the blonde grasped Ross's hand her skin was smooth and soft, but there was a notable strength present, too. With her lean figure and taut neck, she gave the appearance of someone very athletic.

"You're the first people I've heard speak of Dr. Post in years," she said. "Mother used to mention him all the time. And Mexico—she used to speak of there all the time, too. I believe that was her favorite place. Probably because of me coming from there."

"So you know where you . . ." Bailey started. She had mentioned to Ross she wanted to be careful in what she said. She didn't know what the girl's mother and father had told Apache, and Bailey didn't want to be the one who blurted out something that was a family secret—maybe even from the twenty-four-year-old standing in front of her. "So you were born in Mexico?"

"Mother went there to be under Dr. Post's care. All the doctors until then had told her she couldn't have a child—it would be too dangerous. But she had such faith in Dr. Post. The birth went fine." Apache smiled. "Though mother liked to complain about how bad the morning sickness was. Do you know Dr. Post well?"

"Yes," Bailey said. "We found your name in his personal effects. We thought maybe you—"

"Personal effects?" Apache questioned.

Her uncle spoke now. "He's dead, honey."

Apache's pleasant smile went away. "I knew how old he was," she said. "I'm sorry."

"He was murdered last night," her uncle said.

She looked at him.

"He was here on the coast, honey, in Ocean Springs. These people were funding research he was preparing to do. Someone broke into the house while he was alone in his laboratory. It's been on all the TV stations."

"Why would anybody kill him?" Apache asked. She looked at Bailey.

"The police suspect someone trying to steal something broke in on him," Bailey said. "Since your name was in his personal effects, we knew there must be a strong tie. We wanted you to know."

Apache was silent a moment. "I'm glad Mother doesn't know," she said.

"Where is your mother?" Bailey asked.

"She and Father drowned."

"Oh, I'm sorry."

"It was a long time ago," Apache said, "though I'll admit it still bothers me—I was there."

Apache's uncle laid his hand on her shoulder. "They were out in a sailboat. Apache was only six. They were anchored in the Gulf, swimming. The wind came up. Apache had already swum back to the boat. Evidently—"

Apache didn't let her uncle finish, speaking herself.

"I'm not certain it wasn't my fault. I pulled myself on board by the anchor chain—"

"No, honey," her uncle said. "You didn't weigh fifty pounds. You couldn't have dislodged the anchor. The wind blowing against the boat pulled it loose. I've had it happen to me."

Now her uncle looked directly at them. "Apache tried to turn the boat around and go back to them, but she was just a little girl. She was still trying to turn it around when the Coast Guard found her."

During the drive back into Ocean Springs, Bailey said, "Her mother never told her how she was born. I wasn't going to tell Paulie until he was old enough—maybe high school or college. But her parents never had that chance, did they? She obviously was close to them, talking about how it still bothers her. And she seems to have developed a loving relationship with her uncle."

She stared ahead of them through the windshield. "But I still wish I could see one of the children with their mother; see how they interact." She raised the pages of stapled papers in front of her and looked at the second page, and then the third.

No reporters were parked at the head of the drive this time.

Mary waited at the French doors. "Was she the one?" she asked.

"Yes," Bailey said. "A beautiful young blonde. Dr. Post would be proud. She spoke quite kindly about him. She said that her mother spoke of him often." Bailey paused a moment. "She didn't know how she was born. Her mother told her that she was delivered naturally."

Mary said, "She's living with an uncle?"

Bailey nodded. "Her mother and father drowned when she was a child."

Mary normally didn't betray her feelings with her expression. But this time a noticeably sad look crossed her face. She looked past them toward the bay for a few seconds, then turned and walked silently back to where she had been working around the artificial womb. Bailey stared after her for a moment, then walked toward the lounging area.

Inside it, she glanced at the telephone on the coffee table. "I'll look the numbers up," she said, "while you call them."

They started with the Barneses.

In the middle of the calls, just as Ross pushed the cutoff button before starting to punch in another number, the telephone rang.

It was McLaurin. He had seen the news of Dr. Post's death on CNN.

"Damn, Ross, what in the hell happened?"

"Somebody broke in on him."

"Have the police got any leads?"

"They found some boot prints."

"That's what they said on the news. How's Bailey taking it?"

"Mary's continuing with the work."

"You mean she can still . . ." McLaurin was silent for a moment. "Guess I better be careful what I say on the phone. Never can tell who might be listening."

Ross smiled. "If anybody is listening they'll be back out here questioning us about the murder after hearing you say that."

"I was thinking about the bonus we get paid if the word about Bailey doesn't get out," McLaurin said.

"Strike two," Ross said.

"Yeah, it doesn't sound good to say it like that, does it? Well, are you two on your way back here?"

"Bailey wants to stay here a few days."

"Yeah," McLaurin said, "I imagine she wants to see if Mary really can . . . you know."

"Mac, don't ever offer to be a defense witness for me."

"Let's hope it doesn't ever come to that. By the way, Ross, Henry sent you over another DUI case. A friend of his. Well, guess I'll go—phone bill's running up."

"Mac, let me give you some names and see if you can help me out. It's two guys I'm interested in and their parents. I want you to call Ted at the resolution office and see if you can catch him before he leaves for the day. Tell him I don't have any social security numbers on them, but I have everything else—birth dates on the two guys, full names on them and their parents. I would like for him to look for matches to see if they might still live close to this area. Tell him to check . . . let's say in Mississippi, Alabama, and Louisiana. Tell him I'll call him around ten in the morning, his time."

"What are you doing?"

"Looks like Post did this three times instead of once."

"Three? Ross, what does it look like? I mean does it look like it does when it's growing inside a woman? Well, I guess you wouldn't know that, would you, unless you've seen some pictures? And Mary's able to do it in a room in that house? I would have thought of a . . . you know, some kind of high-tech laboratory. It's really something, isn't it?"

"Yeah, it is," Ross said, and then gave McLaurin both Billy's and Justin's names, including their middle names, their dates of birth, and their parents' names.

In the lab, Mary lifted the small glass container full of a milky-colored fluid from the cabinet above the artificial womb. She replaced the container with another one, closed the cabinet, then walked down the counter to a stainless-steel sink and emptied the milky fluid down the drain.

She looked down at the slim book of fetal photographs lying on the counter. She stared at it for a moment, then glanced toward the door to the lounge. Looking back at the book, she opened it, turned it to a particular page, and left it open on the counter.

Outside, the sun had dropped below the tops of the oaks to the west. A red Camry stopped at the entrance to the dirt drive. Braxton Bradford, tall and thin and dressed in jeans and a hooded pullover, opened the driver's door and stepped outside, staring across the door toward the house. Beside him on the seat was a 35-mm camera with a telephoto lens. It was the same camera he had used to photograph Bailey weeks before when she left the building housing the McLaurin/Channing bail-bond business. The photographs he had taken then had been sold for five hundred dollars. They were currently lying in his editor's office waiting for a reporter to think of a story to accompany them. Now there had been a murder—some doctor whose research she was funding. He hadn't seen any reports actually stating its purpose. Research not at some institute or scientific center but at an old house damn near in a swamp. And there was also one of the owners of the bail-bond company with her now—Braxton had heard the guy was serving as a bodyguard. There might be a real story or a close-to-real story to learn. Photographs accompanying such an article could be worth thousands—tens of thousands.

The sound of a car coming along the gravel road to his left caught Braxton's attention, and he saw a white Maxima. It stopped before reaching him, and a young blonde looked at him through the windshield. She was beautiful, her hair bright and shiny. He smiled at her and held his stare as the Maxima began to back down the road. He thought about driving after her car and inquiring if she were lost as a means of meeting her.

But business first.

He looked back toward the old house.

CHAPTER 27

I'm trying to locate a Billy Johnson or his parents, Richard and Cheryl Johnson," Ross said into the telephone receiver. "Billy would be twenty-two."

"Do you know what time it is?" the old man answered.

Ross glanced at his watch. It was ten P.M. He had been making calls for four hours now.

"Yes, sir, I apologize for bothering you at home at night, but this is important."

"Sleep's important, too, mister—especially at my age. And you've woken up Alison, too. She'll be taking more of those pills now to get back to sleep—and then she'll grunt all night."

"No, honey, I don't mind none if you grunt," the man said away from the phone. "'Course I don't, baby."

The man's voice came back to his receiver now. "Now see what you've up and done. Alison's mad at me. No, I don't know no Billy or Richard or Sherry or whoever it was you said."

The man hung up the phone.

Bailey waited.

Ross shook his head. "He didn't know them either.

I guess it's getting late enough we need to break off calling. That's all the Johnsons anyway."

"And all the Barneses," Bailey said. She looked disappointed.

"We'll try the numbers that didn't answer in the morning, then see what Ted comes up with."

Bailey nodded. "I don't think I can go to sleep right now. You mind if we watch television for a while?"

"Fine."

"I'm going to take a shower first," she said. "I feel like I've been in an oven all day."

Braxton's red Camry sat a hundred yards down the gravel road from the old house. He had come back on foot and now walked slowly through the dark shapes of the oaks lining the edge of the marsh. Ahead of him, no lights shone on the home's second and third stories and the windows on those levels were without curtains or shades, giving him the impression those areas of the house were unoccupied. The two big windows directly behind the wide steps leading up to the home's second level not only showed curtains, but bright lights glowed behind them. One of the curtains was gaping open. It was the window he walked silently toward now.

It was to a bedroom. The headboard of a queen-size bed sat to one side of the windowpanes while a door in the wall to the window's other side was open. He felt his stomach tighten with excitement when he caught a glimpse through the door of bare skin—and Bailey Williams stepped momentarily into view before disappearing behind the door facing again.

He quickly raised his camera lens to the glass. Looking through the viewfinder, he waited. An arm holding a towel came into view inside the door and he snapped a shot of that.

Bailey moved past the opening again and he depressed the shutter. The camera gave off a series of clicks. He looked over its top through the glass. Had he caught a shot of her or had she moved too fast?

His finger trembled at the shutter button as he lowered his eye back to the viewfinder and waited. Then, wrapping a towel around her body, Bailey walked from the bathroom into the bedroom. The series of quick metallic clicks started, and continued. Braxton took a photograph of her as she stood beside the closet with the towel tucked tightly above her breasts. He took a shot when she pulled a negligee from the closet. He took a shot when the towel dropped to the floor. He took a shot when she raised her arms to slip the negligee down over her head. The camera ran out of film.

Braxton fumbled inside his pocket for another canister.

Inside the room, Bailey pulled a white terry-cloth robe out of the closet, slipped it on, and began rolling up its long sleeves. Stepping toward the door, she raised her hand to the wall—and the light went out. Braxton moved to a side of the window.

Where was she going? he wondered. A one-sided smile crossed his face. He already had film of the nude Bailey Williams in his camera. No photographer anywhere had been so lucky—the photographs would be worth tens of thousands of dollars. Yet that would only be a pittance compared to what he could get if he caught her in bed with somebody—whoever else was inside the house with her. He only knew for certain that the bodyguard was there. God, wouldn't that be a scoop if he caught her shacking up with a damn bodyguard? The guy had been good-looking, in an everyday sort of dark-haired stud fashion—he might be a lot more than just her bodyguard.

Braxton looked at the darkened window again. Where was there another bedroom in the house, the one where the bodyguard slept . . . and, by now, maybe Bailey with him?

Maybe they had left the lights on.

Braxton looked toward the side of the house, and moved in that direction.

CHAPTER 28

The windows across the rear lower level of the house all showed light, though the curtains were tightly pulled, and Braxton couldn't see past them. He glanced up at the wide wooden deck extending out from the second level above his head, and moved around the house toward its far side.

Bailey had stepped from the bedroom and walked to Mary, who was standing beside the artificial womb. Mary had glanced back at her, but hadn't said anything. Bailey had looked at the book of fetal photographs lying a few feet down the counter, and walked to it.

It was open to a page containing a photograph of a newborn child. A partial Bible verse was written in scribbled handwriting to the side of the photograph. Bailey read the passage. A smile crossed her face. She lifted the book from the counter and, turning through the pages as she walked, moved slowly to the lounging area.

When she stepped inside the room, Ross looked at her robe with its sleeves turned up her forearms in thick rolls and its bottom nearly dragging on the floor.

"It was my father's," she said, "so don't laugh. It's my comfort blanket—my lucky piece. I carry it with me all the time."

"Whatever keeps you warm," he said.

"Warm I don't need. We should have had somebody overhaul the air conditioner. I like it cold when I sleep." She turned the book so he could see the color photograph of a fetus labeled "ten weeks old."

"We start off smart," she said. "Look at how much room there is for the brain." The fetus's head was about half its total length.

She turned to the next page. "She's cute," she said, looking at a photograph of a fetus with prominent dark eye spots.

"You've gone from a he to a she now?"

"Oh, so you think Paulie's going to be a boy, Ross? You think your genes are stronger than mine? We'll see." She grinned now. "I'm not even certain your muscles are stronger." She pulled the rolled robe sleeve up her arm to display her bicep, and curled her fist back toward her head like a bodybuilder posing for competition. "I work out three hours a day," she said. "You better be careful."

At the side of the house, Braxton tried to fit his lens to the crack between the curtains showing light from the lounging area. He cursed silently to himself in frustration, stared through the crack at Ross and Bailey a moment more—they were only talking—and cursed again.

The television displayed a scene of a lion chasing a zebra on an African plain. The lion was about to catch the terrified animal. "I don't like to watch something like that," Bailey said. She sat on the couch with her leg crossed over her knee. She had the volume of fetal photographs open in her lap.

Ross sat a couple feet away from her with his feet up

on the coffee table. He pushed his thumb against the channel changer. The scene on the television changed to Andy Taylor talking to the mayor of Mayberry.

Bailey slipped the stapled papers from her robe pocket. She unfolded them and looked at the second, then the third sheet.

"Three children," she said, "and then they burned the clinic. If they hadn't, think where the process might be today. Every hospital might be capable of doing the same thing."

Ross laid the channel changer back on top of the coffee table. "What are you going to tell everybody when you suddenly show up with a child?"

"I'm not going to tell them anything—about this, anyway. Ten million reporters would be standing around the house every day, trying to get a glimpse of her. It would be worse than the first quintuplets. They'd hound her for the rest of her life. I'll tell them I adopted. They'll go crazy trying to find out from whom."

She opened the slim book again. "Look, at three months the embryo starts sucking its thumb." She scooted closer and held the book for him to see. Her perfume was pleasant. Her shoulder pressed against his arm and her knee touched his. His gaze went from the book to her eyes. She caught his look, stared back into his eyes for a moment, and scooted a few inches away.

"Sorry," she said.

He couldn't help but smile. "I can take it."

"Ross, don't be mean." She laid the book back in her lap. "You don't have anybody special?" she asked.

"Not at the moment."

"Me neither. Really never have. When you're in my business, you don't know who really likes you or who just wants to be seen with you."

"Poor little rich girl, huh?"

She smiled. "Uh-huh." She turned through the color photographs in the book. When she stopped on a page containing the photograph of a newborn child, she repeated a verse written next to the photo.

" 'And God blessed them, and God said unto them, be fruitful, and multiply, and replenish the earth . . .'

"Isn't that a sweet thought?" she said. "It's from Genesis. Somebody was thinking about the blessing of a newborn child, I'll bet. Bet it was Mary instead of Dr. Post." She smiled. "We women are more romantic."

Ross looked at the scribbled handwriting, which was not much more than barely legible. It reminded him of the writing he had seen in the folders from Post's briefcase and on the notepad. "Looks like Post's handwriting. Somehow I don't picture him as being a big one on quoting the Bible."

There were initials under the quote.

"Says it's by U.A.V.," Bailey said.

The initials were written in such an exact hand it almost looked as if they had been done by some kind of mechanical device. Bailey stared at the photograph of the child for a moment. Then she closed the book and they began conversing again, mostly about light-hearted subjects, some about their backgrounds. Bailey had grown up as an only child on her uncle's ranch in Arizona—and once won a roping contest for under-eighteens at a rodeo. "I was only thirteen," she said proudly.

After saying that, she was silent a moment, then looked directly into his eyes. "Ross, when I was talking to you about the acoustical feedback the child receives in the womb . . . Well, I can't help thinking about other things, too. The warmth. The fluid Post has circulating around the placenta is warm, but it's not . . . a snuggle-y warm. Do you know what I mean?"

"You said *homey* warm the last time—and that's only in your mind."

"Yes, I know. But I still feel . . ."

"Guilty?"

"About us doing this? No. What choice did I have if I wanted a child? The doctors said I could die. One said I would die. But I would like to know that the children had no trouble bonding—that it didn't make a difference."

"Bailey, bonding comes after a child is born."

"Don't be condescending, Ross—I know that. But . . . you don't know what I mean."

He glanced at the TV screen, now displaying an old Western movie staring Audie Murphy. Bailey reached into the robe pocket and pulled out a pack of Virginia Slims. She held the pack in front of her for a moment, then slid it back inside her pocket. "I'm trying to stop smoking," she said. "I don't want to be smoking around Paulie. Don't want him . . ." She smiled as she paused. "I've gone from *he* to *she* to *it* back to *he*—I'll be happy when I know. Mary said soon."

She looked toward the TV, but her expression said she wasn't watching what was on the screen so much as looking in its direction while she thought.

Once, she glanced down at the slim book again.

"You want to go walking?" he asked.

She smiled at him. "To get my mind on something else?"

When he didn't say anything she said, "That's sweet. Yes, I do." She stood. "If you don't mind the bears or alligators or whatever it is that runs around out here at night seeing you with me in my robe."

"You'll pass." He came to his feet.

Seconds later, Braxton watched Bailey Williams and Ross Channing step outside the French doors and walk toward the bay. He looked at his camera. His film was high-speed enough to have taken clear shots in the bedroom light, but it wouldn't do in the dark. He watched the two, walking close together to the shoreline and then stopping and staring out across the bay.

He looked down at his camera again.

He already had the nude shots worth a fortune. He guessed he could give Bailey Williams and her body-guard a little privacy—he wasn't a Peeping Tom.

His film wouldn't work in the dark anyway.

Smiling to himself, he glanced back at the two, then turned and moved toward the front of the house and his car parked on the gravel road.

Bailey stared out across the bay. A shimmering mist hung above the water. In the distance, the bright lights of the Biloxi casinos and their hotels rose into the air.

"It's a pretty view," she said. "And you are sweet," she added, turning to face him. "For a bail bondsman."

He could smell her perfume again. Her gaze stayed on his. She stepped closer and kissed him softly on the cheek. Then she pulled her face back from his. "Me having to pay you to come with me," she said. "I feel like I just kissed a gigolo."

"And I don't know if I like having an unwed mother come on to me," he said, smiling.

"I can prove it's yours," she said. She laid the side of her face against his chest. "Any extra charge for being my comfort blanket?" she asked. "The robe only goes so far."

He wrapped his arms around her back. He could feel the smooth softness of her skin beneath the robe. Her hair smelled sweet. "Mary's been sitting in Post's wheel-chair," she said against his chest. "I keep feeling sorry for her and I keep thinking about Apache and her parents never getting to tell her how much they wanted her." She was silent for a few seconds.

"And I keep thinking about the other children and their mothers." She pulled her face back from his chest and looked into his eyes. "You remember when I said I touched the Plexiglas and it didn't feel *homey* warm? I don't know if it was Dr. Post's death or what that started me thinking like this. You know I wanted a baby so badly I just jumped into . . . I'm glad I did. I mean I wouldn't stop now for anything in the world. I wouldn't stop Paulie for a hundred worlds. But I'm worried about . . . I hope I haven't done something wrong for his sake, Ross, I . . . Why am I so nervous about it now? I called Dr. Presnell—the researcher I told you I had been speaking with in California. He would have thought I was crazy if I told him about Paulie. I spoke in hypothetical terms—about the possibility of a baby born through artificial birth not bonding with the mother. About other things that might go wrong. I wish I hadn't now. He told me about a condition called displacement disorder. It occurs in children in orphanages who get little or no care when they're babies. Places like Bosnia where the orphanages were flooded by children who are war victims, and China, where the government takes newborn children away from parents who already have one child. Their orphanages have hundreds of thousands of children and almost no staff. Some of these children aren't touched except to be given a bottle and occasionally changed. They simply lay there. Dr. Presnell said that some of these children, when they've been adopted, can't seem to express love. Some of them don't want to be held. Some of them even become violent. Dr. Presnell says they have lived so long without anybody taking care of them that they won't accept anybody else's help, anybody holding them, accept anything. Orphans have been institutionalized forever. Yet it's only now that doctors are realizing what can happen to them when they're not nurtured. I started thinking about the artificial womb—the only sound is the motor, there's no physical contact with the mother's body . . . no softness. I know it's before the child's born; it's not the same as the children being neglected in the orphanages. But how do we know if the gestation not being inside the woman creates something that's not good? It's never been done before. And then I said to myself, yes, it has been done before. Ross, I know I'm silly, but I want to find those other children. I want to find them because I want to know Paulie is all right. Isn't that silly?"

"Everything is going to be fine," he said.

"We are going to try to find the other two children though, aren't we?"

He nodded.

"Good," she said. She laid the side of her head back against his chest.

They stood that way for several minutes, close together, his arms around her, the warm breeze coming across the bay flowing gently against them, the sweet scent of her hair and her perfume in his mind.

Then she raised her face and smiled. "It worked," she said. "I'm sleepy. Thank you, Mr. Douglas Ross Channing."

And they started back toward the house, Bailey holding his arm and leaning her head against his shoulder as they walked slowly in its direction.

Ross looked over at her. She smiled back at him. Her kiss had only touched his cheek. They had only stood close together. Yet he couldn't remember any woman leaving him with the same warm sensation he was feeling now.

Later, lying under his blanket on the couch in the lounging area, he thought of that sensation again. He looked through the doorway into the darkened laboratory at the bedroom door.

To this point, he had thought of Bailey only as a semi-spoiled celebrity bent on having her way.

Now he was suddenly thinking of her in a different way..

And he hadn't had too much wine this time, he thought, and smiled.

He slipped his hands behind his head on the pillow and stared at the ceiling.

It was a pleasant sensation.

CHAPTER 29

Braxton, still in his hooded pullover and jeans, walked among the gamblers milling around the roulette, dice, and blackjack tables. He was in the Grand Casino in Biloxi. Unlike Las Vegas and Atlantic City, where casinos forced their hotel guests to pass through a gambling area to reach the check-in counter, the Mississippi casinos kept their hotels and casinos separate. Only a passageway connected the gaming area with the tall hotel at its side.

Southerners probably think that's more dignified, Braxton thought. He knew there were a lot of strange beliefs down here. He hefted a stack of hundred-dollar chips in his hand. Much more than he would normally dream of gambling, but he now had guaranteed tens of thousands of dollars in his jeans pocket in the form of nude shots of Bailey Williams. He could afford to celebrate a little.

He started to step to an open spot at a craps table— and saw the blonde staring his way.

She was the same one who had driven the Maxima down the gravel road when he had stood at the entry drive to the old house. He would notice her face among any crowd of starlets he had ever seen. She rivaled Bailey Williams in looks, and that took some doing, he thought. Her main edge was in her much more prominent breast works. She had dropped her gaze, but now raised her eyes again—and smiled in his direction.

He looked at the hundred-dollar chips. Beginning to toss them lightly in his hands so that the blonde would be able to see how much he was capable of spending, he walked in her direction.

She stood by herself a few feet from a roulette table. He stopped in front of her. He only smiled, waiting for her to speak first.

When she didn't, he said, "You from around here?" He'd think of a cooler line as he went on.

She acknowledged his question with a yes.

"My name is Braxton."

"My name is Apache."

He thought that a great name. His real name was Bob Jones—Robert H. Jones, actually. He had changed that to Braxton Bradford when he became a reporter because he thought it looked better over a byline, with the two B's slanted and larger than the rest of the letters.

"Are *you* from here?" she asked.

"No."

Apache, he thought again. He imagined that name probably wasn't a real name either. Maybe a stage name. "You in show business or anything?" he asked. He was thinking *strip club*. The name fit. The tight dress did. The body under the dress certainly did.

"No," Apache said.

Slow start to the conversation, Braxton thought. Obviously he wasn't looking at a big conversationalist. He needed something to loosen her up. He looked around for one of the cocktail waitresses. He kept juggling the hundred-dollar chips.

"What are you doing here?"

At the blonde's question, Braxton looked back at her. "I'm on assignment for a . . . magazine."

Magazine always sounded better than a supermarket newspaper.

"What kind of assignment?"

He looked at her swelling bustline. He decided to give it his best shot. "On assignment accompanying a big name here in town for a few days."

"Bailey Williams?" Apache asked.

Braxton was taken aback at her guessing who he had referred to. But of course, what *bigger* name would be in Mississippi right now? He was certain everybody knew.

"You said you're accompanying her?" Apache asked.

There was something about the way the blonde was looking at him. He didn't know what, but he had a sixth sense about things. There was also an unusual tone in her voice—pleasant, but something under that pleasantry.

"No," he said. "Not really accompanying her, actually. Just along to get a story about what she's doing here."

Apache looked into his eyes, as if she were reading him.

An unnerving thought passed through his mind—maybe she was a cop. Nobody had seen him prowling around the old house, taking pictures through a window. He thought about a Mississippi jail. He pictured a low-lying place, damp and smelly for sure, probably with rats. He knew there would be roaches. He pulled his billfold from his hip pocket. There was always the freedom of the press to fall back on.

He held out his ID card, the one that had the name of the tabloid for which he worked clearly printed across the top in gold block letters. "Simply a reporter doing my job." And then, to not lower himself too far in her eyes if she wasn't a cop checking him out, he said, "Big bucks in what I do." He juggled the chips in his hands.

Apache quit looking at the card. Whatever she was, she was satisfied with what she saw.

She turned away from him.

"Hey," he said, reaching out to clasp her arm, "why are you in such a hurry to—"

"Don't touch me!"

Braxton jumped backward at the sudden, loud outburst. Around him gamblers stared from all the tables.

CHAPTER 30

Ross woke early. The first thing Bailey said was that she didn't mean to be clinging when they were out by the bay the night before. He said he didn't mind—he liked it. She smiled and offered to fix him a breakfast of bacon, scrambled eggs, and toast, or bacon, fried eggs, and toast. The bacon because that was the only kind of breakfast meat in the refrigerator. The eggs because that was the only breakfast she knew how to prepare, she said, other than pouring milk over cereal. She prepared the eggs on the hotplate and the bacon in the microwave. Mary ate in the laboratory, what little she ate—only a piece of toast and none of the bacon or eggs. They ate in the lounge with the television off and only the sound of an occasional speedboat passing on the bay. Ross had to wait until eleven o'clock Mississippi time for nine A.M. to roll around in California and Ted to arrive for work at his office. Then Ross waited for another hour to give Ted time to find the names McLaurin would have called in.

How many Jonathan and Elizabeth Barneses and Richard and Cheryl Johnsons would there be in the area he gave Mac? Dozens? Scores? More? But the list should be considerably smaller with Billy and Justin—

maybe only one each with the exact same name and date of birth. He was put on hold by a bored receptionist at the IRS office and it took Ted several minutes to answer. When he did, he said he hadn't finished running his check yet—and also said he didn't remember even so much as being taken out for lunch since providing the last information he had been asked for. Even lunch, he repeated.

"I'll have a surprise for you as soon as I get back to Los Angeles," Ross said.

"Of course," Ted quickly said, "I'm only talking about a friend taking me out to lunch. No money changing hands. Ha-ha. Call me back in about an hour. This is going to take a little more time."

Ross could hear another voice, faintly, and knew somebody had stepped into the office with Ted. He replaced the receiver.

While Ross waited for Ted to finish gathering the information he needed, he once again tried Billy Johnson's number in Biloxi.

Again an answering machine answered his call. This time he left his name and number and asked for the Mr. Johnson who lived there to please return his call. He waited thirty minutes more and rang the Los Angeles IRS office again. Ted told him that in the three state areas he had requested that IRS records showed there were a half dozen Johnsons and Barneses with the correct full names for the parents. There were no Billys who matched with both his full name and birth date. One Justin had matched.

"You can fax the names and numbers to me," Ross said.

"Are you kidding?" Ted said. "With the IRS letterhead on the fax—you want us both to end up in prison?"

Ross began to copy down the information. The Justin Barnes that matched lived in Mississippi, in Wiggins, a small town of around three thousand, thirty miles up Highway 49 from the Gulfport/Biloxi area. Ted had said for some reason there was no accompanying phone number on the computer.

"He's going to be the right one," Bailey said. "I can feel it."

Surprisingly, no reporters' cars waited at the head of the drive leading from the old house. The trip to Wiggins took about forty-five minutes. A bald-headed man in bib overalls sitting in a chair at the front of a service station told them the address was five miles west of the town. Bailey looked through the passenger window as they slowed to turn beside a mailbox at the entrance to a gravel road running across a large section of pastureland. A white wood-frame house loomed atop a small hill a quarter mile's distance back from the highway.

A short, gray-haired woman sat in a rocking chair on the home's front porch. The afternoon sun shone under the roof overhang, heating her with its bright yellow light.

The woman continued rocking slowly in the chair without looking at them as they came across the grass toward the two steps leading up onto the porch.

"Excuse me," Ross said. "Is there a Justin Barnes here?"

"Will be soon," the old woman said. She nodded toward the highway. "Gone to town to get a part for the hay baler. Broke down about an hour ago."

"He wouldn't be the son of Jonathan and Elizabeth Barnes, would he?" Ross asked.

"Once was," the old woman said. "They're passed on."

The disappointment showed in Bailey's face.

"You want to wait and meet him?" Ross asked.

She nodded.

Ross glanced toward the road. She did, too. The

woman continued to rock, again not looking at them.

"I guess we can wait in the car," Bailey said.

They started toward the Lincoln.

"Care for a glass of tap water?" the old woman asked.

They waited for over two hours. Ross sat on a corner of the steps. Bailey paced the porch.

"Probably had to drive into Hattiesburg," the old woman said, looking toward the highway. "But I can hear him coming now."

A broken cloud of dust trailed an old pickup coming up the entry road. Bailey moved to the edge of the porch. Ross came to his feet. The pickup slowed when it was still a hundred yards away, then drove on toward the house.

When it stopped beside the Lincoln, a large, young man with blond hair, wide shoulders and a thick chest stepped outside. He wore Western boots, a leather belt with a Western buckle at the waist of his jeans, and a plaid shirt.

Ross stepped forward to meet him. "Mr. Barnes, I'm Ross Channing." The man's big hand enveloped his as they shook hands.

Then Justin looked at Bailey as she came toward him. They shook hands, too. The old woman on the porch said, "They wanted to see you, Justin. Didn't say what for and I didn't ask."

Ross had planned what he was going to say this time. "We're doing a newspaper story on a Dr. Sebastian Post and his research. Your father and mother were supposed to be friends of his."

"They were," the old woman said. "Back when they lived in Biloxi."

Justin stared toward her. "Mary Beth," he said. "They're here to talk to me." The woman turned her face away and stared off the side of the porch into the sunlight. Justin's eyes came back to Ross's.

"I was adopted in Mexico. Dr. Post made the arrangements."

Bailey looked at Ross. Justin didn't know that he came from the artificial womb any more than Apache had.

"I didn't know my parents very well," Justin added. "They died when I was nine."

"Gas leak in the house," the old woman said without looking their way. "They never woke up. Justin came running over to my place—little bit out of it himself from the gas—and told me he couldn't get them awake. He needed somebody to bring him on up, and I needed somebody to provide for me with my husband just died the month before. Justin's family owned this place. We came here. Been here ever since. I keep the house clean and he does the field work and we just stay out of each other's way, mostly."

As Ross drove the Lincoln back out onto the highway, Bailey stared through the windshield. "I should be as sorry for him as I was Apache," she said, "and yet I'm angry. Angry with myself. Both of them have been sweet. Why do I keep worrying?" She glanced back over her shoulder toward the wood-frame house. "You know, in a way it's sad that neither Apache nor Justin knows the truth about how they were born—how badly their mothers really wanted them."

She looked across the seat. "Maybe we can find the other boy—Billy."

When they returned to the house, Bailey excused herself, saying she was unusually tired. Ross used the telephone in the laboratory to try the number of the Billy Johnson listed in Gulfport.

The answering machine came on again.

After replacing the receiver, Ross stood in thought for

a moment. He knew Billy's age from Dr. Post's papers. With Billy's parents having lived in the Gulfport/Biloxi area he would have attended school there. In one of the grade schools or high schools in the area there would be an old class yearbook with Billy Johnson among the photographs. There would also be photographs of classmates who had attended school with him.

One of them might know where he was now.

Ross sat down on the couch, picked up the TV's remote control, and pushed a button.

A station in New Orleans was giving the news. A photograph of the old house filled the screen. The anchor was talking about Dr. Post's death—that no arrests had yet been made by the Ocean Springs police.

Lieutenant Browning appeared on the screen.

He said the killer might well be a large man, with his weight in the two-hundred-twenty to two-hundred-thirty-pound range, and probably over six feet. If anyone knew of someone who fit that description and drove a van, a dark red or dark brown, maybe, and a newer model, maybe a Nissan, they should call the Ocean Springs police and give them that information.

What a waste of time, Ross thought. There could be a hundred vans like that driven by a similar-sized person along the coast. The department would be flooded by calls—and literally hundreds of hours wasted if the police followed up on all of them.

Yet what else did the lieutenant have? He was trying.

Browning ended his interview by saying that if any kids happened to be out parking on that road that night, they should call and let the police know. Their parents wouldn't be told.

Then the television screen filled with shots of Bailey Williams walking down runways in exquisite gowns, posing on a sandy beach—the bikini she wore allowed every one of her perfectly formed curves to show. Ross knew that at that moment there would be hundreds of men along the coast leaning closer to their television sets.

He wondered if the man who had committed the murder was watching—and what he was thinking.

Apache stared at the television screen in the living room of her uncle's house. Her lips tightened as Bailey Williams waved from a sandy beach toward the camera lens. Apache clicked the remote control, turning the set off.

Her uncle leaned out of his easy chair and looked back at her.

She didn't cover up her anger well, staring back at him, her lips still tight, then coming to her feet and striding toward her bedroom.

Her uncle watched her go. Then, a questioning expression on his face, he leaned his head back in the chair.

He had never seen her with an expression like that. He looked at the blank television screen.

Cribs in an orphanage floated above Bailey's bed. The tiny babies in them rolled and turned and wailed. Nobody would come to comfort them. She could see the damage already done in their twisted faces, the damage growing worse the longer they went unnurtured. She saw the barrel-shaped womb floating between the babies. She could tell it was cold. A different kind of cold. She tried to say "no" but her lips couldn't form the word. Justin and Apache stared down at her, their features as large and developed as they were as young adults now, but their bodies small, childlike. Around them, other faces began to materialize. One was that of a doctor. "Brain damage," he said solemnly. "A child born in this manner certainly will have brain damage." *A second, older, man's face framed by flowing gray hair hanging down to his shoulders was that of a philosopher. "No cons<u>c</u>ience," he was saying. "The child will certainly be born without a conscience."*

A priest's face materialized. He looked sad as he looked down at her and spoke in a voice so low it was hard to hear him.

"Born without a soul," he said.

Bailey's eyes popped open and she sat up abruptly in her bed.

Beads of perspiration dotted her forehead.

After a moment she took an audible breath, lay back on her pillow and stared at the bedroom ceiling.

CHAPTER 31

Bailey wore a simple, black linen dress. The closest thing to appropriate Ross had brought with him from Los Angeles was a dark gray sport coat and navy slacks. Above them the sky over the cemetery had darkened with thick clouds rolling in ahead of a storm front moving down from the north. It was almost as if Heaven itself was making a gesture of sadness at a human's passing, Ross thought. He looked at the shiny coffin Bailey had purchased. Thick Spanish-moss-draped limbs of a giant oak hung out over the grave site. Fifty feet away, a bluff dropped off to the calm waters of Fort Bayou, sweeping out into the distance past tree-covered islands and swaths of virgin marshland dotted with the white shapes of herons feeding in the shallow waters. Post had lived his last twenty years with the pain of his burns, then died a horrible death. Now, at least, he would finally lie in peace. The pastor the funeral home had obtained started his prayer.

As Ross lowered his head, he caught the fragrance from the flowers on top of the coffin. The scent made him think of the roses he had placed on Estelita's grave, and the wreath he had left on Manuel's. He opened his eyes to try to drive away the thought—he wanted to remember them both as they had been when they were alive, not in their graves. He looked at the flowers on the coffin. They had likely been provided by the funeral home—or Bailey again. Nobody was present for the service except for her and him and Lieutenant Browning.

Especially noticeable by her absence was Mary, he thought, and thinking that drove his mind to something else. Her not coming had caused him to wonder again.

She had said she wanted to remember Post the way he was, not at his burial. The same way he thought about Estelita and Manuel. But he had come to see them. How could Mary not come to see her husband?

There was something about her that just didn't make sense. More than one thing about her didn't make sense. Then the pastor ended his few words. Bailey said, "Amen," stepped forward, caught a handful of the dirt mounded beside the grave, and pitched it gently atop the coffin.

Browning spoke in a low voice. "Nothing yet, Mr. Channing. From the depth of the boot prints we estimate the killer was around two-hundred-twenty to -thirty pounds. And that he could have very well used the van you saw—but that's it. You haven't thought of anything else you forgot to tell me, have you?"

Ross shook his head.

Bailey stepped up beside them.

"I wanted to afford you some privacy," Browning said to her, then glanced toward the narrow, tree-lined entrance to the cemetery. An Ocean Springs city police car sat sideways across the drive. An officer stood beside it. Two cars and a van with WLOX-TV emblazoned across its side were stopped on the far side of the officer. A man pointed the lens of a shoulder-mounted TV camera toward the grave.

"Thank you," Bailey said. "Is there any way you can hold them there when we leave—so they can't follow us?"

Browning smiled. "Sure. They can't get any madder at me than they already are."

As the lieutenant walked toward his car, Bailey slipped the folded telephone directory page from her purse.

The circled name on it was Billy Johnson. His address was underlined. As she looked at it she took an audible breath, causing Ross to look at her. She glanced at him, smiled feebly, and then folded the paper in her hand, holding it tightly.

The home of Billy Johnson, a small one-story with an orange tiled roof, sat at the rear of a lawn dotted with thick bushes and bordered by a tall hedge. Ross stepped onto the shallow porch at the home's front and pushed the doorbell button.

"He's not there."

The voice came from a man in the adjoining yard.. He stood at a break in the hedge. He was an older, gray-haired man dressed in a pair of slacks and a dress shirt. He smiled pleasantly in Ross and Bailey's direction as they walked across the yard toward him.

"I'm Ross Channing. This is Bailey Williams. We're trying to locate a Richard and Cheryl Johnson, or a Billy Johnson, their son."

"You've got the right place," the man answered. "Billy's out of town until tomorrow. He asked me to keep an eye on his house until he got back. 'Course Richard and Cheryl are dead."

Ross caught Bailey's glance. Other than that, she didn't show any emotion. But a thought passing through his mind gave him a strange feeling. "How did they die?" he asked.

"Richard was killed in a car wreck," the man answered. "Around the time Billy was two . . . no, about three, I think—time gets away from you. Cheryl died in a fire in her home when Billy was seven. I remember his age then for certain—it was fifteen years ago, same month my divorce was final, August. My name's Jerry Richards." He extended his arm through the gap in the hedge to shake hands with each of them in turn. "Do you want to leave a message for Billy?" he asked.

There was still the thought in Ross's mind. "Mr. Richards, you said a fire . . . do you know any more than that?"

"Yeah, sure do. Everybody in the neighborhood does—at least those that was living here then. Getting a lot of retirees coming down here the last few years. Some say she had been painting the inside of the house, was using a can of gasoline to clean tiles where she'd spilled some paint, and the gas fumes must have got to the water heater's pilot light. But others said that didn't happen."

"What do you mean, didn't happen?" Bailey asked.

The man looked around him as if he didn't want anyone to overhear what he was about to say. "Well, might have been the pilot light all right—that touched off the gas. But it's the rest of it that some say don't sound right. Cheryl was burnt up in the bathroom. First of all, I say despite her body being charred to a crisp—and they said it was—that if she had been wearing clothes at the time there would have at least been some trace of them still on her, and there wasn't. Number two, they say that the can that blew up was in her bedroom—not the bathroom. The door between the two had been shut according to what I heard. Billy was burned a little—hands and his face. I, and a few others, say she left the can in the bedroom while she was getting ready for a shower, probably already had her clothes off—that's why none of them were burnt into her skin. Maybe she was already taking the shower—they say the water was running. 'Course the investigator said that the fire melted the pipes to cause that. Could have."

The man looked out at an eighteen-wheeler rumbling noisily by on the highway. "In any case," he said as his face came back to theirs, "some of us think that Billy knocked the can over—probably roughhousing, and the gasoline spilt under the door and hit the pilot light. If so, then Billy caused it, didn't he? One thing's certain, a neighbor saw Billy come running out of the house just after the explosion. He stood there—must have been in shock—without running to anyone for help. When the neighbor came chasing over there, Billy suddenly broke into screaming for help—like the neighbor coming up popped him out of his shock. Of course no one would want a boy to have to carry that with him—that he was responsible for his mother's death—so most people don't say nothing about it. But that's what I say."

Richards smiled politely after finishing his story. Ross saw the gesture, but didn't respond. The thought that was bothering him was still in his mind. If anything, it was stronger now that he had heard the man's story.

As they walked back toward the Lincoln, Bailey looked at his face.

"What?" she questioned.

"Nothing," he said.

"What, Ross?"

"Nothing."

As he opened the Lincoln's door and slid behind the steering wheel, Bailey came in through the passenger door. She looked across the seat.

"What is it, Ross?"

"That makes all three of them with dead parents," he said.

Bailey nodded. She looked at him, waiting for him to make his point.

"All three of the children with dead parents," he repeated, "and with the children around when they were killed. The children the only ones around when it happened."

Bailey's eyes narrowed. "Ross, you're not saying you think . . . you're not thinking that the children might—"

"You kept asking me."

"You *are* thinking that. Ross, that's crazy. They were all little children when it happened."

"Yes, when their parents died under unusual circumstances and the children were the only ones around to see it happen," he repeated. "I'm just telling you what went through my mind. That's three of them—and all three the same. It's crazy—but you asked me what I was thinking."

"Ross, my parents died when I was a little girl. That doesn't mean I killed them. There *are* coincidences."

"I know. I told you it was crazy."

"It is crazy, Ross."

"That's what I said."

"Ross, Billy couldn't possibly have killed his father—not at three years old."

"He didn't have to. Only his mother was left."

"Damn it, Ross, that *is* crazy."

He turned the ignition key and began to back the Lincoln from Billy's drive.

"Ross, you know I was already thinking crazy things. And now you start this."

He looked over his shoulder and backed out onto the highway, then started the Lincoln forward.

"Ross, what are you going to do?" There was a tentative tone to her voice.

"I'd like to know more about the circumstances of the fire," he said. "Especially with what Richards told us."

"Ross, you're not going to the police, are you?"

"No."

"How can you find out any more without going to the police? Ross, I don't want you going to the police."

"I said I'm not. They would think I was crazy. Billy was seven when his mother died. Apache was six. Justin was nine. Who is going to believe kids that age were

murderers? There's damn sure not going to be any way
to prove it."

Bailey stared at him.

He glanced at her, and faced back to the windshield
again.

Her voice was low. "I don't want it to be," she said.

He looked back at her.

"Ross, I mean I don't want it to be because . . . because of Paulie. Do you understand that? Because I
don't believe I could bear the possibility that something . . ." She shook her head as she paused. "This is
crazy, Ross. You take any hundred people the age of
Billy and Justin and Apache and a lot of them are going
to have parents who are dead."

"But not all of them," he said.

"Ross there *are* coincidences."

"I know."

A few minutes later Ross stopped the Lincoln in the
Gulfport Library parking area and walked toward the
building.

A woman behind a counter inside the library pointed
them to the area where past issues of newspapers were
stored on microfilm.

"Ross, what are we doing?" Bailey asked.

He located the reels of microfilm he sought, the ones
containing the copies of newspapers printed fifteen
years before. Then he pulled a straight-back chair in
front of a viewing screen and began searching through
all the editions printed after the first of August, the
month Billy's neighbor said the fire occurred.

He found the story in a *Sun Herald* article dated August seventeenth. Almost fifteen years ago to the day.

A Biloxi woman was killed Tuesday morning when
an explosion ripped through her home.

Cheryl Johnson, 34, died while she was apparently doing some work in a downstairs bathroom about 8:30 A.M., police spokesman Todd Taylor said.

"It looks like she was painting and had carried some gasoline into the bathroom and cleaned some spots off the tile and an explosion occurred," Taylor said. The explosion which was heard and felt by residents a dozen blocks away remains under investigation.

Johnson is survived by a son, Billy, 7. Her husband, Richard Johnson, died four years ago in an automobile accident. He was 30.

"It was an accident, Ross," Bailey said.

He ran the microfilm slowly forward, watching the images of the pages moving across the screen as he searched for any follow-up story that might add additional details to what he had read.

He stopped once when he saw the word "tragic" in a headline. But it concerned an accidental shooting where a man mistook his neighbor for a burglar and shot him to death in his backyard. The police had charged the man with manslaughter.

Each page of *The Sun Herald* blurred, then refocused, then blurred again as he jumped from section to section in the newspaper.

Three days after the fire, and, except for a funeral notice, he had found no further mention of the woman's death. He was about to quit his search when the name Trehern appeared in a small headline:

TREHERN CHILD
DIES FROM FALL

Five-year-old Walter Trehern of Gulfport died Thursday when he apparently fell from a second-floor window at his family's home. "We're not sure how it happened at this time," Gulfport City police spokesman Joseph Orr said. "All we know is that the youth died from a fall and we are continuing the investigation."

The only person in the home with the boy at the time of his death was the victim's eight-year-old cousin, Apache, who has been living with her uncle, the boy's father, Gerald Trehern, since losing her own parents in a swimming tragedy two years ago.

A baby-sitter, whose name is being withheld by authorities, was supposed to be in the house, but had gone next door to talk to a boy she knew there.

"This is so sad," said Susan Haley, who lives next door to the Treherns. "He was the cutest little thing you've ever seen, and it's sad for Apache, too. My daughter, Mandy, is the same age she is. I look at Mandy and I wonder how any child that age could endure such tragedies only two years apart. It just makes me sick at my stomach, for the father and Apache as well as little Walter."

Bailey had been reading over his shoulder. She had caught her lip in her teeth as she read. She stared at him now. He came up out of his seat.

"Bailey, a five-year-old child. Apache killed a five-year-old child."

"You don't know that, Ross. You are just speculating because something looks . . ." Bailey turned and walked away from him. He knew she couldn't say anymore or she would start crying.

"Somehow, there has to be more," he said.

The librarian allowed Ross to use a telephone behind the counter. The byline over the newspaper articles showed they had been written by the same reporter, a

Flora Sweeney. He telephoned the newspaper, was told the woman still worked there, and was put on hold while his call was transferred to the paper's Jackson County bureau.

Mrs. Sweeney had a pleasant-sounding voice. She didn't remember much about Cheryl Johnson's death except it had been caused by a fire. She did remember the five-year-old Trehern boy's death. She particularly remembered Apache Trehern. "She was such a beautiful little child. Intelligent, too. Too intelligent, in a way. The baby-sitter said that Apache had just fought with her little cousin over a teddy bear he had received for his birthday. When the police got there, she was holding the teddy, crying, saying that her being angry with her cousin had caused his death. It's like when you have an argument with somebody, feel like you hate them because you are so angry, and then when something happens to them you feel guilty. That's a concept you wouldn't think a child her age would have been able to grasp. Yet she did. It was pitiful—her guilt. When I arrived at the home she was staring back and forth at everybody; you could tell she thought everybody was blaming her. I don't believe I'll ever forget it."

Ross thanked the woman and replaced the receiver. He looked at Bailey. She had caught her lip nervously in her teeth again, waiting to hear what the reporter had told him.

"Ross?" she said.

"Apache killed him over a teddy bear. Over a damn teddy bear she wanted."

CHAPTER 32

As Ross switched on the Lincoln's headlights and drove out of the library parking lot he said, "We have to have something more—a lot more. The police would still think we're crazy."

"Ross, I don't want it to be," Bailey said again.

All he could say was, "I know."

Bailey stared silently through the windshield, then, closing her eyes as she spoke, she said, "I want to know for certain. I wouldn't want Paulie to be like that. I wouldn't want to have him born—for his own sake—if he was going to be like that. I have to know."

Ross stared ahead of them. The dark clouds rolling in ahead of the storm front were growing thicker. All the cars were turning on their headlights now.

"The notebooks in the lab," he said, looking across the seat. "All the papers Post had. Maybe he observed something that would help us. Maybe give us some proof. At least add to what we know—one way or the other."

Thirty minutes later, Ross stopped the Lincoln at the rear of the old house. The clouds completely obscured the moon now, and when he turned off the Lincoln's headlights the darkness was nearly absolute. He held the French doors open for Bailey and they walked inside the laboratory.

The bedroom door was closed. He knocked on it, then opened it without waiting for a response. The bathroom door was shut and he could hear the shower running. He walked to the closet and looked inside it. "Post's briefcase isn't in here," he said. "But it was. That's where Mary got the pages with the children's names."

He walked back into the laboratory and to the counter where a notebook lay next to the artificial womb. It contained only the step-by-step guide as to how to care for the fetus.

Ross laid it back on the counter and opened the cabinet underneath it. It contained jars full of liquid nutrients and chemicals. The next cabinet was empty. He moved down the counter, opening each of their doors in turn.

Bailey opened the cabinets running in the opposite direction.

"Ross."

The briefcase, standing upright, was scooted into the cabinet in front of her.

She pulled it out onto the floor. He turned it on its side and opened it.

The first few stacks of material consisted of the folders stuffed with the pages he had been reading when Mary surprised him in the lounging area. Underneath the folders were some notebooks, then an old gynecological manual. Its cover was slightly charred, obviously having been removed from the clinic after the fire. Beneath it were a half dozen notebooks and pads with wire bindings.

He thumbed through the first notebook. It was full of Post's scribbling. Daily notations were made. Small anatomical sketches of embryos, fetuses, and day-old babies appeared throughout the pages.

The second notebook contained similar notations and sketches.

Bailey knelt beside him and lifted a small notepad from among the other materials and began looking through it. He finished thumbing through the pages of the notebook, laid it on the floor, and lifted another one into his hands.

Bailey moved a stack of notebooks and folders aside, and lifted a small book with a leather cover from the briefcase.

She opened it.

"Ross, this is a diary."

The penmanship, done in a dark ink, was so precise they could have been looking at a medieval text painstakingly written by a monk a thousand years before.

"It's Mary's," Bailey said, handing it to him.

The first page was dated the day Mary stepped off a commercial airliner in Mexico City after graduating from nursing school. She wrote how Dr. Post met her at the airport and took her on a tour of the city as a present for her graduation.

Ross turned the page.

Mary wrote that after two days they quit their mini-vacation and drove west toward Taxco.

He started going quickly through the pages.

"Wait a minute," Bailey said. She reached across him and turned back a couple of the diary's pages. "There," she said. "About a baby."

Dr. Post's and Mary's baby.

The child was named Aurondo.

Another child from an artificial womb that they didn't know about? Ross wondered.

He turned the page backward to the preceding date.

Mary did write about the pregnancy. *Her* pregnancy.

The child had been born through normal childbirth, carried to term in her body.

"What are you doing?"

The voice came from the bedroom doorway. Mary, wearing houseshoes and a white robe hanging to her ankles, stared at them. She walked forward.

Ross came to his feet. "The children murdered their parents."

At his words, she stopped.

"Murdered their parents, and one of them killed her cousin," he said. "A five-year-old boy. I don't know what else they might have done. You knew."

There was the barest shake of Mary's head, and then her low voice. "No." She looked at the diary in his hands.

"Ross," Bailey said, "we don't know."

Mary's gaze had dropped to the floor.

"What don't we know, Mary?" Ross asked. "What am I going to read in here?"

Mary raised her eyes. She looked at the diary, stared at him for a moment, then spoke in a low voice.

"When I arrived in Mexico City, Dr. Post gave me a grand tour. It lasted two days. Then we left for the mountains and the clinic. When we neared Taxco, I saw the first little Indian children and their mothers, selling iguanas on the roadside. The Indians were thin, some of them nearly starving. Chickens ran freely about. The Indians' religion forbade them from eating them—and they would starve before they would betray their beliefs. Though they were poverty-stricken, you could lay a bill-fold filled with money on the sidewalk and it would still be there a week later. They were good people, proud people, suffering people. I knew I had come to the right place to make my life's work. I visited the great Church Santa Prisca in Taxco and prayed for God to give me guidance. I had arrived like a tourist. Now my life's work lay ahead of me."

Mary paused a moment. Her gaze had been expressionless, with almost a blank look in her eyes as she talked, as if she were reminiscing as she spoke. Now her eyes came up to Ross's.

"Sebastian and I were married soon after that," she said. "It all started then. If I had known, I wouldn't have let it. But how could I have known?"

CHAPTER 33

As Mary continued to speak in her low, barely perceptible voice, Ross had to concentrate hard to catch every
word, and the effect was mesmerizing, almost as if he
were there in the mountains while it was happening.

Mary had immediately fallen into the work of ad-
ministering to the sick and injured, working harder than
she had ever known it was possible to work. Not only
working as a nurse, but cooking and washing and
cleaning when there was time to cook and wash and
clean, sitting next to patients' bedsides all day and into
the nights. Most of the Indians in need of care walked
to the clinic that had just been finished, some of them
coming from days away. She drove the old Jeep Dr. Post
owned through rutted roads and passageways that were
not much more than trails to transport the sickest cases
back to the clinic on stretchers lying across the rear of
the Jeep. More than once a patient had died on the way.

But she hadn't worked as hard as Dr. Post. There
were literally days and nights at a time that he did not
sleep, not even a nap. But always the pleasant smile and
the words of encouragement to her and the Indian volunteers at the clinic when they were so tired they didn't
know if they could go on.

Then it happened. She became pregnant. She hadn't been certain what Post's reaction would be; he had told her he wanted to wait awhile before having any children. But when she told him the news his response was one of unbridled joy. They decided to name the boy after one of the volunteers who had worked with them from the beginning and lost his life in a mud slide when he had gone out after a patient in a tropical downpour.

Mary's labor was difficult and intense. She writhed in the pain of childbirth for over twenty-four hours. Post wanted to perform a caesarean section. She didn't know which way to decide.

Her back raw from squirming on sheets that had begun to feel like sandpaper, perspiring as if she had been immersed in water, the pain to the point she was almost delirious, she called for Post to perform the caesarean.

But before he could begin, the baby emerged.

The boy came headfirst. Post had worried about a breech baby. But that was not what he should have worried about. The baby was disfigured, his head swollen out to one side, an eye fixed and glazed, staring blankly.

Mary had felt the disfigurement her fault. She had always been scared of pain. She felt that in her fear of the cramps of childbirth she had held back, keeping the child from emerging, causing the irreparable disfigurement.

To Post that was ridiculous; Mary should know as a nurse that she couldn't have held the child back if she had tried. The problem had been in the living conditions she had endured at the clinic, he said, the arduous work she had done, the drinking water that was delivered in barrels not always free of bacteria, the food she ate sometimes affected by insect-borne contaminants.

It was no fault of Mary's.

But there was fault. There was the fault of the young children as the boy began to grow. The stares, and the

cruel, oh, so cruel taunts. The child, destined to be unusually large as a man, quickly outgrew the children his
age, towering over them, and that alone silenced them
as he stared with his one good eye in their direction.

But there were always older children, and by virtue
of their older age, bigger. The child fought some, but
mostly became withdrawn. At ten, he disappeared. He
left a note behind, saying he was going into the trees to
die.

Dr. Post and Mary, and all the help they could sum-
mon, searched the mountains for days.

But to no avail.

Dr. Post had fallen into a deep depression, not only
at his child's running away, but at what the boy had
suffered to cause him to leave.

When Post emerged from that depression, he began
researching. Babies should never again be born deformed, like their child, but perfect, he said. During
their gestation they should be provided with the exact
amount of nutrients they needed, and those nutrients
should not only be uncontaminated, but sterile. The fetus should not have to endure any stress while the
mother worked, but be kept cushioned softly in a perfect, stress-free environment, and at a temperature perfect for its growth. Nothing that would harm them in
any way should be present during their gestation. Post
was convinced that if this were the case they *would* be
born perfect.

And he set about making that possible.

First came the experiments with egg clusters grown
in petri dishes on various mediums and kept alive for
as long as possible. Then came animal experiments.
Wombs from small mammals of all kinds were dissected, providing growths of tissue kept alive by a constant infusion of blood. Tissues were rooted in
mediums, then in all possible surfaces, kept oxygenated
and moist with varying mixtures of nutrients.

All of this was crude, very little was successful, and what was successful often rotted the next time it was tried.

Post began to retreat more and more into isolation in a section of the clinic he took over for his work, devoting little more than a fraction of his time to the patients who still flocked to the clinic. He gradually began to lose weight. His blond hair, thick and shiny ever since Mary had known him, began to dull and started graying. She began to worry about his mental health.

Finally, she took it upon herself to remind Post of the patients who needed him, and whom he was neglecting. He replied that while a few of the patients were indeed not receiving all the attention he could give them while he worked trying to perfect artificial birth, tens of thousands would benefit if he succeeded.

Meanwhile, the months he predicted it would take him to succeed in his work turned into years. He retreated more and more into seclusion, rarely venturing from his laboratory, going weeks at a time without shaving, months without taking the time to allow Mary to cut his hair.

It was almost a shock to Mary when one day he stepped from the area of the clinic he kept locked and smiled at her. He was clean-shaven. His hair, uncut for months and hanging down over his shoulders, was now freshly washed. He wore a clean pair of khaki pants and a white shirt buttoned at the neck.

"I have succeeded," he said, and started crying.

In his lab, a newborn pig lay on its side, pink and glistening, hardly breathing, but alive. It had been brought to term outside of its mother's womb, from a placenta rooted in the dissected tissue from the womb of another pig and kept alive in a container filled with sterile liquid nutrients supersaturated with oxygen. Dr. Post had shown Mary how he had not only kept the tissue alive, but how it had grown into a larger section than he had first started with.

Ross thought of what Bailey had told him about the artificial skin now being grown by scientists in California. The technique more than likely had many similarities to what Post had done in growing the womb tissue. But he had accomplished his feat alone in a small clinic and without the great infusion of money the California researchers would have had at their disposal. Post was a genius, unchecked in his brilliance—or his madness.

Mary continued speaking. She said that after the birth of the pig, Post had almost completely quit seeing patients. She told how she busied herself teaching the volunteer aides to give shots and treat all but the most seriously ill cases—and there were even some of those Post refused to take the time to see.

Then there was the day he emerged from the lab again. "I know the way," he said.

He had succeeded in keeping a section of human tissue alive, and growing. The tissue had come from the uterus of an Indian woman who had died three months before. Post hadn't asked permission for its use. "The Indians wouldn't understand," he had said.

Eggs and sperm were gathered from a couple who had worked the longest at the clinic, an Indian woman and her Mexican-mestizo husband, a man of mixed European and Indian blood. They hadn't been able to conceive children. For their devotion and long duty, theirs would be the first reward.

The egg cluster aborted soon after it attached to the tissue mounted at the rear of the artificial womb. That had not tempered Dr. Post's excitement. Women miscarry often.

A second egg cluster was implanted.

It lasted for two weeks.

Then a different couple's egg and sperm were tried. It also failed to produce a cluster that worked. Post kept using different couples, each time also making subtle adjustments in the nutrients, the oxygen flow, the process of waste removal, and a dozen other small changes that seemed almost insignificant.

Then an egg cluster produced an embryo, and it kept growing. The embryonic stage passed. The fetal stage began.

At week nine, the fetus was nearly two inches long and beginning to take noticeable human shape, its ears having moved up from its neck to its head, and its prominent dark eye spots beginning to shift toward the front of its face.

Then a second head began to grow.

Post aborted the experiment.

The next try produced a fetus with two arms on one side and none on the other.

Each try produced a succeeding deformity.

Post grew noticeably depressed. He called the original Indian woman and her mestizo husband back in, took their sperm and eggs again, and retreated into his laboratory once more.

Six months later he succeeded.

But since he had succeeded before, and had then seen the deformities form after several weeks of growth, he waited to show Mary until the fetus was in its fifth month.

This time nothing went wrong—until the seventh month, when it was noticed that one hand of the child was suddenly growing much faster than the rest of the child's body, becoming swollen and misshapen. Post had wanted to abort the experiment. Mary had begged him not to, saying it was too late.

The child was born with the much larger, misshapen hand, but with nothing else wrong.

Post had a mixed reaction, pleased with the birth, but disturbed by the deformity, even if it was only minor compared to his past failed trials. "Nothing is lacking in the procedure," he said. "The child should be perfect."

It was the Indians, he decided. There was so much intermarriage among them that even with the Indian woman's egg being fertilized with the mestizo man's sperm, with any man's sperm, it had been impossible to produce a normal child, much less a perfect one.

He contacted friends back in Mississippi.

Three weeks later Carl and Carol Trehern from Biloxi arrived in Mexico City. Post insisted on meeting them at the airport by himself. When they arrived at the clinic, he introduced them to Mary, but then moved them into the area he kept locked for his work. They emerged rarely during the next two weeks, and then only in Dr. Post's company.

Then, suddenly, he left with them during the middle of the night. Returning, he said only that they had flown back to Mississippi. Mary had known that the couple could only have been there to produce eggs and sperm for a new attempt at artificial birth—eggs and sperm that didn't come from the Indians.

That was the time of the beginning of the trouble with the Indian volunteers. Some of them left. All had seen the mutated attempts with the animals and later the even worse mutations that had occurred while trying to bring a human into the world. The child with the deformed hand now lived among the Indians. All knew Post continued his strange experiments in the lab.

Soon the clinic was down to two old women and a young boy as the only volunteers.

Nine months later the first perfect child was born.

"See," Post said, pointing a trembling finger at the child crying in the bassinet that the remaining volunteers had fashioned. "See!" The child was proof that his procedure hadn't been wrong, it was the eggs and sperm tainted with the Indians' blood that had caused the previous deformity.

The child was observed for months, and then another couple arrived from Mississippi. Nine months later a second perfect Caucasian child was produced.

The same procedure was repeated once again—a husband and wife arriving from Mississippi to stay a couple of weeks at the clinic, and a new gestation period started—a third perfect Caucasian was produced.

Now Ross stared into Mary's eyes as she suddenly quit telling her story.

She was silent a moment longer and then said, "By then it was apparent the three children had cold personalities. Sebastian at first thought that their seldom crying as young babies meant they were even more nearly perfect than normal, satisfied more, lacking nothing. He had kept them isolated in the laboratory with him, caring for them himself, recording everything moment by moment.

"I felt that their behavior, their lack of emotion, their often recoiling from touch or trying to hold them, was due to him observing them as subjects, rather than showing them warmth. I felt that they needed the nurturing a loving mother could give them. I persuaded him to give them up, for their own benefit. And who better to give them up to than the original mothers who had donated the eggs that had led to their birth? Who deserved them more?

"He called the mothers back, one at a time. They were irate at first. He had deceived them, told them that the experiments hadn't worked. But he persuaded them that he had good reason, that he wanted to make certain the children were perfect first.

"He swore them to secrecy. There would be other mothers he could help, he explained, if they didn't let it be known what he was doing. Some government agency, prodded by those who would not think what he had done was normal, might step in and stop him from helping any other mothers.

"Because the mothers had ached so much for children, it was an argument they could understand. They agreed, and each in turn left with their own child."

Mary shook her head. "So it was my doing then. Again, I thought the three children were only cold. I was glad their real mothers were finally receiving them. Who else could better bond with them? I had begged him for that. How could I have known?

"But maybe Sebastian knew at that time. He said he wanted to research more before he produced another child, and didn't produce another in the two years after the adoptions.

"Then the child with the misshapen hand killed his mother. The Indians came to the clinic. They barricaded us inside it and they burned it. Sebastian, trying to save the records of his research from the fire by throwing them out the window, was burned horribly.

"I saw my son then. Not in a vision. I saw him through a section of a fallen wall, standing outside, staring into the fire. He was leading the others.

"I pulled Sebastian outside. They surrounded us. I knew we were going to die. My son stopped them. Only Sebastian was to die, for producing the demon children, as the Indian mother had died for allowing the boy to be born in the artificial womb. I threw my body on Sebastian's to try to protect him. I said they would have to kill me if they killed him. My son stopped the others. Even though he was filled with hate for what he was, I had done nothing intentional to him. And Sebastian had allowed him a normal birth, despite what he had done with the others. My son told me to go and take Sebastian with me. He said if Sebastian survived his burns, he was never to perform his experiments again—no other child was ever to suffer another demon birth.

"At the hospital in Mexico City, when it was apparent Sebastian would survive, my son visited us again.

He stood at the end of the bed and told Sebastian that he had prayed for him to live so that he could suffer the pain of his burns like the mestizo child was suffering with the pain of his affliction. He told us not to come back to Mexico and reminded Sebastian that he should never attempt the experiments again, that nobody should ever attempt the experiments again. That he would know."

As Mary finished her story, she looked toward the artificial womb. Bailey was shaking her head. "Why didn't you tell me, Mary? For God's sake, why didn't you tell me?"

"I didn't know," Mary said. "It was my son with his condition, and the son of the mestizo man and Indian woman who had come out of the artificial womb with his deformity, who were filled with hate. But the three children of American parents had come through their birth perfectly. I thought they only lacked nurturing. How could I know—until you told me now?"

Ross said, "You did know."

Mary's gaze came to his.

"You knew, Mary. You gave us their names so we would discover the truth for ourselves. Why didn't you tell us before we started the fertilization?"

"I didn't know for certain. I had not seen the children since they left Mexico. When you said Apache's mother and father were dead, I realized then that my suspicions were correct."

"Your suspicions?" Bailey questioned. "Why didn't you tell us about the things that had gone wrong in the past?"

"Gone wrong?" Mary said. "Sebastian found my diary after we returned to Mississippi. I had written in it about the children's coldness as I have told it to you. He was going to destroy the diary. I pleaded with him. It was the record of my child and of my thoughts of my child as he grew up and all that had surrounded him, what he used to be—before he had run into the mountains. Sebastian said he would not destroy it if I would swear to him on my child's soul that I would never speak of what had gone wrong. I swore that. I wouldn't have sworn if I had known anything was wrong with the children more than coldness. But I didn't, and I did swear on my child's soul, and I wouldn't violate that oath. I won't violate that oath."

Bailey had a questioning look on her face. "But you the same as told us when you gave us the children's names," she said. "You knew we would find out."

"I didn't tell you," Mary said. "I didn't because of the oath on my child's soul."

"It's not on your child's soul, Mary," Ross said. "It's you and Dr. Post who have done this . . . who are doing this now."

Mary shook her head. "No," she said. "I would have never allowed it to go forward if I thought something would happen to your child. I wouldn't allow that to happen again. But I knew it wouldn't go wrong. For my own sake, in my allowing you to go forward with this, I made certain. Sebastian promised me, and I *knew* it wouldn't happen again."

"My God, Mary," Bailey said, "How could you keep believing after so many . . ." As Bailey's voice broke, she looked toward the artificial womb. "It's Paulie now, too."

"No," Mary said. "It's not. It's only the other children. I should have known at the time. They were cold even as little babies. They resisted touch and would fight against being held. But they would sit close together with each other, the baby boy, his older brother, and the girl, often sitting so close they pressed against each other. Sometimes the mestizo boy with the malformed hand cried until his mother brought him to see them. They came to him as they would nobody else. Whatever it was they suffered, coldness, hate, whatever, somehow they realized each other's needs or pain. They came together with each other maybe because they felt they were the only ones they could come together with. I saw that. It was right before my eyes, and yet I didn't realize."

Ross looked at Bailey. "I have to call the police now," he said.

"No," Mary said. "Let the child be born first. It will be perfect. I do know. The child will be perfect this time."

"Damn you, Mary," Bailey said. "You're as crazy as Post was."

"The child will be perfect," Mary repeated. "Let it be born for you . . . and for Sebastian. Let him have this one time." She paused for a moment. "And, in a way, for me. Please."

Ross walked to the telephone on the counter. He laid the diary next to the telephone and lifted the receiver. He glanced at Bailey. She had walked to the artificial womb and was standing with her hand pressed flat against its Plexiglas front.

He lifted the receiver to his ear.

There was no dial tone.

He jiggled the cutoff button and listened again.

"The line's dead."

Bailey stared at him. Mary looked toward the French doors.

The lights went out.

CHAPTER 34

As the lights went out in the old house, the generator in the laboratory jumped to life with the sound of its loud motor. Ross had his automatic in his hand. "We're going to the car," he said.

Bailey looked in the direction of the artificial womb, hidden in the darkness, with only the sound of the generator motor to tell where the barrel-shaped container sat.

"Bailey," he repeated.

She started toward the French doors. Mary didn't follow them. Bailey looked back at her. "Mary?"

Mary didn't move. Ross reached for the doorknob. "Stay close to me," he said to Bailey. He eased the door open slowly.

The automatic held ready, he leaned his head forward and glanced to his right and to his left. He stepped outside. Bailey moved close behind him. The front of the Lincoln was only a few feet away.

He angled out to its side until he could see no one crouched behind it. He pulled Bailey around him and pushed her toward the driver's door.

As she slipped inside the car, he swept his gaze back and forth to the rear corners of the house.

There was no sound of the Lincoln starting.

Ross looked back at Bailey turning the ignition key. She turned the key again.

"Get back inside the house," he said.

Braxton had watched the lights suddenly black out in the lower level of the old house and, a couple of minutes later, Bailey Williams and her bodyguard step outside. They had walked close together like lovers to the driver's side of the Lincoln. Bailey had slid inside behind the steering wheel. A moment later she had jumped back outside the car and they had walked hurriedly back to the house—like they had suddenly changed their minds.

No lights had come on.

Changed their minds to do what? he thought and smiled. He looked toward Bailey's bedroom windows, glanced up at the heavy clouds overhead, dimming the moon, then, camera in hand, started forward through the trees toward the house.

It was almost completely dark inside the laboratory, only the faintest gleam of moonlight filtering through the windows. Ross could barely see Bailey beside him.

Then, even over the loud sound of the generator motor, they heard something bump against the wheelchair.

"Mary," Bailey said.

Ross pointed the automatic in the direction of the sound.

"You should leave," Mary said. Her shape materialized out of the darkness. Her white robe reflected what little light there was. She looked like a ghost. "They won't harm me," she said.

"They?" Ross said. "It's your son, isn't it? He left the boot prints, the prints of a heavy man, the prints of a child you said towered over the others when he was young. He said he would know if Post started his experiments again. How did he know? One of the children from here told him, didn't they?"

Bailey shook her head no as she looked at him. "He didn't know them, Ross. They were sent here before he came back from the mountains."

"Did he know them, Mary?" Ross asked. "Did he . . . No. No, it wasn't him. It was the mestizo boy who knew them, the one who killed his mother, wasn't it? He knew them and he was with Aurondo when the clinic was burned. The shoe prints Lieutenant Browning found around the van—that's who was waiting there for Aurondo. But there were more than one set of prints around the van, and one of those sets a small man's or a teenager's or a woman's—Apache?"

"If you do not leave they will kill you," Mary said.

It was so dark Ross couldn't see the door to the storage room or the lounge or the staircase leading up to the main level. Anyone could silently come down the steps and he would never know it. He walked slowly to the artificial womb.

He felt along the counter, found the light switch and flipped it on. The blue-green light inside the Plexiglas came on, illuminating the laboratory in a faint glow, spreading out to the door to the storage area, to the bedroom door, to the lounge door, and to the spiral staircase leading up to the main level of the house.

The briefcase lay open a few feet in front of him.

He took Bailey's arm and moved back into the shadow at a corner of the lab where he could see, but not be seen.

Braxton waited beside Bailey's window.

He heard the footsteps.

He jerked his head toward the corner of the house. His heart nearly stopped when he saw the dark figure walking toward him.

He started to run. A passing gap in the heavy clouds overhead let a dim shaft of moonlight through. It illuminated the blonde hair. *The woman he had met in the casino.* Still, he stepped backward. What was she doing . . . ?

He suddenly realized what she was doing, and relaxed. A smile crossed his face. So he had indeed been seen by someone when he had taken photographs through the window two nights before. The police had waited for him to come back. It would only be a trespassing charge. A misdemeanor, probably dropped when his editor called and raised hell.

He raised his hands and the camera over his head. "All right, you've got me—the jig is up." He grinned.

He heard the footstep behind him. A much heavier footstep.

He looked across his shoulder at the swollen face.

One glazed, blank eye stared at him.

Ross heard the faint scream, muted through the walls of the house. Bailey's fingers touched his arm. He held the automatic in front of him, looking back and forth from door to door.

McLaurin, dressed in khaki slacks, a dark sport coat, and a beige shirt with its collar unbuttoned, drove a rented Taurus along Highway 90 in Biloxi. He had taken the scenic coastal route from the airport in New Orleans rather than the interstate to see what the Mississippi Coast had to offer. At Bay St. Louis the casinos had begun. The first really luxurious gambling complex he had seen was the Gulfport Grand with its sweeping lights and gaily illuminated signs. A tall hotel rose into the sky next to the casino. An enormous parking garage appeared full and a line of cars waiting to get into the valet parking area trailed back out onto the highway.

Now he passed the President Casino and its accompanying yacht marina. He looked at the wide yacht berths covered with concrete roofs to keep the vessels out of the weather. Sleek speedboats from as small as fifteen feet to luxury vessels a hundred feet long lined the box-shaped enclosure.

He passed a cluster of towering, brightly lit casinos a few minutes later, then crossed over the long Biloxi Bay Bridge to Ocean Springs and drove into a service station to ask for directions.

The sound of the generator filled the laboratory, dimly lit by the soft, blue-green glow coming through the Plexiglas. Ross and Bailey stood in a dark shadow at a corner of the room. Mary stood a few feet away.

"Go sit down, Mary."

At his sharp tone, Bailey looked at him. "Ross?" she questioned in a low voice.

"She's his mother," he said. "I don't want her close to me if he comes inside."

Bailey looked at Mary as she walked toward the wheelchair. "Ross, she wasn't making any sense. She said she didn't tell us what was wrong with the children right after she told us. She's as insane as Post was, isn't she?"

Ross didn't answer. He had felt a moisture-laden draft flow across his face from the side. He looked toward the bedroom. Only a dim illumination extended though the doorway. He stepped in its direction, stopped just short of the doorway, lowered himself into a crouch, and suddenly dove inside the room, hitting on his stomach and yanking the automatic back and forth around him.

He came to his knee. The curtains moved in the gentle breeze coming through the window that had been opened between the nearest bed and the bathroom. The bathroom door was partially cracked. He slowly stepped in that direction.

Bailey's shadow appeared in the doorway behind him.

She screamed as the shape of a man lunged from the side of the room. His thick shoulders bunched, he held a section of steel pipe above his head.

Ross fired, the loud crash of the automatic deafening in the enclosed space. The slug jolted the figure to a stop. He stumbled backward, then came forward again. Ross fired a second time, then a third, then a fourth.

The pipe fell to the floor. The figure swayed backward, then forward, then backward again, and collapsed in a heap. He grunted and was still.

"*Aurondo!*" Mary wailed, and hurried past Bailey into the room. She dropped to her knees. She grabbed the sides of the wide face and turned it toward her.

Ross stared into Justin's wide, young face.

Bailey stood with her hands over her mouth.

"It's all of them," Ross said, looking down at Mary. "It's all of them together, like you said they were as children. Three from here, and maybe the mestizo boy— and your son. They knew each other in Mexico, and they knew each other after they came back here. It is all of them, isn't it, the only ones they care about—each other."

Mary raised her gaze to his. "They only want the growth stopped," she said in a voice so low it was hard to hear. She released Justin's face and slowly came to her feet. "And to see that it doesn't happen again. That's all my son wanted when he burned the clinic— he didn't want it to happen again. I will tell them it won't happen again."

"Mary," Bailey said. "What do you mean it won't happen again?"

"Sebastian knew what was wrong with the children. Your child will prove that. I will tell them that."

"It's the artificial womb," Bailey said. "It's a child being born from there. It's what's happening to Paulie now."

"He will be perfect."

"Mary." Bailey's voice was low now. "You're helping to produce a child this time. It's not only Dr. Post."

"My son will not harm me," Mary said. "I am his birth mother. And, I told you, it will not go wrong this time."

Ross closed the window beside the bed, locked it, and pulled the curtains tightly together.

"Ross," Bailey said.

Mary was walking toward the French doors.

"Mary," he said.

She stopped in front of the doors and opened them. Ross pointed the automatic past her toward the darkness outside the house. Mary stared back at them. "I didn't break my oath," she said, "and I won't. And I give you my oath now—the child will be perfect. I will tell them that."

And she stepped outside, disappearing from sight.

Ross hurried across the room and closed and locked the doors. He didn't know if Mary was trying to help them, or joining her son and the others.

"Ross," Bailey said.

He looked at her.

"Ross, it's me they're really after, isn't it?" Bailey said. "I'm guilty of the same thing their mothers were."

McLaurin turned the Taurus onto the dirt drive lined with thick trunks of shadowy giant oaks. Before him, an aging, three-story antebellum house glowed in the Taurus's headlights.

He parked in front of the inclined steps leading up to the doorway on the second level. Every window was darkened. He glanced at his watch, then opened his door and stepped outside onto the damp ground. He slipped his coat off and laid it back on the car seat, then shut the door. The night air was warm, humid, but not as thick as it had felt when he stepped off the plane in New Orleans. There was a soft breeze. He looked up at the house again, dark and stark against the cloudy sky. *Appropriate setting for a murder*, he thought, thinking about Dr. Post's death. Then looking past the near side of the house, he saw a light in the bay. It was given off by a small aluminum boat a hundred or so yards out in the water making its way slowly in the general direction of the shoreline.

Ross kept his eyes moving, looking at one moment in the direction of the bedroom, the next toward the storage room, and back to the lounge. His gaze fell on Justin's body once again. Dimly illuminated by the light from the womb, it lay just inside the bedroom door. Ross looked down at his automatic. He had never fired it at anyone before. He could feel the strange mixture of regret and fear in his stomach, regret that he had taken a life, fear that he could have lost his own, or Bailey's. He saw Bailey staring at his face.

A sudden loud thumping sound startled him.

It came from the second level of the house. Bailey touched his arm. He tightened his grip on the automatic.

The thumping came again—a loud knocking.

McLaurin knocked loudly on the door frame again. Still, no lights came on inside the house.

If the service station attendant hadn't drawn a map for him he would have wondered if he had the wrong place. But it was the right place. It had to be—there wasn't any other house in the area. He reached for the doorknob, turned it, and the door swung open. He looked into the darkness.

"Ross?"

He stepped inside the foyer. In front of him a barely visible staircase rose toward the third level of the house. To his right was the entrance to a shadowy small area that must have once been a sitting room. To his left, there was a wide opening to a bigger room. Passageways led around both sides of the staircase. It was totally dark behind the stairs.

"Ross," he called louder. A gust of wind blew against his back and he glanced over his shoulder.

"Ross, damn it, will you answer?" Maybe they had gone to one of the casinos or something, he thought.

"Get over here!"

McLaurin jumped at the sudden voice coming from the darkness behind a side of the staircase.

"Here," Ross repeated.

"Ross, what in hell are—"

"Damn you, Mac, get over here—the killer's in here."

McLaurin hurried forward, then slowed as he moved into nearly complete darkness. "What do you mean, he's here?"

"Where's your gun?" Ross asked. His dark shape appeared directly in front of McLaurin.

"I didn't bring it on the flight. What do you mean he's—"

"Damn, Mac, they're here. Four of them, maybe. Bailey, come on, let's get to the car." Ross reached back for her arm and stepped toward the door.

"Ross, damn it, would you mind telling—" McLaurin stopped his words at the sight of the Taurus's hood raised into the air.

Ross quickly shut the door. He looked at McLaurin. "Why are you here, Mac?"

"Hell, Ross, Dr. Post is murdered, and then you call wanting names of others you say he's produced, and I'm wondering what this womb looks like and . . . hell, I got curious. Now I wish I hadn't even thought about it. And what do you mean might be four of them? Killers?"

Ross looked toward the spiral staircase.

Bailey shook her head. "I don't want to go back down there," she said. "I don't want to move."

Mary stood in the darkness at the side of the house. Aurondo faced her a few feet away. Apache and Billy stood at his sides.

"Leave," she said. "Leave before it is too late and go back to your homes. The child will be perfect this time."

Aurondo didn't answer.

"I give you my oath," Mary said. "Your mother's oath. He will not suffer as you have. Dr. Post knew what was wrong."

Aurondo turned away—she was his birth mother.

Billy stepped forward.

Mary saw the long knife.

CHAPTER 35

The girl was sixteen, thin, and had long brown hair. For the warm Mississippi night, and where they were going, she had worn only a pair of slacks and a blouse tied by its ends at her midriff, exposing a strip of firm tanned skin across her middle.

The boy moved her arms from around his neck and looked around her toward the shoreline. He had curly dark hair that hung casually down across his lean face and wore a pair of jeans, tennis shoes, and a long-sleeve white shirt rolled up his forearms. He cut the throttle on the outboard engine and the small aluminum craft coasted forward, bumping its bow gently against the damp mud.

A couple of hundred feet back from the shoreline, the old house loomed faintly visible in the dim moonlight filtering through the thick clouds overhead. He stood up in the boat, cradling a six-pack of beer under one arm and a blanket under the other. Charlene hopped to the soft ground and smiled back at him.

Seconds later, she spread the blanket on the dry ground back from the shoreline. Johnny picked up one of the empty beer cans they had left there the week before. It was a Budweiser can, the brand he carried with him now.

He held up the empty can. "Ours or somebody else's?" he asked in a theatrically deep voice.

"Don't start that," Charlene said.

Johnny smiled. "Maybe some old drunk, his brain eaten up. Hasn't shaved in weeks, teeth stained black and he's sitting over there . . ." He nodded toward the thick stand of shadowy oak trunks to their side and lowered his voice again, "staring at you."

"Johnny, I mean it," Charlene said. "You aren't scaring me, but I still don't like it." She sat down on the blanket and held her hand out. Her voice was softer. "Come here."

He pitched the empty can to the side where it bounced against the ground and rolled into the darkness. He knelt beside her. She reached her hand up and caught the back of his neck, lying back onto the blanket, pulling him down on top of her. He drove his face into her neck, nuzzling it. She enjoyed the sensation and turned her head to the side.

She saw a lightning bug, the insect's luminescence flashing softly off and on as it moved through the darkness a few feet away.

The bug came slowly down toward the ground, and settled on Braxton's chin, lighting it with a soft glow.

Charlene screamed.

Johnny jerked his face back as she clawed his chest to get up from under him.

He saw the body laying partially concealed behind an oak trunk—Braxton's blank face staring toward them.

"Oh God," Charlene muttered through her hands as she came to her feet. "Oh my God. Oh God."

Johnny steeled his nerves. He took a hesitant step toward the body, and then another. Leaning his head backward even as he reached his hand down, he touched the pale face with his fingers. He saw the dark blood covering Braxton's neck and puddled around him.

"*Damn,*" he said, yanking his hand back. "He's not a drunk. He's dead."

"Come on," Charlene said. She was already moving toward the boat. "Come on."

Johnny walked backward, looking at the corpse as he did, then turned and hurried knee-deep into the water, leaning to swing the boat's bow out into the bay as Charlene jumped into the craft.

He climbed over its side into its rear and reached for the starting rope. He saw the figures coming from the direction of the house toward the water.

His heart felt like it stopped. He yanked the rope. The motor roared to life. Charlene saw the figures and screamed. He jammed the steering arm to the side. The bow swung around and jumped forward as he twisted the throttle open wide.

Charlene was thrown backward to the side of the boat, her legs lifting into the air, her back going toward the water. Johnny grabbed her by her tennis shoe and hung on. Her upper body splashed backward into the water. The boat tilted and, with her body creating a drag, turned in a circle.

Johnny cut the throttle and pulled on her legs. Screaming, splashing, she was dragged feet first back into the rocking craft.

From the bank, three shapes came out into the water. Then a fourth figure raced toward the three from the trees. A break in the clouds allowed a shaft of moonlight to come through, showing that the figure approaching the others had the slim build and long hair of a woman. The figure pointed back toward the house.

The other figures looked in that direction, then back at the boat as Johnny opened the throttle again.

The craft, its motor roaring, Charlene lying in its bottom screaming, sped toward open water.

The figures moved toward the house.

They were hurrying now.

Seconds later, three of them scaled up the thick supporting posts at the rear of the house toward the wide deck that extended out from the living room toward the bay.

The fourth figure, the largest one by far, moved around a side of the house toward its front.

Ross stood with his back against the staircase running up above them. He held his gun in both hands, his gaze alternating between the opening to the spiral staircase leading down to the laboratory, the beveled glass door a few feet away, and the dark opening into the dining room. Bailey stood beside him, her hands touching his waist. McLaurin stood as close as he could get. They had heard the screams, and the loud roar of an outboard motor.

That had come a few minutes before. And since, only a deep silence.

McLaurin looked up the rail bordering the stairs running to the home's third level. Ross glanced in the direction of the large living room to his right. Above them, in front of them, behind them, down the spiral staircase—everywhere was darkness.

"I don't think they have a gun or we'd already know it," he said. "We do have one. If we go out the front and stay together in the drive, then in the middle of the road out of here, they couldn't get to us without us seeing them."

McLaurin shook his head. "I'd rather wait until morning," he said.

"Wait for what they're going to do next?" Ross asked. "They know exactly where we are. We don't know where they are. We're going to make the move. We're going to go out the door, stay close together, and keep moving where they can't get ahead of us. You in the back and Bailey between us, right in the middle of the drive."

"I don't know, Ross," McLaurin repeated.

Above them a figure launched itself off the staircase, crashing down into Ross, driving him into the floor. A tire tool slammed into his back. Billy raised the steel weapon to strike again. Ross twisted onto his back and fired twice. Billy was knocked backward against the side of the staircase, the tire tool flying out of his hand.

Bandez rushed from the darkness in the dining room, diving into Ross, grabbing the hand with the gun. McLaurin started toward them. Apache screamed from behind the stairs and charged Bailey. McLaurin stepped to the side and met Apache head-on, slamming his body into hers and driving her backward to the floor. Billy, bleeding, struggled to his knees. Bandez twisted Ross's hand. The automatic clattered to the floor. Bandez hammered his thick fist into Ross's head. Billy pushed himself off the side of the staircase, reaching forward with his fingers spread like claws, digging his fingernails into Ross's cheeks and eyes. Ross grabbed for the automatic. Bandez hit him again.

McLaurin screamed in pain and rolled away from Apache. Blood poured from the side of his neck and his shoulder. He tried to stem the flow with his hands. Apache, her face and blouse blood-smeared, came to one knee, a razor blade clamped in her fingers. Bailey yelled and stepped forward and kicked for Apache's face as hard as she could.

The toe of her shoe caught Apache in the throat, slamming her backward against the wall. Apache gasped, grabbing her neck, and made a gurgling sound. Bailey kicked again and then again and again, bouncing the back of Apache's head off the wall with each blow. Apache's eyes glazed over. Blood ran from a corner of her mouth. Bailey kicked again. Apache's head snapped backward one more time, and she toppled over onto the floor on her face.

A shot sounded.

Bandez groaned, sat up off of Ross, and fell backward. Ross twisted to his stomach and pushed his pistol toward Billy's face. But the clawing fingers had quit digging. The arms were still. Billy's eyes stared blankly without seeing.

Ross sprang to his feet. He looked at Apache lying on her side, unmoving. Bailey knelt beside McLaurin. He had sunk down the wall next to Apache. His beige shirt was in tatters across his chest. Blood seeped through his fingers. Ross knelt beside him.

"It didn't get my jugular vein, did it, Ross?" McLaurin's eyes were scared.

"You wouldn't be talking if it did, Mac. You're going to be okay." He pulled McLaurin's shirt back from his chest and looked at the long cuts. McLaurin looked toward the bodies lying in front of him. "Is that all of them?"

Bailey stood and struck her lighter. In its illumination, Bandez's light-brown face stared blankly toward the ceiling.

"Ross, that's the man I told you came by the office asking for you," McLaurin said.

"Look at his hand," Ross said. "He's the first one born from the womb."

The hand was swollen, with thick fingers. Bailey's eyes moved to Billy. He lay on his stomach, his face staring toward the staircase.

Bailey looked at Apache. The young woman's blonde hair covered her face from view. Blood ran from the corner of her mouth. Bailey's lip trembled.

But Ross felt no regret this time. Not for the ones lying dead before him. Not even for Justin anymore. For as he actually saw in person the mestizo man who as a boy had killed his own mother, and then traveled here to kill again, Ross knew that Manuel hadn't died in a car accident, and that Estelita hadn't been killed by a thief, but that they had paid with their lives simply because they crossed paths with the children of the artificial womb. He looked at McLaurin.

"You're going to have to come with us, Mac. Mary's son's still here somewhere."

McLaurin took a deep breath and pushed himself to his feet.

"You're going to bleed a little bit," Ross said. "But none of the cuts are very deep—you'll be okay if we take it easy."

Bailey, the lighter still glowing in her hand, kept staring at Apache.

"Bailey," Ross said.

She looked back toward the spiral staircase now.

"Bailey," he said again.

Her face came around to his, then she let the lighter go out and started toward the door.

The police car raced along the highway though Ocean Springs toward the road leading in the direction of the old house, the vehicle's lights flashing but its siren off.

Lieutenant Browning folded a stick of chewing gum into his mouth. "The kids said the blood was fresh."

The car's nose dropped and its wheels screeched as the sergeant behind the steering wheel guided it bouncing off the highway onto the blacktop road. A couple of miles ahead they would intersect with the gravel road.

"When we turn off, cut the lights so they don't see us coming," Browning said.

Who would see them coming? he wondered. The killer returning? Another killer? Or what he had wondered from the first—the possibility of Bailey Williams and Ross Channing and that old woman involved in something more than had met the eye?

They hadn't been overly open in what they said the night Dr. Post had been killéd. That had been obvious in their silence when he wasn't asking them a question.

Especially obvious in the old woman's lack of emotion—when it had been her husband who had been murdered.

Bailey helped McLaurin down the steps in front of the house. His cuts barely seeped now. Still, he left bloody shoe prints with each step. Ross felt the aching in his back where he had been struck with the tire tool. He stepped to the ground first. They started past the Taurus.

"Oh my God," Bailey said.

Through the Taurus's rear window Mary could be seen lying across the backseat. The front of her white robe was red with blood. Her arm hung down to the floorboard, her head twisted at an awkward angle and her eyes stared blankly up into the air.

"He killed her," Bailey said in a low voice. "Her own son." She looked back toward the house. Ross pushed her forward. She looked at McLaurin, holding his shoulder.

"I'm okay," he said.

Bailey moved closer to Ross's side. "You don't look as pretty with a busted lip," she whispered and smiled feebly.

Ross couldn't believe she was trying to make a joke. He couldn't believe she went after Apache in the foyer. He couldn't believe how she appeared calmer than he felt at this very moment. He looked back at McLaurin. McLaurin nodded he was okay.

In a couple of minutes they neared the head of the drive. The gravel road running to their right was cast in nearly absolute darkness with the tall trees close to its sides cutting off what faint moonlight there was filtering through the clouds.

McLaurin had begun falling behind. "I believe I'm going to make a fool out of myself and pass out," he said.

Bailey slipped her arm around his back. Ross moved to give him support on his other side.

It was only a mile or so to the blacktop, and then only a couple of miles more to the highway. There would be houses there. *If Mac can make it that far,* Ross thought.

An unusually large oak grew next to the head of the drive. As they passed by it, Ross, his attention drawn to McLaurin, never saw Aurondo's thick shape behind the tree's trunk. A section of limb the size of a baseball bat cut the air with a whisper and slammed into the side of Ross's head. The automatic dropped from his hand and he crumpled to his knees and pitched over onto his face in the dirt.

Bailey grabbed for him and then jumped away as Aurondo stepped forward. McLaurin tried to defend himself by raising his arms in front of him, but a second hard swing of the limb crashed through his forearms into his face, knocking him backward, unconscious, to the ground.

Aurondo stepped after Bailey.

She whirled and ran toward the front of the house.

CHAPTER 36

Bailey ran wildly toward the house. Aurondo took long, loping strides behind her, closing the distance between them with each step. She reached the side of the Taurus, and he grabbed her shoulder. The material of her dress ripped in his hand. She stumbled forward. He grabbed her hair and yanked her back to him. In one motion he lifted her off the ground, turned her lengthwise in the air at his chest, and slammed her down against the Taurus's trunk. The wind was driven out of her with an audible sound and she rolled off the trunk to the drive. He quickly picked her up again, turning her dazed face to his.

"No more," he said, and lifted her feet off the ground. "No more," he said again and threw her backward against the trunk. Her head bounced off the metal and her eyes rolled back under her eyelids.

"No more." He slammed her head into the trunk. Blood splattered. He slammed her again. Blood matted her hair and ran down the back of her neck. He slammed her again into the trunk, but she no longer was feeling the pain.

The sound of a car caused Aurondo to look across his shoulder. It was a police car. Its headlights off, it came rapidly down the gravel road toward the entrance to the drive. Aurondo released Bailey's body and she crumpled to the ground. The car's headlights flashed to life as it turned rapidly into the drive. The driver spun the steering wheel to the side, narrowly evading Ross and McLaurin's forms lying on the ground, and the car slid to a stop. Its doors flew open and Lieutenant Browning and the driver jumped outside.

Aurondo ran for the far side of the house.

Browning saw him and sprinted after him.

Browning's driver hesitated a moment, looking at Ross and McLaurin, then ran toward the house. A second police car skidded into the drive, cut around the stopped car and raced past the driver. Sliding to a stop behind the Taurus, the car's doors opened. Two officers jumped out and darted toward each side of the house.

Browning came around the rear of the house and stopped. To his right, the tall oaks spread out into the darkness. A couple of hundred feet in front of him the bay's waters were calm and dark. There was no sign of a person fleeing in any direction.

An officer came running around the other side of the house. Browning's driver came up behind the lieutenant. Browning looked at the open French doors to his side and walked toward them.

The laboratory was faintly lit from within by the blue-green glow coming from the barrel-shaped container on the counter near the front wall. Browning could hear the sound of the generator motor. His driver switched on a flashlight and played its beam through the doorway. Browning, his automatic clasped in both hands, stepped slowly inside the laboratory.

The driver centered the flashlight's beam on the generator, then swept it across the far wall. He stopped the flashlight when its beam revealed Justin's body, lying on the floor just inside the bedroom.

* * *

At the front of the house, another police car slid to a stop and two officers jumped outside and hurried up the steep steps toward the beveled-glass door at the second level.

In the bedroom, Browning knelt on one knee beside Justin's body. The driver pointed his flashlight toward the open bathroom door, and moved toward it. Browning looked at the circles of blood surrounding the holes across the breast of Justin's shirt, and then rose to his feet. His driver shined his light inside the bathroom.

To the far side of the laboratory, a young officer, flashing his light before him, walked partially down the spiral staircase. Browning stepped from the bedroom. The officer centered him in a circle of light from his flashlight.

"Lieutenant, we got two bodies up here. There's blood coming down the steps, and a bloody shoe print—like a third one's walking around down there."

Browning's driver stepped from the bedroom to the lieutenant's side. "The one in there didn't walk anywhere," he said.

Off to their side the generator continued its loud noise. Browning walked to the counter and switched the generator off. The blue-green light went out. The faint bubbling coming from the tissue behind the Plexiglas ceased.

Browning moved toward the spiral staircase.

Behind him, the placenta continued its barely perceptible gentle movement for a moment, and then began to slow.

Browning's driver walked to the lounging area and shined his flashlight inside its doorway. The young officer on the staircase focused his light on the steps for Browning to see the trail of blood splatters.

"Comes halfway down and stops," the officer said,

"and then there's the print." He moved the beam of his light to the fourth step down the staircase. A faint sheen of blood outlined the imprint of a man's shoe.

Browning moved up the staircase.

A second officer stood in the foyer. His flashlight displayed Billy's body lying close to the stairs leading up to the home's third level. Apache lay against the near wall. Quite apart from the two bodies, there was a spot where blood was smeared in a wide circle against the hardwood floor. A smudged hand print marked the place where someone had pushed up from the floor.

Bandez waded waist-deep in the tall marsh grass. Blood soaked his shirt and trickled down into the dark water. Broken ends of a rib, shattered as it had deflected the shot fired in the foyer away from his chest toward his side, grated together. Gritting his teeth against the pain, he kept forcing himself forward.

On the gravel road leading from the old house, a police car stopped and shined a spotlight across the marsh. Bandez lowered himself in the grass and waited. The light swept over the top of his head, came back again, and then vanished.

Ross groaned and rolled to his side on the damp ground at the head of the drive. He slowly opened his eyes. An officer touched his arm. A police car sat a few feet away. McLaurin was being helped up by an officer.

"Where's Bailey?" Ross mumbled.

He pushed himself awkwardly to his feet as the officer helped him.

"Where's Bailey?" he asked again.

There were two more police cars at the front of the house, one on each side of McLaurin's Taurus. Their blue lights were rotating. He saw two officers standing in the flashing illuminations.

A figure lay on the ground in front of them.

"No," Ross said.

He took a step forward. Dizzy, he stumbled. The officer caught his arm. Ross forced himself forward again. He swayed, nearly fell, tried to concentrate through the swirling inside his head. He took a step, another, and began trotting.

The two officers at the rear of the Taurus looked toward him.

He slowed as he came closer.

Bailey lay on her back with her arms extended out to her sides. Her dress was ripped, exposing her shoulder and the strap of her bra. Her dark hair was matted with blood. Staring at her open, unseeing eyes, Ross dropped slowly to his knees.

The officer behind him looked at the others.

One of them shook his head. Bailey had no pulse.

Ross reached out his hand and moved a lock of her hair back from her eyes.

A pink bubble formed at the corner of her mouth.

Her lip moved.

Lieutenant Browning stepped out of the laboratory into the darkness behind the house. His driver came out beside him. To their left the shadowy oaks spread out toward the marsh. In front of them was the bay. To their right, still more oaks spread endlessly into the distance until they faded into total darkness.

"Call the highway patrol and get a helicopter out here. We're going to need dogs, too."

In front of the house a siren began wailing.

Browning heard the patrol car racing out of the drive and turning onto the road leading away from the house.

"The woman's alive," an officer called as he raced around the corner of the house.

Aurondo swam the last few feet through the bay water to the shoreline. His eye rotated in the direction of the flashlights sweeping the trees off to his side and coming in his direction.

Dripping, he climbed up on the shore. His weight pressing his hands and knees down into the mud, his body kept low, his wide head moving slowly back and forth as he searched through the trees with his eye, he looked more like an animal emerging from the water than a human.

To his right, another pair of flashlights swept the woods and came in his direction.

He scrambled to his feet and ran into the trees.

At the side of the house, a dark-haired officer in his forties held the end of the cut telephone line in his hands. He opened the large switch box bolted against the wooden siding and shined his flashlight across the wiring. The main electrical circuit breaker was thrown. He reached inside the box and pushed the breaker handle up into place.

Inside the house, the overhead light in the foyer suddenly flashed on, startling an officer shining his flashlight behind the staircase. He switched off his light and looked down at the drops of blood leading from the foyer to the spiral staircase.

In each room, officers, their flashlights off now, went through the closets and the cabinets and even glanced under the beds in Mary's room. In the laboratory, the blue-green light had come back on in the artificial womb. Now, one bubble and then another rose through the clear fluid behind the Plexiglas. A slight humming could be heard in a cabinet above the counter. Now, the placenta slowly became infused with a reddish-pink color, and began moving, ever so slightly again.

At the center of the placenta, a white capsulized form so tiny as to almost be invisible, seemed to stretch, turn slightly, and stretched again.

* * *

The police car, its siren screaming, its blue lights flashing, raced toward the Ocean Springs Hospital. Bailey lay on the rear seat. Ross, on his knees on the floorboard, held her shoulders, trying to keep her from being jolted as much as he could. The young officer driving the car relayed Ross's message for him.

"Yes, get in touch with Dr. Benjamin Channing. Call Tulane Medical Center. Call his home. Get him on the phone wherever he is."

CHAPTER 37

Lieutenant Browning sat in his patrol car, parked fifty feet from the emergency room entrance near the rear of the sprawling, three-story complex that made up the Ocean Springs Hospital. His door was open. His foot was on the curb. He spoke on the car's two-way radio.

"Neither Channing nor McLaurin got a good look at him in the dark, but he's Caucasian, well over six feet, maybe six-foot-three, six-foot-four, heavy build, shoulder-length dark hair. Channing said he would be around forty years of age. Channing also said there would be some kind of deformity apparent in the man—but he didn't know what kind. Just put out the word there is a deformity.

"The one missing from the foyer is a Hispanic male, in his mid-twenties. He has a deformity, too—a noticeably swollen right hand. They're certain about that. Five-nine to five-ten, medium-length dark hair. He has a slug in his chest. I imagine we'll find him dead in the bushes. But for right now, consider two of them running."

Ross stood in the wide hospital corridor. The double doors leading to the area containing the surgical suites

opened, and a short, older nurse with gray hair and
dressed in blue scrubs came toward him.

She spoke in a soft voice. "You're Dr. Channing's
son."

"Yes."

"He's been speaking from the helicopter radio to Dr.
Pennington. He said to tell you Miss Williams' blood
pressure and pulse are stabilized. She has a skull fracture but it's linear—not depressed—so they're not going
to have to operate. Her CAT scan was non-contrasted—
so there's no bleeding from the brain. She's still unconscious. Dr. Channing said you would know that the
main danger now is the possibility of the brain swelling.
But there's no evidence of that happening yet."

"Thank you," Ross said in a low voice.

The woman laid her hand softly on his forearm. "My
name is Helen. As soon as I can I'll give you another
report."

The ambulances carrying the bodies from the old house
drove slowly out of the drive onto the gravel road leading toward the highway. Inside the foyer, a police photographer took shots of the pool of blood where the
man named Billy had lain, then turned his camera toward the line of red drops sprayed up the wall, flicked
there by the violent jerks of Apache's head as Bailey
had kicked her repeatedly.

Outside the house, flashlight beams swept back and
forth through the trees as officers continued to look for
the body of the man who had risen wounded in the
foyer and made his way down the spiral staircase.

Aurondo's thick upper body was bare. He held his arms
out in front of him. A long lock of Mary's brown hair,
thickly streaked with gray, lay across his palms. He had
threaded it through her wedding band. He knelt down
on both knees, continuing to hold his hands out, and

began his prayer. Six tiny crosses, fashioned from twigs, were stuck in the ground in a circle before him. But it wasn't a Christian prayer he offered.

His words continued softly, in a low voice reminiscent of Mary's.

He ceased speaking.

He laid the lock of hair in the center of the crosses, stared down at it and the ring for a moment, then rose to his feet.

Walking slowly now, he moved to a bush where his shirt hung from a branch. But he didn't put it on. Instead, he pulled his knife from his waistband, and reached back and began cutting off thick handfuls of his long black hair.

The first reporter to arrive at the hospital was a young man from *The Sun Herald*. He became irritated when a police officer wouldn't let him go any farther than the front lobby, and walked back outside and went around to the emergency room entrance. An officer stopped him there. Shortly after that, a female reporter and a cameraman drove up in a van with WLOX-TV emblazoned on its side and were restricted to the lobby, too. Now another reporter came through the front door into the hospital.

The hospital administrator, having hurried from his home, read his hastily prepared statement.

"Miss Williams is in serious but stable condition with a skull fracture and multiple head lacerations. She remains unconscious. Mr. McLaurin and Mr. Channing suffered concussions resulting in unconsciousness, but regained consciousness while still at the site of the attack. Mr. McLaurin also suffered lacerations to his neck and shoulder."

A pay telephone on the wall next to the gift shop at the rear of the lobby rang. A reporter looked toward the sound. A police officer stood next to the phone, and

lifted the receiver to his ear. Then he called toward
Lieutenant Browning.

"They found the mayor."

Browning walked to the officer and took the receiver
into his hand.

"Mayor, you're not going to believe this."

The mayor said something and Browning listened for
a moment, then interrupted him. "No, not the killings,
but what they were over—an artificial womb. . . . Yeah,
an artificial womb, you're hearing me right—they were
growing a baby in a barrel out there . . . Yeah, that's
right, a human baby."

Near the center of the first floor of the hospital, Mc-
Laurin sat in a wheelchair in the corridor outside the
entrance to the surgical suites. He wore a loose hospital
gown and had pulled it out from his neck to look at
the line of stitches running across his chest toward his
shoulder. Now he let go of the garment and looked up
at Ross, standing next to the wall a few feet away from
the wheelchair.

"I've been thinking about what's going to happen to
the fetus now, Ross. You said you thought Bailey could
face it being aborted—for the child's own sake. But it's
going to become a political question now, isn't it? If
Bailey makes it through this . . ." McLaurin looked toward the double doors. "*When* she makes it through
this, she's going to get smacked again, isn't she? She's
going to find that any decision concerning the fetus is
going to be taken out of her hands. There are going to
be those who want to abort a monstrosity, and those
who want to let it come to term. You been thinking
about that?"

Ross had. Whatever had gone wrong with the children Dr. Post had produced, they were nevertheless the
product of a scientific procedure that was already being
researched with animal subjects in laboratories all over

the world. Many scientists, given the opportunity to study an actual human fetus being grown outside the womb would clamor for it to be spared. There would be others who would consider the whole process the horror McLaurin spoke of and would want the fetus's growth stopped immediately. But nothing happened quickly in the political world. In the end, Ross could see only two possibilities. The fetus would be studied and then aborted shortly before it came to term or, even worse, allowed to come to term and then the child institutionalized all its life while it was studied. In either case, Bailey would be torn back and forth by the arguments that would rage between the different factions, tormented for months, maybe years, with the fetus, and then maybe the child, constantly on her mind.

Then a third possibility passed through Ross's mind. As an attorney, he should have already thought of it. No person could be condemned for a family history. A person could only be held responsible for his own acts. If the fetus was brought to term, it would be an innocent child in the eyes of the law. The child might be observed for a time—there could be some excuse made to allow that. But Billy and Justin and Apache had been observed all their lives, first by their schoolmates and teachers, then by their relatives and neighbors who had taken them in after their parents had died. And none of the three had been thought of as anything but normal.

Had they not attacked and were not now lying dead in the hospital morgue, they would still be normal as far as anyone knew. Bailey's child would be considered normal, too, and then turned loose on the world to do what it wished.

McLaurin spoke again. "In a way, it would have been better if there hadn't been a generator when the electricity went off. It would be over with now, wouldn't it, Ross?"

Ross looked at him. McLaurin glanced toward the

surgical suites again. "I know you, Ross. That's why I've been wondering if you've been thinking about that. I know you have. You're not going to like Bailey having to agonize over something like that, are you?"

Before Ross responded, an officer called down the hallway. "Dr. Channing's coming in."

Ross turned toward the side of the hospital and hurried down the hall.

"Ross," McLaurin called after him, "we already had one person playing God. You see how that backfired. You want my opinion, Ross, let what happens happen. Leave it alone."

McLaurin started his wheelchair down the hallway after him. "You listening to me, Ross? I know you're not."

Ross never did when he had his mind made up.

Aurondo, his black hair cut jagged and short around his ears and high on the back of his neck, came silently through the giant oaks. They were spaced farther apart now, with wide patches of mowed grass between the thick trunks. Camping vans and mobile trailers dotted the area, maintained by the government as one of the many public camping areas spread throughout the hundreds of thousands of acres running along the coast from Louisiana to Florida as part of the Gulf Islands National Seashore Preserve.

One small trailer was still attached to the pickup truck that had towed it to a camping pad shortly before the park had closed for the night. Its narrow rear window, stretching all the way across the back of the trailer, was propped open. The screen behind the window kept the insects that swarmed these lowlands from bothering the sleep of Otho and Edna Edginton, a couple from Pennsylvania who had driven the last twelve hours nonstop before arriving at the campground to begin their vacation.

Aurondo caught the molding around the screen. The screen was the type that would also lift out, and it was unlocked. He pulled it up.

The bald spot in the center of Otho's head softly reflected what dim moonlight was filtering through the clouds passing above the treetops. Edna slept five feet across from Otho, on the bed on the left of the trailer. Aurondo ran his thick hands past Otho's face and clamped one of them over the man's mouth, and pulled his knife across the man's throat.

Otho kicked. His hands flailed the air. Aurondo held him on the bunk by pulling back on his head. Otho's frantic movements began to slow. His hands fell back to his sides. Aurondo pulled him slowly out through the screen.

A few seconds later the procedure was repeated on Edna. Her body was laid across Otho's, and Aurondo walked to the narrow door at the trailer's side.

It was locked. He jimmied his knife down in the crack between the door and the trailer frame and pulled on the handle. Metal screeched lightly, there was a click, and the door popped open.

Aurondo lowered his head and stepped inside the small quarters.

Having to lean forward because of the trailer's low ceiling height, he began to search for the key to the pickup, rifling first through Otho's pants, folded on the small dresser at the head of the trailer, and then through Edna's purse.

CHAPTER 38

There it is!" an officer shouted.

The small helicopter, a bright light rotating rapidly beneath its fuselage, broke through the cloud cover and swept down toward the concrete landing pad behind the hospital.

As the craft touched down, the door at its side flew open and Dr. Benjamin Channing leaped outside. His body leaned low under the spinning rotor blades, he rushed toward his son.

"She's still unconscious," Ross said.

They were already trotting toward the emergency room entrance. "I've been speaking to the surgeons on the radio," Dr. Channing said. "They're doing everything they can. You know I'm going to do all I can."

They hurried through the double doors into the hospital.

The pickup towing the camping trailer turned slowly off Highway 90 in Ocean Springs into the parking area in front of a small strip mall. Aurondo turned the steering wheel, circling the truck back to where it faced the highway again. Only an occasional car sped by on the lanes of pavement in front of the windshield. Aurondo

adjusted the rearview mirror where he could see the reflection of his face. He raised a broken piece of glass.
It came from the bottom of a jar of homemade apricot
preserves, now smashed in a sticky yellow-orange
mound on the floorboard. He pressed the jagged glass
against his forehead. A drop of blood, then a trickle,
smeared the glass and ran down his face.

He pulled the glass slowly across his forehead and
around it into his black hair. The blood ran down his
temple, and seeped around his ear.

He drew a shallower cut across his cheek, and another at a side of his eye.

Now he moved the glass back into his lap. The blood
dripped from his chin across his white shirt. He turned
his face and stared to his left up the highway.

A set of headlights came into view. They grew quickly
larger as the driver of the car coming from that direction increased his speed.

Aurondo continued to stare.

The car grew closer.

The driver flicked on his vehicle's high beams.

A hundred feet away now and coming faster.

Aurondo pressed the truck's accelerator to the floor.

The pickup lurched forward, faltered for a moment
as its rear wheels spun, then jerking the trailer along
behind it, shot forward out onto the pavement.

The driver of the car yanked his steering wheel to the
left to try to avoid the accident. The front of the pickup
caught the smaller vehicle on its passenger door. The
rear of the car came around, slammed into the trailer,
then rebounded. The car spun out of control into a
complete circle, then tilted and flipped over, rolling into
the median in a cloud of smoke and dust.

The trailer had torn loose and tumbled back into the
parking lot. The pickup, its front smashed, skidded to
a stop along the pavement.

Aurondo stared down the highway in front of him,

then raised his hand, clasped it into a fist, and drove it through the windshield in front of him, shattering the glass.

A moment later he smeared the blood from his forehead across his face and over his glazed eye. He sat silent for a moment, then pulled his head back and suddenly drove his forehead forward into the steering wheel with such force that the steering wheel bent— then he lay over in the seat, and was still.

A young black man crawled out the driver's window of the overturned car, stood and stared at the pickup with his hands on his hips.

A quarter mile away, a police officer turned his car's blue lights on and raced toward the two vehicles, one turned upside down in the median and the other sitting smoking from its radiator in the lane ahead of him.

He was already calling for an ambulance.

An artificial womb?" the governor questioned. The concept was difficult for him to grasp. He was speaking from his bedroom in the Chief Executive's mansion on Capitol Street in Jackson.

"I knew you would want to know before the media got hold of it," the Ocean Springs mayor said. "It has a damn baby inside it. A fetus, I guess you call it. It's there anyway, growing like a flower in a hothouse, Lieutenant Browning said. He's got a couple officers out in front of the house. We can keep everybody out for a day or two. But you better decide what you want to do about it before long. Especially if you want to keep it alive—I don't know how you feed the thing."

"I'll call Washington," the governor said.

Dr. Benjamin Channing stepped outside the intensive care unit and walked past the police officer on guard at the double doors to Ross and Lieutenant Browning, standing in the corridor.

"There is still no indication of swelling," he said. "They have her intubated, but I think she's able to breathe on her own—there's been some movement of her head and arms. They'll start weaning her off the sedative. I think we're going to have a lucky lady here. In fact, I'm almost certain of it."

The relief Ross felt washing over him left him feeling weak. His father patted him on the shoulder.

Helen stepped outside the unit. She pulled her surgical cap off and ran her hand through her gray hair.

"Helen, is it?" Dr. Channing questioned.

She nodded.

"Helen, is there anyplace I might find a cup of coffee around here?"

"Certainly. I can brew you a cup in no time. You ever try tea? I already have the hot water on. I was just going to fix myself a cup. With honey."

"You know, that doesn't sound bad at all."

"Fine, Doctor—with honey?"

"Yes, that would be nice."

"I'll bring it back to the unit for you."

"Thank you."

Dr. Channing looked back at Ross. "It's going to be at least a couple of hours before she's fully conscious, son, so why don't you get a little rest? I'll call you as soon as she's able to speak." His gaze went to the side of Ross's head. "You need to get that gash treated."

Browning looked down the hall at a tall young man who had just stepped from the intersecting corridor. He was dressed in a white shirt, open at the neck, and dark slacks. His brown hair was mussed, as if he had just climbed out of bed. He glanced toward Browning, then turned and stepped back into the intersecting corridor.

"Excuse me," Browning said, walking in that direction.

Ross followed him.

The man stepped back into view. Browning stopped in front of him.

The man smiled politely.

"I'm Lieutenant Browning. Ocean Springs Police. I'm sorry to bother you, but we're checking the IDs of anybody on this floor."

The man reached into his rear pocket and lifted out his billfold. He opened it to his driver's license.

"I'm a reporter—from the *Mississippi Press* in Pascagoula."

Browning raised his gaze from the license. "The hospital's keeping the media updated at the front entrance."

"I heard there were several people killed," the reporter said.

"I'm not going to comment until the morning," Browning said, "other than for the descriptions we've already given out on the men we're looking for, a Hispanic male in his mid-twenties and a Caucasian in his forties with shoulder-length dark hair. Like I said, you can get whatever medical information is available on Miss Williams and the others at the entrance."

The man nodded, glanced at Ross, and slipped his billfold back into his pocket, then turned back into the intersecting hallway.

Browning, sliding a stick of Wrigley's Spearmint from its pack, watched him walk toward the front of the building. Then the lieutenant faced back to Ross.

"So do we flinch every time we see someone come down the hall, Mr. Channing? Are there more of them—ones we don't know about?"

"No."

"Because Mary told you so?"

Everything Mary had said had been different each time she had spoken, Ross thought. First there was only a single child born of the artificial womb. Then she had shown him the stapled papers naming Apache, Billy, and Justin as three more. She had said that even with her giving them the names she hadn't broken her oath to Dr. Post. Was there something else? Something that was still protected by her oath? What could Post reveal that she hadn't if he were still alive?

Maybe Post had already revealed more—and they weren't aware of it yet.

"There's a briefcase in the laboratory."

Moments later, Browning guided his patrol car away from the curb near the emergency room. At the traffic signal guarding the exit from the hospital onto Highway 90, Browning stopped the car, waiting for an ambulance racing toward them with its red and white lights flashing.

As the boxy white vehicle turned off the highway and sped past them, Browning pressed on the accelerator, and the patrol car shot across the four lanes of pavement onto the blacktop road leading toward the old house.

Behind them, the ambulance braked to a stop in front of the emergency room entrance. Two white-coated ambulance attendants hurried around to the rear of the vehicle, threw open its doors and pulled the stretcher containing Aurondo's large form outside.

The jagged ends of his black hair hung barely to his ears now. His face was coated with a thick, dried smear of blood. With his eyes closed, the glazed eye wasn't noticeable. But the police officer standing at the emergency room doors did see the swelling at the side of Aurondo's face, and turned away to avoid looking at the damage the wreck had caused. He wondered if his daughter, on her way back to the University of Southern Mississippi at that very moment, had remembered to wear her safety belt.

The attendants hurried the stretcher past the officer into the hospital.

CHAPTER 39

The young police officer centered the beam of his flashlight on the six crosses made of twigs. They were stuck into the ground in a circle surrounding a long lock of brown hair heavily streaked with gray. An ornate wedding band glinted in the light.

"Hey, Brosh, come and look at this."

A second young Ocean Springs officer came through the trees.

He looked down at the circle of light—and what it displayed.

Only minutes before he had slipped his automatic back into his holster, tired of carrying it in his hand, and certain that whoever they were looking for had cleared the area.

He pulled the weapon back out of the holster now.

Windows glowed on the lower level and second level of the old house, but the third story was darkened, black against the cloud-filled sky. The tall oaks nearest the house were dimly illuminated in the light shining from the uncurtained second-story windows. Spanish moss hanging from the thick tree limbs glowed a silvery gray. Farther from the house the oaks darkened, and then were lost in their own thick shadows as they filled the distance. A night bird squawked as it flew overhead in the direction of the marsh. The two young officers standing next to the Ocean Springs police car parked across the head of the drive looked into the sky at the sound.

Then they looked up the gravel road at Lieutenant Browning's patrol car coming toward them.

The car slowed, turned into the yard, and drove past them to the rear of the house.

Two officers standing by the French doors nodded as Browning stepped outside the car and walked toward them. Ross was the first one into the laboratory.

The briefcase lay open in the middle of the floor.

Ross looked at the artificial womb glowing with its blue-green light, glanced at the closed bedroom door at the back of the lab, then walked down the counter to Mary's diary, lying where he left it next to the telephone.

He began quickly thumbing through the pages, all filled with Mary's perfect handwriting. He stopped on the mention of Aurondo being born, then flipped through the pages again.

Browning had knelt next to the briefcase. He glanced in Ross's direction, then lifted a legal-size notebook from among the other materials in the briefcase, and began going through it.

Halfway through the diary, Ross saw a mention of the experiments. He turned the pages more slowly now. There was the work with animals. He came to where the pig had been born. Mary began to mention her frustration with Dr. Post's ignoring the patients. Ross stopped on the page written about the first child born of the artificial womb—the mestizo boy with the misshapen hand. The one who now as a man had pushed himself wounded up off the foyer floor and was yet to be found.

Browning laid the legal-size notebook on the floor and lifted a folder into his hands.

Ross stopped again on the page where Apache was born.

In yearly successions, the others came from the womb—Justin and then Billy. Ross scanned every paragraph carefully now, trying to see something that might give him a hint of another child, even if the birth wasn't specifically mentioned.

And if there weren't any other births in the intervening two years between when Billy was born and the clinic was burned, why had Post stopped using the process? Had he noticed something? Maybe something he had recorded; something that would explain why the births from the artificial womb had created children not much different from the demons of the Indians' superstition.

A few pages more and the writing stopped abruptly in mid-paragraph, almost twenty years before to the very month. Ross stared at the incomplete paragraph and wondered if Mary had been writing in the diary the day the Indians came to burn the clinic—with Aurondo as their leader.

The remainder of the pages were blank. She had written nothing more after she and Post had come back to Mississippi.

Ross wondered how she had saved the diary from the fire.

He wondered how any of Dr. Post's notebooks and folders had been saved from the fire.

He remembered Mary saying Post had been throwing his research papers outside as the clinic went up in flames. Somebody had to go back and get them for them to be in his briefcase now. *Mary?* Had she put her life in danger once more for the man she worshipped?

Or had she gathered them before the military helicopter had arrived to take Post to Mexico City?

Ross pushed the idle thought from his mind, and walked to the briefcase and knelt down on one knee next to Browning. He lifted a legal-size notebook from the briefcase and opened it.

It was one of those he had hurriedly looked through the day Mary had come in and caught him going through the briefcase, the one with only one page used, containing the letters that didn't appear to be scientific symbols.

        UAV-AL
        SL-MA
        GR-LM
        LX-MZ
        CW-BZ
        EO-GP
        DC-NR
        SL-LM
        SL-CA
        SL-EA
        SL-CE

He lifted another notebook from the briefcase. It was full of the names and addresses of chemical and drug companies throughout Mexico, Central America, and South America. There was a section of pages where blood, blood plasma, and platelets were discussed.

He flipped slowly through the section, again looking for a hint of something that might lead to answers. Then he laid the notebook aside and lifted a folder from the briefcase. Browning flipped through another notebook.

The folder contained loose sheets describing a variety of chemicals and formulations. Most of them were crossed out by a single scratch of a pencil.

Ross reached for another folder.

In a half hour, the brick floor around the briefcase

was littered with the several notebooks, pads, folders, and manuals. There had been no reference to any other births. No hint of anything specific that had gone wrong with the children other than a notation as to their apparent coldness. Post had written that he agreed with Mary that the children did need parents who could spend the proper time with them.

"So is that all of them?" Browning asked.

The French doors behind them opened. A young officer stepped into the opening.

"Lieutenant," he said, "we found something in the trees. Some kind of setup on the ground with a lock of hair and a ring surrounded by little crosses made out of twigs. I don't know if it has to do with this or if it's something some kids were playing with and left there."

Ross came to his feet. "It has to do with this," he said. He had thought of Estelita, and what she told him about what Manuel had found at the clinic. "A friend of mine found a shrine in the clinic's ruins fashioned out of some of Dr. Post's instruments surrounded by crosses."

"Let's take a look," Browning said and walked toward the doors.

Ross started to follow him, then glanced at the barrel-shaped artificial womb. "I'm going to stay here," he said.

Browning looked back across his shoulder.

Ross nodded toward the materials scattered around the briefcase. "I'm going to go through these again. We went through them so fast we could have easily missed something."

The young emergency room physician used a syringe filled with lidocaine to deaden the borders of the deep cut across Aurondo's forehead in preparation for stitching it closed.

"CAT scan turned out fine," the doctor said. "But

you took quite a lick. I'm going to keep you overnight for observation."

The doctor, not wanting to cause his patient to be self-conscious, had to continue to resist the urge to glance again at the swelling at the side of Aurondo's face. It was one of the most dramatic birth deformities he had ever witnessed.

Aurondo stared impassively toward the ceiling.

But his hands remained clenched tight.

The doctor thought it was from nervousness.

Ross waited until the French doors closed behind Lieutenant Browning. Then he turned his gaze to the counter. Behind the artificial womb's Plexiglas front, the placenta moved slowly, infused with a pinkish-red color. A bubble slowly traveled up through the clear liquid.

Ross's thoughts went to how Dr. Post had stood in front of the Plexiglas. Not in this laboratory, but in his own laboratory in Mexico—the first time. As McLaurin had said, *playing God.*

Or had Post not been doing any more than any other scientist would do given the knowledge he possessed?

Was the only difference in what Post had done and what others would someday do—as his father had said would happen soon—the fact that Post's experiments took place in a small clinic in an out-of-the-way place rather than a state-of-the-art facility given government approval?

Ross thought back to when Bailey had asked to use his sperm to accomplish the fertilization. He had felt reluctant. At the time he had thought the feeling was due to his not wanting to be part of bringing a child into the world who might not be loved. Had his hesitancy also been in not wanting to be part of something that wasn't natural?

Scientists would laugh at that, he thought, compare

him to the superstitious Indians who burned the clinic. His father would certainly laugh. No neurosurgeon would want to go back to what was normal in the past, give up all the modern techniques and state-of-the-art medical instrumentation and procedures that were available now. After all, that was what progress was, moving from what was natural in the past to something new and better. The cycle never stopped; discover something new, then discard that when something even newer was learned, time and time again. Progress.

But was there a time when somebody should scream stop, even when, technically, another step could be taken? Even when, theoretically, great good could come out of not stopping? There would always be those who would say great good could come out of anything. Ross looked at the electrical splice wrapped with black tape running into a fuse box in the wall at the womb's rear.

The splice connected an electric line to the generator and then the line ran from the generator to the womb. If the electricity shut off, the generator started. But the generator switch was turned off now. If the splice was unwrapped and the wires pulled apart, both sources of power to the womb would be gone—and Bailey wouldn't have to face the anguish of uncertainty over the fetus's fate. For weeks, maybe months, he thought once again as he had thought at the hospital, with the end result being the fetus aborted anyway—or worse, he thought again, brought to term. He could wrap the tape back around the loose wires, and nobody would know he had done anything.

He felt hesitant about reaching for the splice. And he didn't know why. He had never fired his automatic in anger before that night, and now he had killed two people, probably a third. Though he wished it hadn't happened, he knew that faced with the same situation, he wouldn't hesitate to pull the trigger again.

And yet he did feel hesitancy now.

Was it because he could see the life in front of him, and it threatened no harm?

But it would threaten. Soon after birth it would.

He knew this, and yet still he paused.

Because the fetus was part of him?

He knew that his reluctance was for all of those reasons, and yet, if he did what was right, he had no choice.

Especially for Bailey.

He looked back at the materials scattered around the briefcase. Bailey had said they had to be certain.

There wasn't any uncertainty.

His gaze fell on the small notepad with the red cover down the counter from the womb—where Post and then Mary had been writing their observations.

He walked to the pad and opened it.

On the first page there were the dates of his and Bailey's birth and their full names, scribbled in by Dr. Post—Bailey Leigh Williams and Douglas Ross Channing.

The next page contained the mention of Bailey's eggs being fertilized.

There was the date the fertilized egg was implanted in the growth at the back of the womb. The words *It is done*, were written by Post underneath the date. Ross saw his and Bailey's initials underneath that—D.R.C. and B.L.W.

Now we shall see was written next.

Underneath that were the words *Thank you*, written in Mary's highly legible script.

Thank you? Post had given Mary the chance to have enough money to live after he was gone. She was expressing her gratitude. The gratitude of a person who knew what horror was being committed in the fertilization, and yet ignored that for money.

However pitiful had been her life, Ross felt more anger at her than Dr. Post. Post had simply been insane. She had sold her soul to the devil.

Ross stared a moment longer at the words *Thank you*, then started turning through the pages in the pad. They contained notations of the embryo and then the fetus being maintained—the checking of oxygen pressures keeping the liquid supersaturated, the disposal of wastes, the addition of blood platelets used in some kind of nutrient osmosis, and the keeping of chemical levels at proper concentrations.

There was nothing that hinted anything might go wrong. There was nothing that hinted anything had gone wrong in the past.

He turned his gaze back to the Plexiglas and the living mass growing behind it. He made up his mind and walked toward the womb.

He stopped in front of the Plexiglas. He reached to the tape and began unwrapping it. His gaze went back to the placenta. The first time Bailey had seen the small, white capsulized form at its center she could hardly contain herself. When they were at Mary Mahoney's and she had asked him what he thought when he had seen the fetus, and he had replied that it was the start of a life, she had been almost irritated at his lack of excitement.

"The start of a life," ran through his mind again.

The beginning.

He stopped unraveling the tape. He looked toward the closed bedroom door, thought for a moment, then walked to the door and opened it.

The small book of fetal photographs lay on the bedside table next to Bailey's bed. When she had carried the book into the lounge, she had opened it to the photograph of a newborn child. There had been a passage scribbled in Dr. Post's handwriting next to the photograph. The passage had been from Genesis—the beginning.

Mary's Bible lay on her bedside table.

He walked to the table, lifted the Bible into his hands and opened it. The passage wasn't in the first few verses of Genesis. He turned the page, and saw it immediately—it had been underlined in dark ink.

And God blessed them, and God said unto them, be fruitful, and multiply, and replenish the earth . . .

He remembered that while the passage that had been copied into the book of fetal photographs had been done in Post's scribbly handwriting, the initials underneath the passage had been written in a painstakingly exact manner.

U.A.V.

The same exacting hand Mary used in her diary.

That Post wrote the passage, but Mary initialed it—and with someone else's initials, passed idly through Ross's mind. But it had no meaning to him.

The letters might not represent initials, but mean something else, he thought, again trying to spark a thought that would give him a hint of the answers he sought.

But, again, that meant nothing to him.

He turned through the Bible, looking for any more pages with passages that might be underlined.

Don't touch it until a photographer gets here," Lieutenant Browning said. He was looking down at the crosses of twigs encircling the lock of gray-streaked, brown hair threaded through a wedding band.

"Lieutenant, over here."

Browning walked toward the officer standing next to a bush a few feet away.

The officer's flashlight illuminated the long clumps of dark hair spread across the ground.

CHAPTER 40

Ross continued to turn through the Bible. There had been no more passages underlined. At the place where the Books of the Old Testament ended was a series of pages with headings and blank spaces to be filled in by the Bible's owner.

The first page listed the certification of the marriage of Antoinette Lee Mobley to Ural Albert Vest Post in Jefferson City, Missouri on May 1, 1925.

The next two pages contained lined spaces for children of the union to be listed. There was only one, Sebastian Lee Post, born in his parents' house in Jefferson City. Dr. Post.

It wasn't Mary's Bible, but rather Post's family Bible.

The next page contained room for the married couples' parents and grandparents to be listed.

Nothing had been written in the spaces.

The New Testament began on the next page.

Ross thumbed through its pages.

There were no more underlined passages there, either.

The New Testament ended.

The last pages included a listing of the Bible index, the Bible atlas, and the maps depicting the Holy Land.

His gaze stopped on the back of the last map.

It had formerly been a page left blank by the publisher.

Now, in writing done in Post's scribbly hand there was the listing of his father's family history that had been absent in the section of the Bible reserved for that information. But more names were listed than simply Post's father and mother. And deaths were listed, too. In fact, as Ross looked down the list he saw that *only* deaths were listed.

Jewell Post—Dr. Post's uncle. The date Jewell died was listed. The place of death was the asylum for the insane in Fulton, Missouri.

Carol Mobley—Dr. Post's aunt. She had died due to pneumonia the year after Jewell's death . . . in her husband's arms at their home in Jefferson City, Missouri.

U. A. V. Post—Dr. Post's father—dead at fifty-five. The place of death was the same insane asylum where the uncle had died.

Ross stared now at the initials U.A.V. Ural Albert Vest Post. Ross pictured in his mind the initials Mary had printed under the passage written by Dr. Post in the book of fetal photographs—U.A.V.

The U.A.V. who had died in an insane asylum. The same insane asylum where an uncle had earlier died.

Down the list were the continuing names.

Antoinette Lee Mobley—Dr. Post's mother—died in her own bed in Sedalia, Missouri.

Lila Mobley Johansen—Dr. Post's mother's sister—died after being thrown from a horse outside of Hannibal, Missouri.

Grover Post—Dr. Post's grandfather—had lived to be ninety-two, and died in the same asylum as the other Posts.

The male Posts—all ending their lives in insane asylums. A family history of madness on the male side of the Post family tree—every one of the males listed.

U.A.V., Ross thought. And another picture appeared in his mind. He looked back toward the laboratory.

Carrying the Bible with him, he walked from the bedroom into the laboratory to the briefcase surrounded by the material that had been lifted out of it.

He found the notebook he looked for, and opened it.

It was the same notebook he had looked inside three times now, the first time when Mary had caught him going through the briefcase, the second time when he and Browning were going through the briefcase a few moments before, and now this time.

He opened it to the first page again.

```
UAV-AL
SL-MA
GR-LM
LX-MZ
CW-BZ
EO-GP
DC-NR
SL-LM
SL-CA
SL-EA
SL-CE
```

The UAV at the top of the column made sense now—initials standing for Ural Albert Vest—Ural Albert Vest Post, the first male listed in Post's family history.

Across from those initials were the initials AL—Antoinette Lee—Antoinette Lee Mobley. The columns weren't a list of symbols but rather the first initials of couples united in marriage in Post's family history.

Ross ran his gaze down the list.

Below UAV-AL were the initials SL-MA. SL—Sebastian Lee. Dr. Sebastian Lee Post. MA—Mary Alexander. Mary Alexander Walker. Dr. Sebastian Post and

Mary Alexander Walker when they were united in marriage.

The next few sets of initials represented names unknown to Ross.

    GR-LM
    LX-MZ
    CW-BZ
    EO-GP
    DC-NR
    SL-LM
    SL-CA
    SL-EA
    SL-CE

He noticed the series of SL's in a row at the left-hand bottom of the columns. Sebastian Lee four times in a row. Each time a different set of initials across from his.

United in marriage?

Suddenly Ross understood.

A cold chill swept up his spine.

Dr. Post was a scientist, not a historian. He hadn't listed marriages. He had listed where the sperm and egg came from as he attempted each of his experiments.

The four SLs in a row—it was clear what had taken place—he had used his own sperm in each and every case of the women who had come to him from Mississippi.

The sperm that had come from a family history of madness.

Then another thought caused Ross's stomach to tighten in a strange mixture of apprehension and hope.

He came to his feet.

He looked at the notepad lying on the counter and walked toward it.

He opened it to the second page—where Post had

written *It is done* and Mary had written beneath that *Thank you*.

Ross couldn't keep a big smile from crossing his face.

Mary *had* known that Paulie would be all right. She had begged Dr. Post not to use his sperm again. He had decided to do as she said. Maybe not agreed with her that a malady carried in his sperm had been what had been wrong with the other children, but he had agreed. He had written *It is done*. What she asked had been done.

And Mary had written *Thank you*.

CHAPTER 41

Bandez's undershirt, torn into strips and fashioned into a compress to stop the bleeding, was pressed against the bullet wound in his chest.

But the worst pain was not there. The slug had left an ever-widening tunnel of torn flesh after it had been deflected off his rib and careened down his side to lodge just under the skin at his waist.

Gritting his teeth against the pain, he stood in the darkness next to a hangar at the Gulfport/Biloxi Regional Airport. He had watched the three couples walk from a large private jet to the limousine waiting to take them to the Grand Casino. He had waited until the jet had been refueled and only the pilot was standing beside it.

Now, he walked forward.

As he neared the sleek plane, the pilot turned and smiled politely at him.

Then the pilot saw the blood-soaked front of Bandez's shirt—and the knife he held in his hand.

When Post first tried to produce a child with the Indian couples he kept having failures," Ross said. He sat in the passenger seat of the patrol car, speeding up the blacktop road as Lieutenant Browning drove them toward the hospital. "He decided that the intermarriages among the Indians with their closely related sperm and eggs had made it impossible for him to produce a child. So on the sixth try, he substituted his own sperm.

"That fertilization proved successful in creating the first child born of the artificial womb. But not a wholly successful birth, not with the boy having the misshapen hand.

"But even with the deformity, the birth would have made Post even more certain of why his earlier attempts at producing a child had failed. In his mind, his sperm had been powerful enough to bring a child to term, but the Indian woman's egg had still harbored defects that couldn't be totally overcome.

"So he sent for the Caucasian couples. To add even more certainty that the births that were to follow would produce a perfect child, he used his own sperm again rather than the women's husbands—the sperm of a genius."

Ross held the notebook toward the lieutenant where he could see the column of initials.

"See, Lieutenant, Dr. Post was the direct descendant of U.A.V. Post, the initials at the very top left. Post wrote them in, then he wrote his and Mary's joining their sperm and egg together. Then came the Indian couples."

UAV-AL

SL-MA

GR-LM

LX-MZ

CW-BZ

EO-GP

DC-NR

SL-LM

SL-CA

SL-EA
SL-CE

"It was a shorthand he used for the mothers—their first and middle names. See, going up the list from the bottom. CE for Cheryl Ellen Johnson, Billy's mother. EA for Elizabeth Alberta Barnes, Justin's mother. CA for Carol Ann Trehern, Apache's mother.

"Post had three straight successes with them—as far as he was concerned. Mary did have her doubts due to the coldness of the children. But, as usual, she relied on Post.

"She later found his shorthand notes and realized that he had used his own sperm to produce all of the children—the three children who were cold from birth and the mestizo child who had killed his mother. She knew Post's family history of insanity. He threatened her with destroying her diary—the only thing she had left of Aurondo—to get her to swear not to tell that the reason the children were crazy was because he had passed his own family's madness on to them. That's all he cared about—in his arrogance. He didn't care that anyone knew that there was something wrong with the children, even that they were mad. He wouldn't have let Mary keep her diary detailing the coldness and the murder of the Indian woman if he had cared that anybody knew that there was something wrong with them. He only wanted her not to tell that the madness came from him. That was her oath—and even though she let us know everything else, she kept her oath.

"But she made certain that Bailey's child would be okay. She was present when Post fertilized the eggs. That's why after he entered my initials listing me as the sperm donor, that she wrote *Thank you* below the entry—to show her gratitude. Why did he write the passage from Genesis in the book with the fetal photographs? I don't know. Maybe as some kind of point directed at Mary. She wrote the initials U.A.V. under the passage—maybe as a reminder to him. Maybe in his arrogance he was using the passage to argue with her that his work was blessed. Maybe Mary's rejoinder was to make a point it wasn't blessed, not with the Post family history. We'll never know.

"How he missed suffering the outward consequence of the madness himself for so long, I don't know. But a genetic trait can be skipped by one generation or more, and still carried by that generation to be passed on. Or maybe his madness was simply in the way he thought.

"And of course Aurondo wasn't driven mad from the taunting of the other children, nor from anything that had to do with whatever deformity it is that he carries, but rather because he is a descendant of the Post family history, too. The artificial womb has nothing to do with the madness of any of them. Bailey's child is going to be okay."

He smiled. "Bailey's child is going to be okay," he repeated. "My child, too. When Bailey hears this she's going to—"

Ross stopped talking when he saw the man walking along the side of the road.

As they flashed by the figure, Browning said, "We occasionally have some transients sleep in the woods down here. Probably walking up to the highway to catch the morning traffic. We're not going to find Aurondo that easily."

Ross looked through the patrol car's rear windshield at the man, then turned back around in the seat.

"We might not have to find him, Lieutenant. With him cutting off his hair, he's hoping he won't be as noticeable. Not noticeable when he's getting away—or not noticeable when he's coming at us."

"And you think it's the latter?" Browning said.

"Each mother of every child born of Post's experiment is dead, from the mother of the child in Mexico to the women here. He's going to come after Bailey either now or later. I hope it's now. Because if it isn't, we're not going to know when he's going to come."

Browning slowed the patrol car at the traffic signal turning red in front of them, looked up and down the highway, and drove through the red light across to the road leading into the hospital complex.

He stopped the patrol car a few feet short of the emergency room entrance and looked across the seat. "There's also the one you shot."

Ross nodded. "They know Bailey was brought here. After the kind of beating she suffered, she could only be in one of three places—the morgue, surgery, or the ICU."

CHAPTER 42

The morgue was located in a narrow wing of the hospital's first floor. A sign next to the door read CAUTION, FORMALDEHYDE IN USE. The door was unlocked. Aurondo, dressed in a hospital robe, stepped into the darkened room and flicked on the light switch at the side of the doorway.

Apache lay on her back on the stainless-steel autopsy table. A sheet covered her from her neck to her ankles. Her long, brilliantly blonde hair, flecked with blood, had been pulled out from under her head and hung over the end of the table. A tag was attached to her right big toe.

Billy lay on a stretcher a few feet from the table. He was naked. Two small, round dark holes centered his chest. The blood had been wiped from around them. Rags dark with the clotted red liquid lay on a small table on rollers next to the stretcher.

Justin's wide body barely fit on a stretcher against a wall at the left of the room. He was still dressed in his khaki pants and blood-soaked shirt.

Aurondo walked to the freezer unit. It was a small one with only two drawers, one above the other.

He pulled the top drawer open.

Braxton's blank eyes faced the ceiling.

Aurondo pulled the next drawer open.

Mary, the cut across her throat gaping, lay in repose with her eyes closed and her mouth slightly parted.

Without closing the drawers, Aurondo turned and walked from the room, leaving the door open behind him.

Four police cars exited one behind the other from the hospital parking lot. A single officer drove each one. Four officers stepped onto an elevator on the ground floor of the hospital. The door closed behind them. Helen, still in her surgical scrubs with her gray hair pinned up under her cap, hurried to the entrance to the surgical suites, pushed the wide double doors open, and stepped through them.

Several reporters now gathered in the waiting area at the front of the hospital. The administrator spoke with one of them, then looked nervously back over his shoulder toward the single police officer standing at the entrance into the hallway leading toward the rear of the hospital.

Aurondo stopped in front of the double doors leading into the surgical suites.

A police officer in his thirties came down the hallway to the side. He had a sandwich and a paper cup of coffee in his hands. He was hurrying, as if he had to get back to someplace quickly. He slowed his pace when he saw Aurondo, in a hospital robe, staring toward him.

The information the Ocean Springs Police Department had put out earlier that night had warned of a tall, heavy man with long dark hair. The man the officer was looking at had short hair. He was also a patient, as evidenced by the robe and the line of stitches that ran across his forehead. But at this time of night he seemed to be out of place standing in front of the entrance to the surgical suites.

The officer stopped in front of him.

Aurondo's long hands shot forward like a snake striking, grabbing the officer's face and smashing his head back into the hard, stucco-covered wall. The coffee cup and sandwich fell to the floor. The officer slid unconscious down the wall to the floor.

Aurondo reached to the man's holster and jerked his automatic out. Then he stepped forward to the entrance to the suites, threw the double doors open and strode inside a wide area with a double door at its far end and another to his side. He walked to the nearest doors and threw them back. Ahead of him down a wide passageway, doors to four surgical suites lined the walls.

He kicked the first door open.

An operating table, big lights overhead, and medical instrumentation arranged around the walls, met his eyes.

He walked to the next suite and threw its double doors open, stared inside the area, then walked to the next doors.

He pushed them open.

Helen, coming toward him from inside the suite, stopped. She held a tray of syringes and small bottles in front of her. She looked at the gun in his hand. She didn't speak. She didn't move.

Aurondo whirled and walked from her sight.

The door to the unit swung closed behind him.

Helen waited for seconds, then a minute, unmoving, the bottles and syringes beginning to make a rattling noise on the tray as her hands started trembling.

She took a step forward.

Hesitantly, she took another step, then another.

She stopped just before the door and waited, then slowly pushed it open with the tray.

No one stood in the corridor leading to the suites' exit. She walked slowly down the corridor.

Stepping inside the wide entry area, she looked toward the telephone there. But she couldn't stand the thought of remaining alone in the area even for the few seconds it would take to use the phone. She turned toward the exit, hesitated a moment, then slowly pushed the doors open.

The police officer lay against the wall a few feet away.

Helen screamed and dropped the tray.

The echo of the scream, followed by the sound of the syringes and small bottles crashing to the floor, traveled up the hall to Aurondo. He increased his pace. Hanging from the ceiling above him, a directional sign's arrow pointed toward the ICU doors, a few feet away.

Aurondo burst through them running.

In front of him was the central area where stretchers and wheelchairs were stored. Beyond it the nurses' station was surrounded by individual intensive care rooms, arranged in a horseshoe shape around the station. Each room's front was constructed entirely of glass, where the nurses could visually monitor each patient.

No nurses sat at the station.

Three of the rooms were empty.

Three were occupied, two at the back of the area, one closer, off to the side. Each of the patients had sheets pulled up nearly to their faces. Two were males. In the room to Aurondo's side, the sheet was pulled up past the patient's chin. Bandages completely wrapped the patient's head. IV tubes snaked from plastic bags of solution hanging from a metal stand to disappear under the sheet.

Aurondo walked silently toward the still figure.

The room's door stood open and he didn't stop, moving to the side of the bed.

The sheet slipped down.

Ross stared into Aurondo's face.

Aurondo's lips tightened.

Ross waited.

Aurondo raised the pistol.

The loud sound of Ross's automatic firing was deafening in the enclosed area. Aurondo was jolted backward by the shot that had come through the sheet. A red circle of blood formed at the center of his chest.

Miraculously, he still stood.

He started to lift the pistol again.

Ross fired again.

The blood splashed from Aurondo's chest. A larger circle appeared next to the first. Aurondo swayed, stared at Ross, then turned a half circle as if he were going to walk away.

Browning and another officer, their automatics in their hands, had thrown their sheets back and rushed out of the rooms at the back of the unit. Aurondo stared at them.

The pistol fell from his hand.

His legs buckled.

He went to his knees.

And toppled forward—his dead weight slamming face downward against the hard floor.

In the makeshift intensive care unit that had been quickly fashioned on the hospital's second floor, the doctors, nurses, and officers alike had heard the muted pop of the first shot—then the second.

The officers who had been waiting at the elevator piled into it. Other officers, their weapons out in their hands, raced down the steps toward the first floor.

In Bailey's room, she was still too groggy to have heard the shot.

But Dr. Channing, standing next to her bed, had.

And McLaurin had.

He rolled his wheelchair out the door past the two officers on guard there and stared at the elevator doors closing behind the other officers.

CHAPTER 43

Bailey, a pair of pillows behind her shoulders, leaned back against the headboard of her hospital bed with the sheet pulled up to her waist. She wore her lucky robe. Her dark hair, what the doctors hadn't cut away, was nearly concealed by the bandages wrapping her head. She held Ross's hand.

McLaurin stood at the end of the bed. He was reading a copy of *The Sun Herald*. Bailey could see the large headlines where he had folded the first page back.

"The media will never leave Paulie alone," she said. "I'll bet it's in every paper in the nation."

The headline stretched all the way across the front page in big, black block letters.

FAMOUS MODEL NEARLY KILLED IN OCEAN SPRINGS IN ATTEMPT MADE TO STOP ARTIFICIAL BIRTH

In smaller print, a sub-headline over the several columns of the article explaining what had happened, read SIX KILLED—ONE POSSIBLE ADDITIONAL FATALITY.

The article listed the names of the dead, and explained that the possible fatality might be a Hispanic originally shot in the old house's foyer—and still unaccounted for. The article mentioned that the Jackson County Sheriff's Department planned to have boats drag the shallow bay waters directly behind the house.

But that information was already out of date. The pilot the Hispanic had forced to fly him to Mexico, had escaped after they landed on a private field close to Taxco. The Mexican authorities would soon have him in custody.

"Ten to one they'll have to kill him," McLaurin mused under his breath. "They are like some kind of crazy damn terrorists. Better to be dead than not do what they set out to do." He lifted the notebook Ross had brought from Dr. Post's briefcase. It was the one that described the oxygen pressure, nutrients, and chemicals needed to sustain the fetus's continued growth.

"Have you read through this yet?" he asked. "It's sort of like taking care of tropical fish. Maybe taking out the waste is more like taking out cat litter."

Bailey frowned.

McLaurin shrugged, "Oh, by the way, Bailey, the officer said to tell you thank you for the flowers."

The officer he referred to was the one who had been attacked outside the entrance to the surgical units. The officer hadn't been on duty. In fact, he wasn't even a member of the Ocean Springs police force, but was from Biloxi. His pregnant wife had been visiting her mother in Ocean Springs when her labor pains had suddenly started. He had rushed over from Biloxi and had just stepped out of his wife's hospital room to get himself some coffee and a bite to eat.

"And in case you don't know, Bailey," McLaurin said, "there are a hundred reporters outside the hospital."

"What are we going to do, Ross?" Bailey asked. "I

don't want my child growing up under the kind of media scrutiny that—"

"Say the fetus died."

"*Ross*, don't say that."

"Why not? Then you can have another baby—as far as the world is concerned."

"Without being pregnant?"

"Who's to know you're not pregnant?—take a few months' vacation away from everybody. When you come back, bingo. You tell everybody you left to have your child in peace."

Bailey glanced toward the room's window. "With all the uproar, you think I'm going to be able to just take the artificial womb with me?"

"Anyone who receives a call from the President of the United States—two calls in less than twenty-four hours—is going to get to do anything she wants."

"I did say I had connections, didn't I, Ross? But how am I supposed to get pregnant—I mean with this child I'm suddenly going to have?"

"How did you get pregnant the last time?"

"By you," Bailey said, smiling.

"Sounds good to me," Ross said.

McLaurin raised his gaze from the newspaper.

Bailey looked at her hand, holding Ross's. "Well, if that's the case," she said, "shouldn't we get a little better acquainted than just holding hands? Kiss me."

"Should I leave?" McLaurin asked.

Ross leaned forward and pressed his lips against Bailey's. When he drew his face back, he didn't draw it back very far, looking into her eyes.

Bailey cupped her hand behind his head and pulled his lips back to hers again.

This time the kiss was much stronger.

"I'm leaving," McLaurin said.

They didn't break the kiss.

McLaurin stepped from the room and closed the door.

Bandez's forehead was dotted with beads of sweat. His shirt was damp. It had been over thirty-six hours since he had been shot. The fever had begun. He cursed the driver of the old pickup truck as he had cursed him many times during the bumpy drive along the rutted road from Taxco. When the pickup stopped, he threw open the passenger door and stepped outside into the bright sunlight that felt like it was two hundred degrees. Bandez moved slowly toward his small home.

The two Indians in front of the house hurried toward him.

"Get a doctor," he growled in Spanish.

The men looked at the blood-soaked front of his shirt, the lack of color in his face. They turned and hurried toward the Jeep parked at the side of the home.

As they drove off, Bandez pushed his door open. His legs already about to fail him after only the short walk from the pickup, he stumbled across his living room, leaving the door open behind him.

In his bedroom, he moved unsteadily toward the wide bed covered with a blanket. He reached out with his hand, placed it against the mattress, and slowly let himself down on the bed, rolling to his side.

Even that slow movement caused pain to course through his body.

"*Mi Tonito.*"

Bandez thought he was hallucinating.

But the voice came again.

"*Mi Tonito.*"

He forced himself to sit up.

The figure standing in the bedroom doorway was blurred. He tried to focus his eyes.

"*Mi Tonito está muerto,*" the voice said again.

Bandez's vision cleared.

Tony's short, stocky mother stood in the doorway. She held a single-barrel shotgun. It was forty years old. It had belonged to her father. Tony had hunted with it. He had learned to stuff the shells with powder and pellets to reload them. He always used too much powder.

The explosion of the firing shotgun sounded like a cannon roaring in the small house. Bandez's body, ripped to shreds by the expanding lead pellets, was blown backward in a somersault off the far side of the bed.

CHAPTER 44

Lieutenant Browning had become Ocean Springs' Chief of Police two years before. He had spent a long and distinguished career as a law enforcement officer. He was proud of his accomplishments. In his home, in one small bedroom his wife had let him turn into a den, he kept much of the memorabilia he had collected over the years. Included among it were several framed newspaper articles.

Hanging on the wall, was the one that had appeared in *The Sun Herald* when he had made his first narcotics arrest as a twenty-year-old rookie, and the one, complete with a small photograph, that had appeared in the same newspaper when he had been promoted to lieutenant, and the article two years before, announcing his appointment to Chief of Police. The most prominently displayed items, though, were those articles and photographs that had to do with the time Bailey Williams's fetus was growing in the artificial womb in the old house on the bay. Sitting on his desk at the center of the den was the *Newsweek* magazine cover when that publication devoted much of its space to a scientific dis-

sertation on the morals of out-of-womb birth, *The Sun
Herald* article about his appearing on *60 Minutes*, and
an article from the Jackson *Clarion Ledger* showing
him receiving a handshake from the governor as a reward for his setting up the plan that trapped the last
killer in the ICU—though that plan had actually been
Ross's idea.

The single thing Browning most often looked at was
not on display, however. It was the letter from the director of the research center in Washington, DC that
had been given a congressional mandate to learn as
much as possible about the artificial womb and how it
worked.

The research center's task had been complicated by
the fact that Bailey Williams, through the McLaurin/
Channing law firm, had refused to turn over the artificial womb for nearly a full year after the fetus had died
shortly after the barrel-shaped container had been
moved to her mansion in California. By the time the
center had received the womb, the embedding tissue had
rotted away and the unknown liquid that had cushioned the placenta had evaporated.

Browning folded a stick of gum into his mouth, lifted
the one-page letter from the director out of the top
drawer of the desk in the den, and read it for the thou-
sandth time.

Dear Lieutenant Browning:
I am writing this letter in the hope that with your
knowledge of the characters surrounding the Bailey
Williams/Sebastian Post incident you might be able
to shed light on a question we are unable to re-
solve.

   Dr. Post's family Bible has its last page torn from
it. Analysis of pressure indentations on the inside
of the back cover show that the missing page con-

tained a date, printed initials, and writing in Dr. Post's hand.

The date corresponds with the eighth day after Dr. Post and Mary Walker moved into the house on the bay. The printed initials have been determined to be E-BL and S-DR. Based on Dr. Post's shorthand elsewhere, and more particularly that the latter identical sets of initials were found earlier among the pages of a notebook, we have logically determined that they refer to Egg—Bailey Leigh Williams and Sperm—Douglas Ross Channing.

Had these initials been different, e.g., Dr. Post's initials used after the letter denoting the sperm, and given his record of having deceived even his own wife, we would assume that he had once more deceived everybody, used his own sperm to fertilize the egg, and then torn the last page from the Bible to keep the knowledge of what he had done secret.

But since the initials used are those of Mr. Channing, this is obviously not the case. Our analysts have hypothesized several possible scenarios for the initials appearing again, and the page being removed. The most likely scenario, and the one we will report to Congress as the most probable, is since this is the approximate date that the egg cluster formed that Dr. Post was simply noting that event and, for reasons unknown, later removed the page.

As I stated in my opening paragraph above, I was wondering if your knowledge of the characters and events surrounding this incident might lead you to any different conclusion.

Of course, it hadn't.

Now Browning looked at the final paragraph in the

letter. The director wrote that the analysts had also been able to determine that a section of a verse from the Bible had been written on the missing page. It was from The Second Book of Kings.

And when Ath-a-liah the mother of A-ha-ziah saw that her son was dead, she arose and destroyed all the seed royal.

Below that, there was the imprint where Dr. Post had scribbled a last thought of his on the missing page.

We shall see.

It made absolutely no sense.

GREATER LOS ANGELES, CALIFORNIA

Bailey reclined in a lounge chair next to the oversized swimming pool behind her house. She wore a modest bikini. The sun glistened against her lightly tanned skin, covered with a suntan lotion so high in protective value it left a faint gray sheen across her body.

But lightly tanned, or faint gray, or any other way, few men would be able to resist the temptation to steal glances at her figure. It was as near to Barbie-doll-like perfection that a human could attain. The media had made a point of mentioning how well she had regained her figure after she had returned with her newborn daughter from the Pacific island owned by multibillionaire movie director Robert Thompson.

There had been a few gossip columnists and, of course, the tabloids, that had maintained the child had been the one from the artificial womb—even though it was well known the fetus Dr. Post had produced for Bailey had aborted in a manner similar to a fetus miscarrying during a normal pregnancy. .

Dr. Presnell, the California researcher most preeminent in fetal development, had speculated that the temporary loss of power to the old house during the night of the murderous attack had been more than the fetus had been able to withstand. Or, possibly, the damage had occurred when the artificial womb had been removed to Bailey's mansion in California.

In any case, the little girl born to Bailey had been perfect. Now six years and three months old, but already showing the beginning of flowing limbs and exquisitely shaped facial features, she was nearly a complete remake of her mother, except for her hair, a bright natural blonde rather than Bailey's dark hair. Nobody could decide where that genetic trait came from, though Bailey did remember hearing that a grandmother on her father's side had naturally blonde hair.

Bailey rolled to her side and looked at Pauline, beyond the far end of the swimming pool, playing with Cooper next to the dollhouse—a full six-feet tall—that they had bought her.

For a moment, an old, slight nervous feeling revisited Bailey. She couldn't help that from happening from time to time. Even with Mary's writing *Thank you* to Dr. Post in the notebook, there was always the possibility he had deceived her once again. That thought had remained in the back of her mind through the birth and even as Pauline had grown into a perfectly normal child.

What would I have done? Bailey thought. The thought used to make her shiver. She was past that now—but it still came back from time to time.

Then she smiled at Pauline gently pulling Cooper's tail, as he whirled and growled playfully.

Ross called from the home's back door.

Bailey rose from the lounge chair, wrapped a towel around her, tucked it above her bikini top and walked toward the house. She was sorry to see Ross leaving town even for a week. They had been inseparable since the night of the attack, through their marriage four months later, and every day since then. But his and McLaurin's growing law practice was very important to him—though, of course, he didn't need the money. Bailey never would mention her thoughts about that to him, but she felt the money he made from his practice was probably a source of pride to him—that he could do well in his own right.

She kissed him on the cheek when she came inside the door.

"A whole week?" she said, part theatrically, and part seriously. "I'll die."

Ross looked past her out the door. "Where's Pauline?"

Bailey smiled. "Mean little thing. She's sulking by her dollhouse. I told her she should join one of the little kids' soccer teams. All the children her age are. She said she didn't like soccer—and she wasn't going to do it."

Ross shook his head a little. "She just doesn't like sports, Bailey. Any kind of roughhousing. She just likes to take it slow and easy."

"She has you wrapped around her finger, Ross. You'll go along with anything she wants. But sports are good for a girl's self-esteem." Bailey smiled as she paused. "Remember I told you I was a rodeo champion. Besides, she's getting where she's spending too much time by herself—it's making her moody. I believe more so every day." She looked back across her shoulder and smiled a little.

"But I know how to get my way. You wait and see. When you get back in town, I bet I'll have talked her into it."

Ross smiled and kissed her on the head.

"No, what you'll have is her agreeing with whatever you say, then her running to me when I get back and telling me how mean you've been."

"You'll see," Bailey said.

They walked toward the front door and McLaurin waiting in his car for Ross to emerge from the house.

Next to the oversized dollhouse, Pauline glanced past the swimming pool toward the back door of the house, and then pulled a pack of matches from her dress.

She lit one, watched it burn and then go out.

She pitched the smoking match to her side.

It landed on Cooper's back, lying there, smoldering.

He suddenly jumped and whirled and tried to look back across his shoulder at what had stung him. Pauline realized what she had done and looked sad for a moment.

And then she smiled.

Six-year-old Paul Haines watches as two older boys dive into a coastal river...and don't come up. His mother, Carolyn, a charter boat captain on the Mississippi Gulf Coast, finds herself embroiled in the tragedy to an extent she could never have imagined.

Carolyn joins with marine biologist Alan Freeman in the hunt for a creature that is terrorizing the waters along the Gulf Coast. But neither of them could have envisioned exactly what kind of danger they are facing.

Only one man knows what this creature is, and how it has come into the shallows. And his secret obsession with it will force him, as well as Paul, Carolyn and Alan, into a race against time...and a race toward death.

EXTINCT
by Charles Wilson

"Eminently plausible, chilling in its detail, and highly entertaining straight through to its finale."
—DR. DEAN A. DUNN, Professor of Oceanography and Paleontology, University of Southern Mississippi

"With his taut tales and fast words, Charles Wilson will be around for a long time. I hope so."
—JOHN GRISHAM

WITH HIS TAUT TALES AND FAST WORDS, CHARLES
WILSON WILL BE AROUND FOR A LONG TIME. I HOPE SO."
—JOHN GRISHAM

Paleontologist Cameron Malone has discovered a
500,000-year-old man, so miraculously preserved that
some scientists call it a fraud. But Malone firmly believes
in his find—and so does another man, renegade scientist
Dr. Noel Anderson, who has plans for the Ancient Man.
Plans that will prove the theory his colleagues ridiculed,
and shatter the very foundations of modern science.

When Anderson steals some tissue from the frozen corpse
and uses the still-viable DNA to create a modern Ancient
Man, his experiment succeeds beyond his wildest
dreams—and transforms into a waking nightmare. Only
one man, Dr. Cameron Malone, can stop these horrors of
genetic engineering. But can he do it before they are
unleashed on mankind?

DIRECT DESCENDANT
Charles Wilson